## "I have something to tell you."

Eliza blurted the words before they could be stifled. Now she was on the front line without a shield.

He studied her. "Okay."

"I have a secret, Pierce. A big one." Clasping her hands together in her lap, she swallowed. In spite of all of the hours she'd spent thinking about this moment, preparing for it, she had no idea what to say.

Her heart pounded while her lungs tightened around the air she couldn't seem to get enough of.

"But before I tell you, I need you to promise me that you won't shut me out. That you won't just go away and refuse to discuss it."

"I'd never do that."

"You have no idea what you'll do. You don't know the secret."

"I know you. And I know how completely I love you."

If only life were

D0822585

Dear Reader,

I feel like I should put a warning label on this one. I sent one to my editor when I turned in the book. She wrote back that she understood why when she sent the revision letter. It's just that kind of book. One I think you wouldn't want to miss. But my advice is to find a quiet place—and some alone time—to read it.

*Her Soldier's Baby* started out as a somewhat typical, exactly-what-you-want romance novel. It has a lot of the elements we most like to read. A soldier. A secret baby. A nurturing woman with a backbone of steel when it comes to protecting her family. A bed-and-breakfast. Add in a little celebrity status when our heroine is chosen to appear on a reality cooking show and it clicks.

This story has all of those elements. It's what Pierce and Eliza did with them that changed everything. I had no idea what I was getting into when I sat down to tell their story. I am still feeling every aspect of their journey, thinking about their choices, wishing they were real and I could invite them over for dinner. Or to be my best friends. I want to follow them into the future...

Instead, I give them to you.

I love to hear from my readers. Please find me at Facebook.com/tarataylorquinn and on Twitter, @tarataylorquinn. Or join my open Friendship board on Pinterest, Pinterest.com/tarataylorquinn/friendship!

All the best,

*Tara*

www.TaraTaylorQuinn.com

# HEARTWARMING

## *Her Soldier's Baby*

———

*USA TODAY* Bestselling Author

## *Tara Taylor Quinn*

Peters Township Public Library
616 East McMurray Road
McMurray, PA 15317

If you purchased this book without a cover you should be aware
that this book is stolen property. It was reported as "unsold and
destroyed" to the publisher, and neither the author nor the
publisher has received any payment for this "stripped book."

Recycling programs
for this product may
not exist in your area.

ISBN-13: 978-0-373-36811-2

Her Soldier's Baby

Copyright © 2016 by Tara Taylor Quinn

All rights reserved. Except for use in any review, the reproduction or
utilization of this work in whole or in part in any form by any electronic,
mechanical or other means, now known or hereinafter invented, including
xerography, photocopying and recording, or in any information storage
or retrieval system, is forbidden without the written permission of the
publisher, Harlequin Enterprises Limited, 225 Duncan Mill Road,
Don Mills, Ontario M3B 3K9, Canada.

This is a work of fiction. Names, characters, places and incidents are
either the product of the author's imagination or are used fictitiously,
and any resemblance to actual persons, living or dead, business
establishments, events or locales is entirely coincidental.

This edition published by arrangement with Harlequin Books S.A.

For questions and comments about the quality of this book,
please contact us at CustomerService@Harlequin.com.

® and TM are trademarks of Harlequin Enterprises Limited or its
corporate affiliates. Trademarks indicated with ® are registered in the
United States Patent and Trademark Office, the Canadian Intellectual
Property Office and in other countries.

Printed in U.S.A.

Having written over seventy-five novels, **Tara Taylor Quinn** is a *USA TODAY* bestselling author with more than seven million copies sold. She is known for delivering emotional and psychologically astute novels of suspense and romance. Tara is a past president of Romance Writers of America. She has won a Readers' Choice Award and is a five-time finalist for an RWA RITA® Award, a finalist for a Reviewers' Choice Award and a Booksellers' Best Award. She has also appeared on TV across the country, including *CBS Sunday Morning*. She supports the National Domestic Violence Hotline. If you or someone you know might be a victim of domestic violence in the United States, please contact 1-800-799-7233.

## Books by Tara Taylor Quinn

### Harlequin Heartwarming

#### *Family Secrets*

*For Love or Money*

#### *The Historic Arapahoe*

*Once Upon a Friendship*
*Once Upon a Marriage*

### Harlequin Superromance

#### *Where Secrets are Safe*

*Wife by Design*
*Once a Family*
*Husband by Choice*
*Child by Chance*
*Mother by Fate*
*The Good Father*
*Love by Association*
*His First Choice*
*The Promise He Made Her*

### *Shelter Valley Stories*

*Sophie's Secret*
*Full Contact*
*It's Never Too Late*
*Second Time's the Charm*
*The Moment of Truth*

### *It Happened in Comfort Cove*

*A Son's Tale*
*A Daughter's Story*
*The Truth About Comfort Cove*

### **MIRA Books**

*The Friendship Pact*
*The Fourth Victim*
*The Third Secret*
*The Second Lie*

Visit the Author Profile page
at Harlequin.com for more titles.

For my Heartwarming sisters and our readers.
Thank you for welcoming me into the family...

# *CHAPTER ONE*

ELIZA CLUNG TIGHTLY to her husband, Pierce, pressing her body against his, thigh to thigh, chest to chest, her arms around his waist, pulling him in. Charleston International Airport was teeming with comers and goers and waiters that Friday afternoon. Businesspeople arriving home for the weekend, and others, like her, heading out.

Pierce gave her a tight squeeze—more akin to a pat on the head than a desperate hug filled with the emotional angst of having gone through this before, pledging to see each other again and then not.

She savored the contact.

"You've got your driver's license, your boarding pass is on your phone and there will be a car waiting for you in Palm Springs. If your name is not professionally printed on a card, get a cab instead..." He'd started walking the five feet to the security checkpoint line. Once she joined the queue, he'd leave her.

"Remember, don't make eye contact with men you don't know, and—"

She shook her head. "I got it, Pierce. I've been keeping myself safe for a long time." Having lived the majority of her adult life alone, she wasn't worried.

"The world's changing, Eliza, and California is not Shelby Island. Not everyone you meet is your friend, nor are they all safe for you to bring home."

She knew that, too. Had a very careful vetting system and security measures in place for the guests she hosted at her successful Shelby Island bed-and-breakfast in an antebellum home just thirty miles down the South Carolina coast from Charleston.

She'd also been doing that alone for the majority of her adult life.

"I promise, I'll stay alert, babe," she told her husband—because she knew that these reminders were his way of supporting her choice to go.

"Just watch yourself going to and from the studio. You're going to be all over national television, and who knows what kind of crackpot could come out of the ozone? You're a beautiful woman and..."

She wasn't. At five-five and a hundred

thirty-five pounds, she wasn't as tall and skinny as the California TV beauties. She wasn't blonde, either. On good days, her brown hair had a bit of a shine to it. Mostly it just fell, all mousy-looking, around her shoulders, wherever gravity took it. But she loved that Pierce found her as good-looking as he had when they'd been an item in high school. Hard to believe that had been nearly eighteen years ago.

They'd reached the end of the line. Which was moving quickly. She stepped to the side to let a family of five pass. Mom, dad and the kids. That would never be her.

She looked up into Pierce's big blue eyes—the only soft part of her military-trained cop husband—and melted when he met her gaze with all of the depth of his heart. That look… some days it seemed it was all that was left of the sweet, sensitive boy who'd left her just-turned-sixteen self to go off to basic training.

"I love you, babe," she said.

"I love you, too."

There. She took a deep breath. Came back to herself.

"I'll see you in two days," she told him. A promise. A pledge. A hope.

And a worry.

"Don't worry about getting your bag when you come back," he said. "I'll park and come in."

She nodded.

He kissed her. Just a peck. She wanted it to be more personal and might have pushed him into it if she hadn't had a guilty conscience.

And off she went. To join the queue of strangers. To fly across the country to meet more strangers, to appear as one of eight contestants—all strangers—on the nationally syndicated *Family Secrets* cooking show—and to search for the one stranger who knew her from the inside out.

Literally.

A stranger Pierce Westin knew nothing about.

FROM A VANTAGE point against the wall, mostly concealed by a pillar, he watched her through security. And for as far as he could see her.

Because Pierce would never get enough of seeing his beautiful wife. It wasn't just her big brown eyes, soft cheekbones, and lips that set the world on fire that drew him—though he loved all of that, too. No, it was just…her.

And the fact that she was in his life again. Married to him.

Some nights he woke up in a cold sweat and still couldn't believe that Eliza Maxwell was his wife. He'd lie there, touching her shoulder, looking at her sometimes for more than an hour, to avoid going back to sleep. When he slept, she was, like the rest of his few good childhood memories, completely out of reach.

The fear that rent his gut when she turned a corner and was out of sight would be with him until her return.

And he would work his tail off. Protecting the people of Charleston, paying it forward— so that the law enforcement of Palm Desert protected her.

He might kid himself that he risked his life every day as a kind of penance—to pay for the sins of his past. But deep down he knew better. There was nothing he could do—ever—to make up for what he'd done. No way his soul would ever be out of debt.

As he reached his patrol car, the fear inside him increased. He wasn't afraid of the job. On the contrary, his time on the streets, looking out for bad guys, taking them on, taking them in, was the only time he ever really felt comfortable.

What he feared was greater than mere

physical death. It was the fear of a man who knew that he wasn't good enough for the woman he loved.

Who knew that…someday…he would lose her. Again.

THERE WAS A little gathering for contestants Friday evening down in the lounge. Hosted by the hotel, there'd be wine and hors d'oeuvres, and a chance for all of them to get to know each other before traveling in the van to the studio the next morning. According to Eliza's paperwork, seven of the eight contestants were traveling in from out of state and would be guests at the hotel.

The eighth, an eighty-one-year-old woman from Utah, had rented a condominium for the next two months in one of the popular senior resort communities for which Palm Desert was known. They'd all had a list of area options. For those who were going to be traveling back and forth for the weekend tapings, the host hotel was by far the best deal.

Eliza would have stayed with the crowd anyway. There was safety in numbers. And convenience in door-to-door transportation.

She took the car she and Pierce had arranged from the airport to the hotel. Paid the driver. Checked in. She was a couple of hours earlier than the three other contestants arriving that day. Three had arrived the night before.

Eliza could have made plans to get together early with them. Could go downstairs on the off chance she'd run into them.

Instead, she grabbed the big black shoulder bag she'd bought to use as a purse for the duration of her time on *Family Secrets*—a minimum of two weeks, a maximum of six—and made sure the folder was inside.

She opened that and looked for the pencil markings she'd made. Just a couple of numbers. A mnemonic device. She didn't need it. The information she needed was etched so legibly on her brain, she was half surprised that Pierce hadn't been able to read it in full.

After his time in Iraq, coupled with his police military training and his time on the job after he got out, her husband could see an ant on a paper plate at a picnic from a block away. His "sniffing out trouble" skills were honed to perfection.

The agency she needed to visit was in Anaheim. A good hour and a half west of Palm Desert. She already knew she could get a rental car from the hotel, and as soon as she'd dropped off her suitcase and quickly freshened up, she went down to the lobby to do so.

She didn't need to look her best. She was going only to the agency. To see if she could get some information.

In deference to the questions she knew her husband was going to ask, she got a car with built-in navigation. And called him as soon as she was inside. Telling him that she'd only rented the car for the afternoon. She had some free time and didn't want to be cooped up in a hotel when she was in sunny California for the first time in her life.

Pierce didn't like her out and about on her own. At all.

But he didn't question her desire to take a look around. He never questioned anything she did. Trusted her completely.

Which made the start of this particular journey that much more difficult.

Pierce didn't trust often, or easily, but he'd always been able to trust her. Since the moment he'd come back into her life, she'd never given him reason to doubt her.

He'd needed that.

And she'd somehow worked it out in her brain that if she did that for him, she could make up for the part of her past that he didn't know about. Make up for the one secret she kept. The one part of her life he wouldn't recognize.

The part after he'd left for the army, and she'd left town—and the high school where they'd met and been a couple—to finish high school in South Carolina. Living with her grandmother.

The licensed nonprofit agency was located in a suite of offices in an upscale professional park. Following the instructions coming over the car's system, she drove straight there. Parked. Stared at the door. This was a long shot. At best.

At three o'clock on Friday afternoon, the employees inside were probably winding down for the week. She knew from their website that they closed at five p.m., five days a week. And were closed all weekend, too.

A couple came out. His arm around her, his head slightly bent toward hers. They appeared to be in their midthirties, well dressed. Got into a royal blue BMW.

And she hadn't come all this way to watch other people live their lives. Truth be told, she hadn't come all this way to compete on a cooking show, either.

She'd auditioned for the show as a means

to come all this way. If she hadn't won the audition, she'd told herself she'd see that as a sign that she was to do nothing.

Likewise, if she got on the show, that was momentous enough to be considered a sign in the other way—it would be sure direction to act.

The fact that winning *Family Secrets* could allow her and Pierce the finances to get him off the streets was added impetus.

She'd been motivated by need and had been given opportunity, and now it was up to her to do all she could to make their future come to fruition.

And added to all of that, the unforeseen aspect... She really needed to win the competition for herself. Needed it badly. These past weeks of living in her future while knowing she was going back into her past had shown her something very clearly. Her whole life she'd defined herself by those in her life— her parents, Pierce, her grandmother and then Pierce again. And she was...weary. It was like she was constantly running to keep up, but never quite catching up because someone always needed something more.

But winning the competition...that was for her. To show herself that separate and apart from everyone else, she was just plain good at something. She was an individual with a talent that had nothing to do with anyone else in her life.

Maybe if she could believe that, if she could show herself that much, she wouldn't constantly feel as though she had to earn the love of those around her. She could just love them. Serve them. And feel…like she was enough.

But first, she had to take care of her past.

# CHAPTER TWO

WHILE THERE WASN'T a lot of crime on Shelby Island, there was plenty of it in Charleston, which was where Pierce worked. With the harbor and the beaches, the moderate temperatures and South Carolina charm, the city attracted all kinds. From drug users to homeless, vacationers to the rich and famous, illegal immigrants to some of the nation's most respected leaders, Pierce, with his fellow officers, walked among them. Determined to keep the peace.

When a call came in, he put himself on the front line as often as he could. He was trained for all kinds of warfare. Had reflexes that outranked those of most officers.

And no fear of dying.

Some thought he was a bit too into danger and shied away from partnering with him. Others put in requests to ride with him.

He preferred going it alone.

And would have liked to stay on for a second shift when his was up Friday afternoon. But instead he parked his vehicle and headed out right on time. With Eliza gone, he had evening social hour welcoming duties at the bed-and-breakfast. He wasn't good at it. Figured he probably put as many people off as he made feel welcome, but his wife didn't seem to get that.

She had a full-time assistant. And a part-time one, too, for times like these when she couldn't be at Rose Harbor B and B herself. The weekend's meals were all prepared and in the refrigerator, ready to heat. As cooking was Eliza's passion, she did all of it herself.

Someone would be at the house to check in guests and tend to unforeseen needs: a pillow that was too hard or too soft, an allergy to a particular kind of soap, menu preferences that a guest might have forgotten to fill in ahead of time.

Pierce's job was simply to be present. To welcome Eliza's guests into their home as though they were friends. To chat with them and assure them that they were happy to accommodate their needs.

And to fix anything that might be broken. A toilet with a flush valve gone bad. A leaky faucet. Things Eliza could do, too, in a pinch.

His wife, a Harvard graduate, had a lot of surprising talents. He thought of her, and the fact that it was still early afternoon in California, as he drove home. Had to toss his cell phone to the backseat while he drove in an effort to stop himself from calling. And he concentrated on the evening ahead.

They had four of their six rooms filled that weekend. Two to families in town for a reunion. One an older couple who visited at least once a year. And the fourth to a recent widow, traveling on her own.

Other than the mingling, Pierce was happy to be a part of Eliza's venture. To contribute.

Mostly he was happy to be her self-appointed sentry. Checking out as many of their guests as possible, assessing, making certain that there were no signs of risk.

And if there were, to investigate further. Without anyone being the wiser, of course.

He was there to serve the woman he loved.

For as long as he could be of use to her.

For as long as he was more help than hurt.

ELIZA WAS SHOWN to a counselor almost immediately. Probably because there'd been no one else in the waiting room that late on a Friday afternoon.

"Mary says you're here to ask about one of our clients?" the woman, Mrs. Carpenter, said as she shook Eliza's hand. She told her to take a seat before sitting back down herself.

The counselor looked to be in her mid-forties, with short, dark hair and a reserved but friendly smile. She was well-dressed in a gray suit with a maroon silk blouse. Eliza hadn't seen her shoes before she sat down behind her desk, but figured them for fashionable heels.

"I received a letter from your office," Eliza said. "Just before Christmas." And that was when she'd started looking around for a reason to visit California without arousing Pierce's suspicions—and had come upon the *Family Secrets* auditions.

Sort of. She was a huge fan of the show. And had been trying to figure out a way to pursue the letter when she'd been watching *Family Secrets* one night and had seen that there were going to be auditions in Raleigh the week between Christmas and New Year's…

She'd seen that as a sign. In her imagination, as she'd watched the show over the past couple of years, she'd fancied herself a contestant many times—without ever expecting the chance to make the fantasy a possibility.

Without ever believing she'd have the moxie to actually pursue such a thing.

Until that letter arrived.

She'd told herself she'd try out. If she did make it, it would be another sign. She was supposed to pursue the letter.

But Mrs. Carpenter didn't need to know any of that. The last thing she wanted was for the woman to think she was some kind of kook.

"I got a letter," she said. As heat spread up her body, causing the outbreak of an instant sweat, she stood up. "I'm sorry, Mrs. Carpenter. This was a mistake. I should never have come. I'm sorry for bothering you...wasting your time..."

The older woman stood, as well. Came around her desk to take Eliza's hand, and then placed her other hand on Eliza's arm. "Please, sit down," she said, maintaining physical contact as she lowered to the chair next to Eliza's. "You aren't wasting my time. This is exactly what I'm here for."

*This.* Eliza hadn't even told her what *this* was. And just as she'd thought, Mrs. Carpenter had four-inch spiked heels on her shoes.

They were gray. Patent leather. And definitely real leather.

Eliza liked shoes. Always had. An inexplicable weakness for one who'd always eschewed her parents' penchant for keeping up appearances in their upper-middle-class crowd.

Pierce, the son of a single father who was a happy drunk, hadn't been good enough for them.

And in the end, Eliza hadn't been, either. The summer after her sophomore year of high school, they'd shipped her, their only child, off to her grandmother and bought a four-bedroom home on a golf course in Florida.

In their defense, they'd expected her to join them eventually. To graduate from high school in Florida. Her mother had decorated a suite just for her, with her own bathroom. Eliza was the one who'd opted to stay in South Carolina. They'd agreed to let her do so as long as she agreed to get good enough scores in high school to be able to attend Harvard.

She just hadn't been able to picture Pierce coming home to that house in Florida.

As it turned out, he hadn't come to South Carolina, either. Not until a long time later.

"That's it. Just breathe. Calm will come," Mrs. Carpenter said. Which was when Eliza realized the woman was still holding her hand.

She felt like an idiot. Slipped her hand out from the counselor's and sat up straighter. "I had a baby."

The sky didn't fall.

"I've...actually never told anyone...not since the day they took him away from me." She'd been sixteen. Had been in labor for almost two days. Had been certain she was going to die—that she was paying for having sinned so horrendously. She'd been delirious before it was over. "I never even saw him."

She'd been told he was perfect.

"Was that your choice?" Mrs. Carpenter's tone was soft.

It had been her parents' choice. They'd also insisted that she be homeschooled during her pregnancy. Which was why she'd been shipped to her grandmother. Her mother's mother had been a schoolteacher before she'd retired to go into the B and B business.

"It was for the best," was all she said. Her parents had given in to her need to stay, permanently, with the grandmother who'd saved her life that year—emotionally if not physically. But their acquiescence had come with cost. After her baby was born, she was never to speak of it again. Not to tell anyone. Ever. When she'd started attending her new school her senior year, she was just a new girl. They said to handle it. Any other way would brand her as someone who couldn't control herself. Who didn't make wise choices. Who was irresponsible.

There was truth to that.

"So…you've never told anyone you had a baby?"

The caring in Mrs. Carpenter's tone brought tears to her eyes. She shook her head.

"I notice you're wearing a wedding ring…" The words trailed off.

Eliza looked over, meeting the counselor's compassionate gaze. "He doesn't know I'm here."

She expected some reaction to that. Horror. Disgust. Shock, at least.

Judgment.

"So, tell me about this letter."

"I didn't realize that Family Adoptions had sister agencies," she said, naming the agency her grandmother had chosen in South Carolina all those years ago.

"We're one of the few licensed nonprofits

with offices around the country. It opens our pool of birth mothers and adopting families to suit everyone better, while still allowing us to do on-site home studies over the course of a couple of months for each one."

Up until a month ago, Eliza hadn't known the ins and outs of adopting a baby. She'd trusted her grandmother to make certain her son had a good home. She'd trusted the agency she'd visited one bleak day that horrible fall.

She knew now how families were vetted. The paperwork and legalities and home visits. The social workers assigned to prospective families. All of it had comforted her. She wished she'd done the research sooner.

And yet, how could she research something that, for all intents and purposes, had never happened?

She'd borne the child but had no rights to him. At all.

"I gave up all rights," she said now. Except the one her grandmother had insisted upon. "Except that he's allowed to know who I am. If he ever asks."

Mrs. Carpenter nodded.

"His family got him through this office," she said.

Feeling slightly woozy, muddled, Eliza stared at the gray patent leather shoes. Wondered how long she'd be able to walk in them if she owned a pair.

"Has he asked to see you?" The soft words broke into her consideration of crunched toes, foot cramps and blisters. None of which were likely to be a problem for her.

Because she'd been wearing heels since she was seventeen. And because she wasn't likely to be wearing four-inch ones any time soon. She was an innkeeper. The owner of Rose Harbor Bed-and-Breakfast. Making a home away from home for hundreds of people every year.

"No," she said now. "The letter just told me that he'd contacted your office to inquire about my identity. I guess I had the right to know that they'd given him what information they had on me. My name, where I was living at the time of the adoption and the office through which he originated."

Nothing else. It was so…open-ended.

But tightly shut, too.

What if he wanted to find her and couldn't? She'd married. Her name was different.

And the address was, too. Back then, her grandmother had lived in a separate house off

Shelby Island. She'd managed Rose Harbor in those days. But the year Eliza had graduated from high school, when her grandmother had turned sixty and had been able to access her retirement fund without penalty, she'd used it to buy Rose Harbor.

What if he found her, came knocking on the door, and Pierce answered?

"I...came here to find out..."

She broke off as she started to shake. And get too warm again.

"If, as you say, you gave up all rights, I can't give you any information on him."

Swallowing, she attempted a smile, one she gave to reassure an agitated guest, and failed. "I know," she managed. "I'm not asking. I just...wanted to know if you could maybe find out...somehow...if he wants to see me."

*Please, God. Yes. Let me meet my baby boy. Finally. Please. Just to touch his hand once. To look in his eyes one time before I die.*

*Oh. God. No. Have him be happy. Fulfilled. In want of nothing. Including the need to see the woman in whose body he was created.*

Mrs. Carpenter shook her head. "If there's something in his file that indicates that he's open to seeing you, I can pass on your infor- mation. But generally, if that were the case, the letter you received would have indicated as much."

The counselor took her name anyway. The case number that Eliza had memorized from the letter that she'd shredded. Taking a bottle of water from the small refrigerator under a counter across from them, Mrs. Carpenter handed it to Eliza, asked if she'd be okay for a few minutes and, at Eliza's nod, left the room.

Eliza wasn't okay. Her fingers shook so badly, she dropped the cap of the water bottle after opening it. And in her black pants and white cropped jacket, Eliza dropped to her knees to reach under the desk it rolled under.

Back in her seat, she pulled out her phone. Read Pierce's text telling her that he was home and that everything was on course for social hour.

He didn't include any silly emoticons or anything that could indicate how very much in love he was with his wife.

But those words, reassuring her, read like an avowal of undying love.

Longing for the life she'd built, the adrenaline rush of being in her own parlor with guests who were happy with her accommodations, happy with the hors d'oeuvres she'd served them, Eliza wished she'd stayed home.

Auditioning, traveling across the country like this…it had been a mistake. She should be home, basking in the knowledge that when her guests retired for the night, she'd be going to bed with Pierce. To fall asleep in the arms of the only man she'd ever loved.

She wanted to answer the text. Typed. Deleted. Typed. Deleted. She couldn't lie to him. Couldn't tell him where she was. Or why she was there.

She hated not being able to tell him.

Fear shot through her as she considered the Pandora's box she'd opened.

But she hadn't opened it.

Her baby boy had opened it. He'd asked about her.

There was no way she could ignore any possibility that he needed her.

No way Pierce would want her to.

And no way she could tell him that she'd given away the only child he would ever father.

## CHAPTER THREE

LILY ELIZABETH MCCONNELL had been married thirty years. "Not long enough," the fifty-something, salt-and-pepper-haired woman told Pierce as she stood, a china plate holding a couple of Eliza's miniquiches in her hands. "You take it for granted, you know?"

Her eyes were glassy with emotion, but her voice was calm. Pierce respected the control. "I do know," he said wholeheartedly. "Sad, isn't it, that you have to lose something to realize what it meant to you?"

He hadn't meant to speak that last bit out loud. But the woman's need tapped into the vulnerability he normally had buried so deep he could pretend it didn't exist.

He was always a bit off when Eliza was gone.

The well-dressed widow tilted her head. "You've lost someone, too?" she asked.

He'd walked right into that one.

Music played softly from good-quality

speakers resourcefully hidden among the genuine antiques that filled—and garnished—the room. Classical piano. He recognized Pachelbel's Canon only because it was Eliza's favorite and she had what seemed like a million renditions of it.

He didn't want to offend the guest, but he wished the couple in the corner enjoying the free wine were more open to socializing. Or that the families he'd been told had checked in would come downstairs.

"I have," he told Mrs. McConnell, taking a sip from the glass of iced lemon water he'd poured before leaving his and Eliza's private section of the mansion to do his duties as host.

There. They could have mutual understanding, as the strangers they were, and move on. Glancing over her shoulder, he noted the still-empty stairway. No families coming down yet.

Lily Elizabeth McConnell seemed as interested in his hand as he was in the staircase.

"You're wearing a wedding ring," she said when she caught him noticing her stare.

Awkward. And the reason he hated these things.

"Yet you're here alone. Did you lose your wife?"

He knew how to parry a come-on. And did. Every single time he was faced with one. This wasn't a come-on. If the woman's tone hadn't told him so, the pain in her eyes did.

"No," he said. No playing with fate on that one. "I just assumed everyone here knew… Eliza's away being a contestant on *Family Secrets* every weekend this month. This is our home, but the bed-and-breakfast, that's all her doing. I'm strictly support staff when it comes to Rose Harbor."

He helped her with the books, too. She ran all decisions by him. But the house was hers. Eliza had been running the successful B and B long before he'd come back into her picture.

Mrs. McConnell nodded. Looked down at her sensible, almost flat black shoes. He wasn't the most sensitive guy around, but even he could tell that her pain, in that moment, was acute.

"What about kids?" he blurted. People her age relied on their kids. Didn't they?

She shook her head. And he'd have gladly escaped to keep from saying anything else that didn't help. "We… Harley and I…we never had kids. It wasn't that we didn't want them. It just never happened. And neither of us wanted to pursue other avenues. We figured if we were meant to be parents, we'd get pregnant."

Were it him, he'd have pursued every avenue there was and any dirt lane, too. But this wasn't about him. "I get what you mean about not being meant to be a parent," he said before realizing that they'd ventured outside guest-welcoming territory.

"You and your wife don't have children?" she asked. And he just stood there. Staring at her.

Eventually he shook his head.

And as though fate had stepped in to save him for once, footsteps bounded down the stairs. Mrs. McConnell took the interruption as an opportunity to move back to the food station that Margie, Eliza's assistant for the past ten years, had laid out.

Maybe she thought he and Eliza had lost a child. He had, after all, told her he'd lost someone.

Lord knew why he'd said *that*. He'd never lost anyone he was close to.

His mother had taken off before he was old enough to remember her. His old man was gone, but since he'd been drunk so much of Pierce's life, that hadn't been a big surprise. At least he'd been a nice drunk.

Pierce had had no reason to commiserate with the woman's loss as though he understood. Living without Eliza all those years—that had been his choice. He'd consciously opted not to contact her when he'd gotten back from the war in Iraq, a changed man. One who'd been hit by an explosive device that left him sterile.

After going by her place in Savannah, where they'd grown up, finding out that she'd moved to South Carolina the summer he left and that her folks were in Florida, he'd gotten on with his life. A life without her. Except for keeping tabs, just to make certain she was thriving. That's how he'd known she was at Harvard while he finished his time in the marines as a cop at Quantico.

And known that she'd graduated and was running a bed-and-breakfast when he'd married a fellow marine shortly after getting out. And that she was still there three years later, when he married his second wife. A waitress from the coffee shop where he had breakfast every morning.

The woman had a young son. Pierce had fancied himself a father.

He just hadn't been a good husband. Too distant. Too many nightmares. No desire to spend his off time with the woman he'd married.

Turned out, he hadn't been a great father, either.

Nope, he hadn't lost anyone. He'd made conscious choices.

And would probably make them again if he had a second go at it. Including the one that had resulted in an inability to father children. Some days he figured he'd deserved that. He'd still choose to join the army, too. If he was going to make anything of himself, get away from the reputation he'd earned as the son of the town drunk, get any kind of education, he'd have had to join up. He'd had no money for college. Nowhere to live, no way to support himself during the four years of attending classes to get a higher degree. No way to support the love of his life, or prove to her father that he was good enough for her, unless he joined the army, worked until every bone in his body ached, and earned not only money but also respect.

No, as hard as leaving Eliza had been, it

was a choice he'd make again. For the same reasons.

Even the worst choice he'd ever made, given the same situation, the same intel, he'd make again, because when you made choices you got only the before, not the after. He hadn't known that that one choice would irrevocably change his world. Change him.

One choice. A split second. The pull of a trigger.

And Pierce Westin had lost his soul.


"I'M SORRY FOR the long wait, Eliza. Thank you for your patience."

Mrs. Carpenter came into the room quietly. Efficiently. All business.

From the chair she was clinging to like a life raft, Eliza nodded. Forced a smile. She didn't do this whole fragile thing well. Her days didn't require it.

Her life didn't require it.

Because she'd kept her secret. Banished it to the past. Made a life without it, just as her parents had espoused.

She was beginning to see why they'd been so adamant. And figured they'd been right.

She watched the counselor take a seat. Fold her hands. And knew.

This wasn't good news.

"I've looked through your file," Mrs. Carpenter told her. "Your adoption was a bit... unique..." she said. "Private adoptions have more leeway as far as terms are concerned. According to your documents, your child is to be given any information we have about you, anytime he asks. But it was further agreed that even if you ask, you are not to be given information about him."

She hadn't known that.

"I'm assuming you knew that. Your signature was on every page."

Okay, so maybe she had known. She hadn't remembered. She'd been just shy of her seventeenth birthday. Scared to death. Heartbroken.

If only Pierce had contacted her. Even once...

If only she'd known then that her father had had a very firm talk with Pierce after he'd joined the army. Feeding Pierce's fears that he wasn't good enough for her. That she was destined for great things, a settled and successful society waiting for her, that nothing about her assets was suited to the moving around required by military life.

Pierce could have told her. Said now that

maybe he should have told her that part. He'd still have joined up—and hadn't wanted to bad-talk her father to her.

And what was done was done. They'd determined before they'd married seven years before that the only way for either of them to find happiness was to let go of the hurts they couldn't change. And be thankful for all the great years they had left to share. To make the most of every minute of those years.

To realize that they, unlike so many others, had a special appreciation of their love that would prevent them from falling into the habit of taking that love, taking each other, for granted like they'd both seen happen with so many other couples.

"I can't even know his name?" she asked, after taking as long as she could to assimilate her situation and pull herself together.

Clearly she hadn't done either, yet.

Mrs. Carpenter shook her head. To give the woman her due, she didn't seem in any kind of hurry to get Eliza out of there.

"You do have the right to stipulate if you'd rather we not give him any further information about you," the woman said after another few minutes of standby.

Eliza knew Mrs. Carpenter was waiting for her to go. She just didn't.

Thoughts of the gathering in the hotel lobby, due to start in less than two hours, skirted across her mind. She watched the other contestants flit about like in some kind of weird movie. A flash of the lobby. A group of strangers.

"Can he give his permission for me to know about him?"

"His parents were willing to give that information at the time of the adoption," Mrs. Carpenter said. "This is a strange situation. Clearly you feared that at some point in your life you'd want to revisit this situation, but from what you knew at the time of the adoption, with everything still clear in your mind, you wanted to protect your future self from the eventuality."

"I was sixteen."

"You'd been counseled for months. And asked your father to sign the papers, as well."

She kind of remembered that.

"You re-signed them when you turned eighteen," Mrs. Carpenter said softly, as though not sure what she was dealing with, a rational human being or a crazy lady. Eliza didn't blame her. She wasn't sure herself.

"I did?" she said.

"Yes."

She might have. She'd been so messed up back then. Hardened. Hurting beyond what she could bear. Her parents—and her grandmother—just kept telling her to look forward. To effect that which she could effect. To use the past as a lesson. To take every opportunity to make a good life for herself.

She'd signed a few things. To be executor of her grandmother's estate in the event that anything happened to her, even though, in Eliza's mother's eyes, she was still just a kid. Her mother had thought she should be the one with power of attorney over her own mother's estate. It hadn't happened that way.

Eliza's grandmother had made a will of her own.

Taken out a life insurance policy.

A readmission of her adoption papers could very well have been one more piece of business to be dealt with and filed away.

Standing, Mrs. Carpenter came toward her. Eliza expected to be shown out. There really was nothing more for them to say. Instead, the woman sat down in the chair next to her and took Eliza's hand. "Were you raped?"

*What?* "No!" Was that what her parents had told people? Was that how they'd saved face?

She'd thought leaving town before anyone had known she was pregnant had done that.

Mrs. Carpenter looked at her in a way that made Eliza feel like she was being professionally assessed.

"I had one very, very wonderful, if completely inappropriate, night with a boy I loved very much," she said softly.

The words wouldn't stay back. Wouldn't remain unsaid. She and Pierce...that night... deserved better than that.

More words flew to her throat as though they'd all been waiting for release.

But with so many years of silence, she managed to contain them. They were making her nauseated, all bottled up in there. But in there they stayed.

Because what would she say? How crazy would this counselor think her if she knew that Eliza was now married to that same boy? But that he knew nothing about the son he'd fathered?

To know would do neither of them any

good. It would be more of the hurt from the past that could prevent happiness in their future. More angst, acrimony. More *why*s without answers.

They couldn't have their son. And Pierce couldn't father another one. It seemed too cruel to let him know what he'd missed. And to what end? So that he could hate himself for not contacting her after he left?

So they could both die of what-ifs?

"I have to ask you again," Mrs. Carpenter broke into her thoughts. Oddly, having come full circle, Eliza felt no more certain of anything, no less vulnerable. And yet she'd found her strength.

"Ask what?"

"At this point, all your son has done is make one query into your information. Do you want to update what we have so that, if he comes back, he can contact you?"

Her heart started to pound again. "Can you contact him and let him know it's here? That I've been here and left updated information?"

She supposed she wasn't surprised when Mrs. Carpenter shook her head. She *was* disappointed. Hugely so. But back in control, she nodded. Took a breath.

Did she want this young man to be able to call her out of the blue? Any time of the day or night or year? Just to show up, unannounced at their door?

*Yes! Of course! Absolutely!*

And what about Pierce? What if he was having one of his bad spells? Or even if he wasn't? Was it fair to him to open the door to this possibility? To the fact that at any moment, he could come face to face with his son without even knowing he had one?

If she did this...gave Mrs. Carpenter her information, gave her son the ability to contact her...she had to tell Pierce that the young man existed.

First.

"Can I call you and do that?" she asked now.

"Of course." Mrs. Carpenter sat back.

Was Eliza no longer sounding like she was about to lose her marbles, then? She still felt like she was.

"You do realize there's a possibility, given the internet, that he could find you anyway, right?"

Fear shot through her.

Mixed with excitement.

"That's why I came," she said. "To find out what the future might hold."

Maybe she'd hoped to be able to see her son on her own. To know if finding out about him would cause Pierce more pain than good. To know if, regardless of the pain, their son needed them.

That had been the closer. If the boy needed them, she and Pierce had to put their own regrets, their own pain, aside and be there for him.

"I want him to have my information," she said. "I want him to be able to contact me. But I need to take care of something first. I will be contacting you just as soon as I've gotten that done. I don't know exactly when that will be...how soon...but it will be as soon as I can get it done." She was babbling. Pedaling forward and back. Afraid for Pierce. Afraid for their son.

Mrs. Carpenter took her hand again. "That's fine, hon. You don't have to do this. That's why you gave him up for adoption in the first place. So that he would be the son— the responsibility—of someone else. Whatever prompted you to do so...you clearly did what you thought best. What your parents thought best, too, based on what I read. You have no reason to feel guilty. Or obligated..."

"Oh, no. I *want* this!" She needed this. And hadn't realized, until just that second, how much.

"It's just...not just me...and I have to tend to others who love and need me..."

The woman nodded. Looking wise and understanding. And for the first time, Eliza felt like she was doing the right thing.

She stood. Walked to the door. And couldn't quite step out. Not yet. Looking at the woman who'd somehow become a friend to her heart, she said, "Is there some way you can make a note in my file...to let him know...in case he comes back before I call...that I will be calling?"

"I can make a note that you said you would be calling."

Eliza got the distinction. Mrs. Carpenter still thought she might change her mind. Or that she didn't know her own mind.

She didn't blame her. History wasn't looking too good for her on that one. Recent history included.

But as Eliza left, as she drove back to Palm Desert and met all but one of her opponents in the contest, she'd never felt more like she and her mind were in sync.

They'd found each other again. Her thoughts and heart.

Somehow she was going to have to find a way to bring Pierce into the mix.

# CHAPTER FOUR

THAT FIRST WEEK there was no televised show he could watch. The contestants would be shuttled from the hotel to the studio for their first taping the next morning, but it was for footage that would be woven in throughout the series as warranted. They were being introduced to each other, shown their kitchen pods, their green room and lockers. And then toured around the studio. Natasha Stevens, the show's host, wanted them familiar with their surroundings when the competition began the next weekend.

For the next five weekends, Pierce was going to be sleeping alone. If Eliza won any of the four weekly competitions, there'd be a sixth trip to Palm Desert for her. And he'd be expected to accompany her in the event that circumstance came to pass. If she actually won the whole thing, he'd be called up on stage to stand beside her as she accepted her award.

Lying in bed alone that Friday night, his arms folded on the pillow, his hands propping up his head, Pierce stared at the ceiling. And pictured his beautiful, vivacious, loving wife up on stage, on national television, announcing to the world that he, Pierce Westin, was her husband.

It was way too early for him to be lying in the dark, too early to have stripped down to his T-shirt and briefs. Guests were still up and about. Someone could need something.

But social hour was over. And if no one had a problem that Margie couldn't handle, he could lie there alone until morning without being missed.

When he'd come in, he'd kind of had a plan to turn on the television mounted on the wall across from their big four-poster bed. Thought maybe he'd take in one of the more violent suspense flicks he liked. The ones that Eliza read through. If she could bear to be in the room with the sound at all.

*Kill 'em and die movies*, she always called them.

He grinned. What did that really mean? If you killed them, you didn't die. That was the point.

He'd brought a fresh glass of iced lemon

water in with him. And a plate of Eliza's macaroon cookies. They were sitting where he'd left them, side by side on his nightstand.

In the dark. Just like him.

He was waiting for Eliza's call telling him her cocktail party downstairs was over and she was up in her room for the night. With the three-hour time difference, it might be a while. Still, he'd wait to speak with her before turning on a light.

Or starting a movie.

With the lights out, he could almost pretend she was there with him.

Not that he'd ever tell her—or anyone—that he had those kinds of thoughts. Doing so would only raise emotional expectations he'd be sure to fail to live up to.

And while he was more comfortable with his wife by his side, he wasn't a sap. Or even a warmhearted guy. He was a man who'd done wrong. Who could never right that wrong. And who was spending the rest of his life serving others to pay an unpayable debt.

He was a man whose heart had ever been completely open only to one other—Liza Westin. She didn't go by Liza anymore. And he wasn't the same man who'd once loved with such trust and abandon. But he remembered…

He must have dozed off—a shock in itself—and sat upright when his cell phone pealed, catching it on the first ring.

"How'd it go?" He'd seen her caller ID with bleary eyes.

"Good!" Her upbeat tone had him on edge. Eliza wasn't one to get overly excited. Not anymore, at any rate.

But then, she'd never been to California, or been about to be on national television before, he reminded himself as he listened to her tell him about the contestants she'd met that night.

A set of identical twin sisters who co-owned a bistro in New Orleans and were both contestants. Neither had ever been married, which Eliza found hard to believe because they were both quite striking, with dark hair and eyes and infectious smiles. There was the computer genius—she called him that because of his glasses, clean-shaved face and haircut—who learned to cook from his mother when he was a kid. He worked in a bank and entered cooking contests. The *Family Secrets* qualifier was his fourth major win, but he'd won hundreds of local contests.

"You'd have hundreds of wins, too, if you'd ever entered a cooking contest before," Pierce told her, stacking their pillows together and settling back against them. Content to sit in the dark and listen to her voice for the rest of the night.

"I don't know about that." She chuckled. "All we really know is that I'm good enough to keep our guests happy."

"You won the first contest you ever entered," he reminded her dryly. "You won the audition contest to be there. That's how good you are."

"Yeah, well, you're good for me, Pierce Westin, you know that?"

He wasn't. But with her so far away, he wasn't going to let on to her that she'd caught the raw end of their deal.

She told him about a man who owned a culinary cooking school in Idaho. Another one with a popular fast food stand on the beach in Florida. And a woman from California who'd confessed that she really wasn't all that great a cook. She'd used a friend's recipe to audition for *Family Secrets* because she was trying to break into the business.

"The cooking show business? If she's not into cooking, why does she want to be in the business?" he asked, grinning. He loved it when Eliza's tone took on that slightly sarcastic note. Not quite poking fun at people, but sounding as though she were asking him, *Can you believe it?* To his knowledge, she'd never used the tone with anyone but him.

Which was probably why he liked it so much...

"I wondered the same thing," Eliza said, "but only to myself. Luckily, Mr. Beach Food Stand wasn't as reticent and was able to ask her questions and draw her out. She's hoping to break into show business," Eliza said.

Pierce wondered what she looked like, but didn't ask. He wasn't going to spend what time he had with his wife talking about another woman's appearance.

"Apparently she's spent the past two years going on auditions, and this is the first gig she got."

A gig that didn't pay unless you won. Which you weren't likely to do if you couldn't cook.

"She's hoping to get discovered when the world sees how *photogenic* she is," Eliza continued. "From what I hear, several former contestants on *Family Secrets* have been offered full-time positions on other shows. One even got a show of her own."

Pierce was ready to move on. Way on.

Eliza was photogenic. Gorgeous, in fact. And a fabulous cook. She could get offers… be lured from their quiet life. The only kind of life he could endure with a reasonable assurance of maintaining his equilibrium.

Was this the beginning of the end for them? Would this be how he lost her?

Shaking his head, he sat up. Turned on the light. Fear was a waste of time. And flights of imagination were not allowed in his world. Were not anything he could afford to indulge in. Ever.

He had a hard enough time keeping the nightmares manageable when he controlled every thought.

"You got the light on?" Eliza's voice broke into the moroseness he'd allowed to enter their room.

"Yeah."

"And the TV?"

"Not yet."

"Sleep with the TV on, Pierce, please? Don't try to prove anything…"

Sweet woman. Didn't get that proving himself was all he ever did. "I won't," he told her.

And then added, "And I will sleep with the television on."

"We've gone almost a year without a nightmare," she told him. "I'll feel awful if they start up again because I'm off having a dream moment…"

She'd done the audition as a lark. Hadn't expected to win. And had offered, many times, to turn down the opportunity when she did win.

"You have nothing to feel awful about, Eliza," he said now, his voice filled with command. "The fact that you put up with the nightmares at all makes you an angel. I won't have them preventing you from enjoying the best life has to offer you…"

Or forcing her to be less than her potential would allow, he finished silently, remembering a long-ago night when his not-yet father-in-law had come to him. Issuing the warning to stay away from his daughter.

"You are the best life has to offer me." Her voice had dropped, and if she'd been there, he'd have taken her in his arms.

God, he missed her.

"So, tell me about the rest of your day," he said, when he should have told her how much he loved her.

His breathing steadied as she talked about the magnificent mountains, the desert landscaping and all of the pristine green surrounding Palm Desert and its Siamese twin, Palm Springs. As she described the huge beds of colorful flowers on every street corner, he tried to picture her there. And wished, for a moment, that he'd agreed to go with her.

He might have gone, except for one key point neither of them had acknowledged— she'd never asked him to. From the moment she'd won the audition, the only question had been whether or not Eliza would take part in the show. Not once had she ever asked him to go with her or given him an opportunity to offer to go.

Right from the beginning she'd assumed he couldn't, citing his work schedule. And the limited time off they had. He hadn't pressed the issue. Partly because the idea of flying to California and hanging around a television studio surrounded by strangers who'd expect him to be social had left him more than a little uncomfortable. And he didn't want Eliza thinking she had to tend to him, or worry about him, while she was there.

And there'd been another risk he hadn't been willing to take—the other reason he hadn't introduced the possibility of him accompanying her to California—the chance that she might just tell him she didn't want him there.

Lord knew he wasn't an easy man to live with. Laughing didn't come as readily to him as it did her. He didn't always have a lot to say. And he was overprotective. He didn't blame her if she needed time away to be carefree and enjoy herself.

"Pierce?"

"Yeah?"

"I was…talking to Mr. Beach Food Stand tonight. His name's Jason…"

The hesitancy in her voice bothered him. More than a little. He waited to see what was coming. Picked up the TV remote and pushed On, watching as the smart television booted up.

"He was talking about his kids," she continued. "He has two of them. Two boys. Seven and nine."

With the sound muted, he scrolled through channels. Waited for mention of a wife. A mother to the boys. Wondered why beach bum Jason had caught her interest enough to talk to him about it.

"Listening to him talk…it just made me

wonder…maybe it's time we talked about our future."

Was she trying to kill him here? She was a country away, getting ready to become a television star, and she wanted to talk about the future, too?

"What about it?"

"I just…we never talk about kids…"

"What's there to talk about? I can't have them. You knew that going in."

"I know."

She was going somewhere with all of this. Pierce settled on a sports station. A rerun of a boxing match. Thought about smashing heads. Or getting his smashed.

Figured it would be preferable to this conversation.

"We agreed, before we married, that we'd both be happy with it being just the two of us," he reminded her. Because it was the basis of their union.

Not because he thought he could hold her to it.

"I know."

Pierce threw a mental punch, felt the satisfaction of it connecting. Took a harder one. And went dizzy.

She wasn't going to say any more. He knew

that. Just as he knew that she needed him to do so. To ask what was going on. To need to know why she'd brought up an already closed subject.

"Are you nervous about tomorrow?" he asked, leaving the boxing ring and landing on a news station. He couldn't hear what the announcers were saying. But headlines flashed up now and then. The stock market had taken a dip.

Something that didn't matter to him directly. Or to Eliza. Their money was safely tied up. Together.

"A little," she said, sounding subdued. "But not nearly as much as I would have been if I hadn't already met so many of the others tonight. I've just never been on camera. I hope I don't do anything embarrassing," she said.

Relaxing back against the pillows, he scrolled through more channels, stopping when he found commercials. "You aren't going to embarrass yourself," he told her. A repeat of a conversation they'd had at least a half-dozen times since she'd won her spot on *Family Secrets*. Most recently on the way to the airport. And before that, the night before when he'd lain in the exact same spot and watched her pack.

"I could trip walking across the stage to my stool."

"Which is why you packed your flat patent leather penny loafers."

"What if I sneeze?"

"Say 'excuse me.'"

"I might get tongue-tied and just stare."

"Then they'll cut that part out. This time isn't live."

"What if I get stage fright when it is live?"

"Everyone will get a chance to enjoy your beautiful face while you stare at the camera."

"I might lose, Pierce."

"Yeah."

"I don't want to let you down."

His heart was racing again, but in a way that didn't strangle him. "You couldn't possibly do anything, *anything*, that would let me down, Eliza," he said. "I love you more than life."

The words weren't clear, sticking in his throat. But he got them out. And felt guilty—like he was holding her to him when he had no right.

"I love you more than life, too. You know that, right?"

"I do." She loved the man she thought he was. The man he'd been. Not the man he'd become, whom she knew nothing about.

"Can we talk in the morning?" she asked. "Before I go?"

"If you'd like."

"I'll call your cell?"

"Yeah."

"Sleep tight, Pierce."

"You, too."

Waiting until he heard her disconnect, Pierce turned off his phone's screen but didn't put it back on the nightstand. He'd sleep with it in hand. Just like he did every other time he spent a night apart from his wife. While she was gone, that phone was their connection. And his comfort.

Not that anyone would ever, ever know that.

## CHAPTER FIVE

ELIZA DIDN'T EMBARRASS herself that first day in the studio. She enjoyed herself immensely. More than she'd ever imagined. Being around professional cooks, meeting Natasha Stevens in person, just looking around her small but state-of-the-art stainless steel culinary space made her feel like skipping around the room.

She was no longer just running a business her grandmother had left to her. Or being her father's daughter who continued to be a disappointment to him. She wasn't even just retired-medal-toting-military-man-turned-respected-cop's wife. Suddenly, and for the first time in her life, she was someone in her own right. A chef worthy of national television. Her love of cooking, her cooking talents, were her own.

As she said her goodbyes at the studio, took a cab to the airport and boarded her plane home Saturday night, Eliza had another problem on her plate. Not only did she have an illegitimate son her husband knew nothing about, not only had she given away her sterile husband's child, not only did she have to tell Pierce both of those things—but also, she now needed to win *Family Secrets*. Needed it with a burn inside that wasn't going to let her rest.

All her life she'd been looking for her way. Her own mark to make on the world. She'd been looking for her purpose. Not her parents' purpose for her. Not her grandmother's. Or her guests'. Not even Pierce's—not that he'd admit to any purpose for her but her own happiness.

Since the day she'd given away her baby, she'd accepted the fact that she'd given away any chance she'd had of knowing ultimate joy. From that point on, she'd been settling. Not allowing herself to want for more than she could have. Content to love those she loved with all of her heart, to serve them. To take her happiness through pleasing them as best she could. To avoid asking for more than she deserved. To be thankful, every day, for what she had. She'd lost her drive to be all she could be. To achieve more than what was placed before her. To pave her own way.

She sat in her window seat and stared out

into the night, scared to death that she'd just found her way and that it might implode her entire world. Scared that Pierce wasn't going to understand. Scared that she'd fail. And that she wouldn't.

And more excited than she'd been in a long, long time.

PIERCE KNEW THE SECOND he saw Eliza walking toward him that things had changed. The lightness in her step, the easy smile on her face, were like a shield around her—keeping him out. Not because she'd had fun or was enjoying the beginning of her television experience. But because, for the first time since they'd reconnected, she wasn't greeting him with a sense of relief.

Relief that they'd parted and made it back together again unscathed.

He almost let himself be convinced that he'd been imagining the difference. And yet, as the new week started—and next weekend's separation loomed—a shadow seemed to lurk over their home.

Maybe that sense of darkness, of doom, was only in him. As Pierce took the Shelby Island exit Monday, he didn't discount that possibility. His first call that day had ended in the arrest of a man for pulling his young daughter's arm out of the socket and then backhanding her when she'd cried about it. He'd gone from there to take a report from an elderly woman who suspected her children were stealing from her. And then he'd been second on the scene at a convenience store robbery. Not exactly a bright, sunshiny day. In spite of the blue skies and seventy-degree weather report.

A few hours alone with Eliza, sequestered in their portion of their antebellum home, would probably work wonders on him. She was making his favorite steak dinner. Though he'd stood in the kitchen talking to her more than once while she'd made it, he knew only that the sauce had about three kinds of mushrooms and whipped cream, and the meat itself was crusted with sea salt. And that it was the best steak he'd ever had in his mouth.

He'd be having it at least twice that week as she timed herself from refrigerator to plate in preparation for the upcoming Saturday's meat competition in Palm Desert. While the whole idea of the show was making him nervous now, he wanted her to win. And figured the steak would do it. At least enough to guarantee her a place in the competition's final round.

The inn's guests for the evening included just two separately roomed businesspeople who were regulars. Social interaction requirements would be minimal.

He was hoping for an evening walk on the beach. Or good tunes on in the exercise room while they took turns with the equipment. Something to use pent-up energy while still having her close.

Pierce had himself down for being the only one aware of any gloom when Eliza met him at the door with a very welcoming kiss. After he changed out of his uniform into jeans and a casual blue button-down shirt, she was actually the one who suggested a walk on the beach after social hour and their private dinner. So much for thinking that she'd been shielded off from him. They were as simpatico as always.

He couldn't help watching her—like a man watched a woman—while she moved about the parlor, welcoming their guests back, asking about their days. In black leggings and a longish black-and-white variegated-plaid flannel shirt belted at the waist, she was the furthest thing from nightmares he could imagine.

The meal she'd prepared was superb, as always, but it was her smile, the warmth in those brown eyes as she waited for his assessment, that really filled him up.

Dishes done, she grabbed her sweater. Pierce might have suggested they stay home instead of taking that walk, but he took her hand as they set out to Shelby Island's long stretch of public beach, content to be by her side in the cool evening air.

Right up until she said, "Can we talk?"

A rendition of "we need to talk." And everyone knew what that meant.

He braced himself.

"Of course."

"I just… I'm thinking about kids a lot these days, Pierce."

*Kids.* He'd been prepared for changes due to television stardom. A need to fly permanently away from their lives on quaint and relatively safe Shelby Island. Her eventual dissatisfaction where he was concerned.

And…kids. Her mention the other night on the phone had not been casual. When she didn't pursue it, he'd just hoped whatever question she'd had had been answered in the meantime.

There was much he might say. Much he probably should say. At least an inquiry into where she was going with this. An indication that he was willing to listen.

He walked beside her. Felt her squeeze his hand and didn't squeeze back. He also didn't let go.

"We said we'd always make space between us to talk about whatever we needed to talk about…"

He didn't disagree. Still said nothing.

They'd reached the beach. Still holding his hand, she slid out of her flip-flops, bent to pick them up, then continued to walk. He'd noticed the hand-holding most.

Took note. Breathed a little easier. And told himself that he'd get through this…whatever it was…for her. And had never been more thankful for darkness. While streetlights emblazoned patches of sidewalk and blacktop up off the beach, nothing illuminated the sand but the moon.

He could see a couple of lights bobbing out on the horizon. And noticed three or four other people sharing the beach with them. All locals, he assumed, enjoying their beach before tourists completely took over. Spring break—the official beginning of Shelby Island's tourist season—was only a few weeks off.

He knew specifically because it would be starting before Eliza finished with *Family Secrets*. She'd almost backed out of the show because of it…

"I know that you can't father children, Pierce. You're right, we talked about all that. And we agreed that just being together was enough for us…"

That was then. This was now. Things changed. People grew. Not always together.

Had Eliza's biological clock started to tick? He thought about her pregnant. She'd be beautiful big with child. And would be an incredible mother, too. The best. Any kid would be lucky to have her.

He even thought for a brief second about asking her what she thought about artificial insemination before his psyche shut down on him. As it did every single time he tried to imagine himself in any kind of situation in which he had a relationship with a child.

The shutdown was his mind's way of coping. And, according to the shrinks he'd seen in the army and again in the police department, it was a good thing. His mind's way of blocking allowed him to be tough under pressure. Made him the go-to guy. The one who got the job done where others might crack.

As long as he understood that he had to deal with whatever his mind was blocking. He always had to remember to debrief in some fashion. Or have nightmares—his mind's way of debriefing on its own.

Possibly both.

"Are you with me?" They'd walked several yards up the beach—far enough from the ocean that he could barely feel the chill coming off it. Sweating, he longed for a naked dive into the highest wave. Longed to conquer it, swim past it and let the ocean wash him clean.

"Yes."

She knew him well. He trusted her to know that he'd listen to whatever she had to say. And do his best to support her in any way he could.

She even knew about the shutdowns. She just didn't know what had triggered them in the first place. Or that there'd been one specific event that had done so.

Only a handful of people knew that. And none of them were talking. Ever. The pact was as rock-solid all those years later as it had been when it was made.

Not to save his butt. In some ways he'd just been the pawn. The one who drew the short straw.

But in the end, he'd been the perpetrator, too.

Because he'd made a choice. One he'd probably make again if faced with the situation again. And one he'd regret for the rest of his life.

And that was the crux of his predicament. You couldn't be forgiven for something you knew you'd do again.

"When we were young, you talked about wanting to be a father."

He didn't miss a physical step, had only a bit of a mental blip.

"You were going to be everything your own parents were not…"

He heard the words. Didn't relate to them. But held her hand. Because doing so was best for both of them.

"I know this is difficult ground, Pierce, considering your injury, but we need to talk about it."

The thing was, the injury he'd sustained that had rendered him incapable of fathering children—it had been just. A man who'd taken the life of a child did not deserve to have children of his own.

He walked beside her. Would remain by her side for as long as she'd have him there. He'd made her that promise.

Of course, he'd promised, when he'd left his sweet young lover all those years ago, that he'd be back for her. He'd been too much of a kid back then to understand that life changed you—sometimes beyond anything that would fit into the life you'd left.

Still…he'd come back to her. Eventually.

"What do you think about adopting?"

Her words stung his skin. Hurt his ears with their volume. Tightened around his chest.

Pierce let go of Eliza's hand.

# CHAPTER SIX

SHIVERING AS SHE walked beside Pierce up the sidewalk that led to their home, Eliza refused to give in to the self-pity that was pushing its way up her throat.

He wasn't cutting her off. Or out. He was experiencing something beyond his control. The result of having been sent, as barely a man, to fight a war that so much of the time made no sense to him. Pierce's time in the Middle East had involved full combat against insurgents. The physical injuries he'd sustained, while horrendous, weren't as horrible as the mental battles he still fought.

Her job as his spouse, his partner, was to understand his silences for what they were. He'd been up-front with her from the very beginning this time around. He'd let her know that he wasn't the man he'd been.

He still didn't get that, to her, he was. The essence of him, the heart and soul, was battered but intact. Pierce was every bit the boy he'd been. And so much more.

"I'm not asking you to bring a baby into our home, Pierce," she said softly half a block from the inn. "Or even telling you, yet, that I want to. I just wanted to talk about kids. About us not having any. About how it's hard sometimes. I wanted us to think about the fact that if we both wanted a child badly enough, we could check into adoption…"

She'd been thinking about it a lot. Anytime her brain hadn't been filled with her son and *Family Secrets* and…Pierce. Her visit to the agency…remembering how it had felt, for those few brief moments, to be a mother. Thinking about the family who got to have a baby of their own through her. Picturing her and Pierce on the receiving side, instead of the losing side—no, not losing, giving. They'd been on the giving side.

For so long, ever since Pierce had come back and she'd known about his injury, she'd resigned herself to being half of a childless couple. Had thought it was her fate for having given away her baby. Pierce's obvious struggle with his infertility had just been the final seal on the decision…

"I don't want a child."

They were the first words he'd spoken in almost half an hour.

"It's just…well…when you married Bonita…it was because of her son. You said you married her because her son needed a father and you wanted to be there for him. Whether you think you were a good father or not, you still wanted to be one…" She was rambling. And he knew her well enough to figure out that she was upset. If enough of him was there with her to notice.

A few yards from home, he stopped, turned her to look at him. "I understand if you feel different, Eliza, but please hear me. I do not want a child."

His words were a death knell to her future.

The deep emotion shining in his eyes, overflowing with all of the things he couldn't say, held her heart tightly, passionately bound with his.

"No." INSTANTLY AWAKE, Eliza lay frozen. She hadn't dreamed the fierce growl.

Was Pierce in the bed with her?

His body wasn't touching hers, and she was afraid to move to find out if he was there. She hardly breathed but couldn't hear his breath.

Pierce wasn't a heavy sleeper. Waking to

find herself alone wasn't uncommon. When his demons were doing their worst, he'd get up and roam. Sometimes just in their suite. Sometimes outside on the grounds. Depended on how much air he needed to clear his mind.

Some nights he turned on the television and lay awake watching sitcom reruns. At first, she'd thought maybe the sound of the television had woken her. But she could tell by the lack of light and shadows on the wall that the TV wasn't on.

"Nooooo." The sound came again. Fiercer this time. And then it was a howl. A wail. No longer in doubt as to its origin, Eliza still didn't move. Her husband was in a hell she couldn't share. But if she startled him, he might mistakenly take her there.

Pierce had never hit her—or even swung her way—during one of his nighttime episodes, but he'd insisted that she go to counseling with him before she'd ever spent a night in his bed. She knew that it wasn't impossible that she could inadvertently be hurt.

She also knew it wasn't likely to happen. Not after all these years. Pierce was diligent with his mental and emotional awareness.

So much so that they'd gone so long without an episode that she'd thought perhaps he was over them.

Had hoped that her love, their life together on the island, gave him enough peace to keep the demons at bay.

It would help if he worked in a field other than the dangerous one he'd chosen. Dealing with thugs and break-ins all day was too reminiscent of battling insurgents. But it had been decided, with professional input, that in Pierce's case, being out on the streets actually helped him work out some of the panic bottled up inside him. He was more at peace when he was doing something to help make the world a safer place.

The bed started to shake and so, then, did Eliza. Alarmed, she held her breath. He'd never convulsed before. Was he having a seizure?

Willing to risk a fist in the face if it meant saving her husband's life, Eliza shot up and turned toward Pierce, ready to cram her fingers in his mouth and hold on to his tongue if need be—something she'd read you had to do to prevent someone having a seizure from swallowing their tongue. Nothing she had any real knowledge about at all.

Before she'd even touched his shoulder, she

stopped. His back was to her. And now that she could see him, she knew he wasn't convulsing.

He was sobbing. Leaning over him, careful not to disturb him, she saw his eyes were closed, but his face was soaked with tears. He was sobbing in his sleep. Something he had never done before.

She'd been told not to wake him when he was in the middle of a nightmare. But how could she sit there and watch her husband's anguish?

She didn't care if he lashed out, if he hit her. But if he did, he'd never forgive himself.

So Eliza lay back down. She closed her eyes and willed her breathing to an even cadence.

And she sent every ounce of love she possessed across the mattress to her husband.

She'd caused this.

It had been either the show, or the talk of children, or both. But there was no doubt in her mind that she'd done this.

Nothing else had changed in their lives. The show. And the kid.

And she didn't think the show had sent him back to hell. He didn't like her to be away on her own, but he'd known about the show for weeks. And had slept great the first night she'd been back. For that matter, he'd said he hadn't had even a bad dream while she'd been gone.

But tonight, when she'd tried to open up the idea of adoptive children to him, he'd started to blip on her. Give her that blank stare that she'd grown to hate. The one that said he was off someplace in his mind where she couldn't go.

Why had even the mention of him as a father set him off like this?

She'd promised herself that she'd tell Pierce they'd had a son before her flight back to Palm Desert on Friday. Telling him had been her primary goal for the week. She wasn't going back if she didn't tell him.

As she lay there, listening to her husband grieve, she made another decision. She wasn't going to tell Pierce about their son until she knew why talk of kids had elicited such a strongly negative response.

Which meant that she also couldn't call Mrs. Carpenter with the okay to release her information to her son in the event that he came looking for her again.

And that opened the door to another possibility…that after a second try, if there even was one, the boy would lose interest in her. There was a good chance he wouldn't come back a third time.

And, based on the papers she'd signed, there was no chance at all that she could ever find him if he didn't.

Pierce quieted. Sometimes his nightmares woke him. Sometimes they didn't. Sometimes they haunted him for days or even weeks. Sometimes he didn't even remember having them.

She'd tell him about the episode. Knowing what was going on inside him was all a part of his accountability to his own health. She wouldn't rob him of that right.

But she needed time to herself first. To figure out what she was going to do with the mess she'd made of her life.

Pierce had paid too high a price already for doing nothing more than serving his country. He'd already lost so much. He wasn't going to lose her, too.

It was a promise she'd made to him. And one she'd made to herself. She'd failed her baby. She wasn't going to fail his father.

By the time Pierce's sobs quieted, Eliza's cheeks were wet with tears.

*Family Secrets*, being a chef, glitz, glamour, awards and the bright lights of television were so far distant, she wasn't sure the whole thing hadn't just been a dream.

Well, she *was* sure. It wasn't just a dream. She could feel the win pushing at her. Needing her as badly as she needed it. But maybe a dream was all it would be. All it could ever be. As her eyes closed and she finally drifted back to sleep, it was with the thought that she'd call Natasha Stevens in the morning and withdraw herself from the competition. From the show.

She cried about that, too. With sobs that shook her body.

But she didn't change her mind.

The family secrets she'd already kept were more than she could handle.

PIERCE KNEW, AS soon as his gaze met Eliza's in their bathroom mirror as they brushed their teeth Tuesday morning, that the fog in which he'd awoken hadn't been because of a deep sleep.

He swore. She nodded.

He'd had another nightmare. After going almost a year without them.

Her look of compassion practically brought him to his knees. He didn't deserve her. And had to find a way to tell her so. To talk of things he'd sworn never to mention. And hadn't. Not to the multitude of professionals who'd helped him over the years. Not to his superior officers. Not even to those who'd made the pact with him.

He'd tell her. But not that day. Probably not any day soon. Someday, though.

After her television stint was through.

She deserved this chance. Deserved whatever came of it. And if it took her from him... she needed to never know the truth about the man she'd loved so purely.

His need to get to work, and hers to serve their guests' breakfast, precluded any conversation that morning. But Pierce came home Tuesday night prepared to do a better job of communicating with his wife before he laid his head down to sleep again. He had to be responsible about the nightmares, stay diligent. To protect her.

And he knew exactly from whence this one had come.

They'd had a third check-in to the inn that day. A woman who was writing a piece of fiction that would feature the B and B. In exchange, Eliza had given her free room and board. She'd been so excited about the opportunity when the author had first contacted her.

Seemed like ages ago now. More than a month before she'd auditioned for, and won, her spot on *Family Secrets*.

If nothing else, the television show was giving her more publicity than she could ever have hoped. The inn was already booked through the summer but was starting to fill up through the fall and into Christmas.

"I just got my first booking for next summer," Eliza told him as she met him at the back kitchen door when he came in from work on Tuesday. She was grinning.

He could feel her joy.

And see the sadness lurking in her eyes, too.

"Can we talk?" he asked, setting in stone the decision he'd made that morning. Several times throughout the day. And again that evening on his way home. "Tonight? After we're through out there?" He nodded toward the door that led into the portion of their home that was open to the public.

He didn't like the way she studied him, eye to eye, but he withstood it.

"Of course," she said. And then she kissed him. Obliterating the world for just a moment in the way only she could. Giving him a different kind of mental blip. One that he could gladly succumb to for the rest of his life.

Life with Eliza required much from him. He'd give everything and more to be with her.

So he socialized with their guests, thankful to be able to look across the room and see her beautiful smile. He carried a box of the author's files up to her room for her. Cleared empty dishes and ran the vacuum in the parlor after the crowd had dissipated. He even stopped by the library to chat with one of the businessmen who liked to spend an hour or two in the evenings sitting in one of the antique leather wing chairs, reading from the collection Eliza's grandmother had amassed.

And when the house had settled, he joined his wife in the kitchen. Eliza was putting finishing touches on breakfast and preparing hors d'oeuvres for the two nights she'd be gone over the upcoming weekend. She'd given Margie a couple of days off to make up for working all weekend, and had spent her day cleaning and refreshing.

"Can I help?"

He couldn't blame her for the surprised look on her face. Pierce's kitchen skills were nil. Boiling water was debatable.

"I can chop," he told her, meeting her gaze head-on. She'd barely slept the night before. He could tell by the shadows under her eyes.

And so, with her careful instruction, he took up knife and onion and set to work, slicing it into precise cubes. And then celery.

He'd come in to have their talk.

They worked in total silence.

But it was a peaceful silence, he told himself. Companionable.

Silence was right up his alley. But it wasn't like Eliza not to fill in his gaps.

Words ran through his mind. Slowly at first. And then more rapidly. What to say? How much to say? When to say it?

He owed her. So much. For the previous night. For the past. And for the happily-ever-after he probably wouldn't be able to give her.

"I did marry Bonita because I thought I could be the father her son clearly needed." Celery stalks, cut into thin strips, took turns beneath his blade. Quick. Precise. Sharp cuts that left no strings.

He'd had some asinine plan back then that it would be his way of atoning for his sins. That he could give back some of what he'd taken. As Eliza had stated the night before, he had, at one time, thought that he'd make a great dad. Had wanted kids of his own almost as badly as he'd wanted Eliza.

Standing at the stove across the counter from him, she'd been stirring. Her hand still on the big metal spoon, she seemed to freeze, her spoon standing upright in the pan.

Pierce had more to say. He just wasn't sure what. He chopped. And eventually she started to stir again, too.

They finished their preparation, classical music playing softly in the background. Did the dishes side by side. And went into their room.

He brushed his teeth while she washed her face. But when she was about to undress and get ready for bed, Pierce took her hand, led her over to the chintz-covered stool at her antique dressing table. He lit candles. Put on Beethoven. Turned off the lights.

And drew her a lavender-scented bath.

Tonight wasn't about him. It was about making it up to her—all of the things she'd lost because of him, the things she continued to sacrifice.

It was about showing her the things he couldn't say.

As his lovely wife sat on the edge of the tub, still in her robe, waiting for the bubble bath he'd started for her to fill, he slipped out to pour two glasses of iced lemon water. Placing them on one of her silver serving trays, he added a small dish of milk chocolate shavings—Eliza's favorite indulgence—and, for himself, a couple of her chocolate cream cookies.

She looked up when he returned, tray in hand, fully dressed in his dark blue pants, shirt and slip-on boat shoes.

"You'll stay with me?" she asked. Even now, she welcomed him.

Pierce swallowed. Shook his head. Set down the tray and handed her a water and the plate of chocolate.

"I wish you'd at least get comfortable," she said, testing the water in the tub with a frown.

He was scaring her. The last thing he'd meant to do.

So he went to change into the blue chenille robe she'd bought him for Christmas, and sank to the floor of the bathroom, his back against the wall.

That was Pierce. Always with his back to the wall. Or against a wall.

Still in her robe, she'd turned off the water, but he knew she wouldn't get in until he'd said what he had to say.

"Two things," he said, keeping his voice low as he invaded the peace with which he'd purposely surrounded her. "First, it took less than a year of marriage for me to know that the man I am today, the man I became in the Middle East, could not ever be a father."

Her chocolate sat untouched on the side of the double-wide cast iron tub—a luxury he suspected had been built in more modern times to emulate a tub of old. It had been holding court in the largely decorated with roses room the first time he'd visited Eliza.

"The responsibility, the constant need to be one step ahead, knowing that someone was relying on me for safety and security on a constant basis, being in charge of someone who could not always fend for himself…it triggered nightmare after nightmare. No matter what I did, how hard I tried, how much counseling I sought…the boy triggered nightmares."

He knew why. His counselor hadn't, not specifically. Because he hadn't told him. But the PTSD professional had known enough.

"Last night was because of me," Eliza said. "Because I wanted to talk about kids."

"It's not your fault, Eliza. And you need to talk about what you want and need. You have a right to. And our marriage needs you to do so. Our relationship needs it." The words flowed freely when he was dealing with her. Loving Eliza was the one thing that had always come easy to him.

Too easy for her own good.

"And we need to deal with the fact that I am not a man who can have kids with you. Not in any way. Biological or not."

Surrounded by roses, cast iron heart shapes adorned with roses, wallpaper depicting rose trellises, he felt like he was spewing ash on her beauty.

She wasn't saying anything. But watching her expression, he knew she was thinking. Knew, too, that he had to nip any hope in the bud.

"It's not just the nightmares," he told her. He'd known that morning that he was going to have to give her more. Because they were dealing with so much more.

He wasn't going to break the pact. Not yet, anyway. He couldn't predict the outcome and was not going to get in the way of her reaching for her dreams. But she deserved the truth he could give her.

"I was a terrible father," he told her. "Jeremiah thought I hated him. He was a good boy. Got good grades. Was respectful. I truly cared about the kid, but my silences scared him. So I'd try to talk and end up saying the wrong thing." Because he'd had nothing to say. "I don't have the ability to nurture a child. One night when I got home, Jeremiah ran up to me and threw his arms around my waist. I immediately dislodged them and backed up. And when I saw what I'd done, saw the hurt on his face, I still couldn't hug him."

He shuddered inside just thinking about that night.

"I was already sleeping in my own room by then, behind a locked door, because of the nightmares. I had to struggle, every day, for patience with Jeremiah. Listening to his boyish chatter, I'd go on a mind freeze and hope that he finished soon." The boy would talk and Pierce would see all of the ways in which he was setting the kid up for hurt. For disappointment. Setting himself up for failure. And know that he couldn't do anything to prevent any of them.

Jeremiah's innocence had not belonged in his world, and he'd known it. Or rather, he hadn't belonged in Jeremiah's innocent world.

He belonged on the streets. Busting criminals. It was what he was good at. The way he could contribute good to the world.

"It got to the point that he refused to be alone with me," Pierce told her the worst of it. "That's when Bonita and I decided to divorce."

He should have left months before then. He'd just hated to walk out on another woman.

And he hadn't wanted to leave that boy.

"Pierce?"

Eliza's soft tone drew his gaze. Her eyes should have been showing him…disappointment…at the very least. Instead, they were glistening with…him.

She'd sat in his darkness.

She loved him anyway. Still.

## CHAPTER SEVEN

ELIZA TOOK A later flight on Friday. She had no exploring to do. Her visit to California had one purpose—competing on *Family Secrets*. Getting the win she so desperately needed. A personal reinforcement that would give her the strength to do the things she needed to do for those who loved her. For those she loved.

Her son, finding him, was on hold. Telling Pierce about the boy who might or might not even agree to meet them couldn't be done just on her own timetable. She had to consider her husband. Care for him.

Love him.

She had to follow through on the commitment she'd made to him. To prove to herself that she didn't always let down the people in her life.

After her flight was delayed in Denver, she missed the car that had been arranged to take her to the hotel and had to take a cab. The lobby was like a morgue. Just she and the desk clerk. The one bellhop on duty was away from his stand, and rather than wait for him, she opted to take her own bag up to her room. One roller. She could handle it.

At just before midnight, her internal clock thought it was almost three in the morning. For Pierce, it was. But she called him anyway.

He was awake. But he sounded drowsy.

"I love you, babe."

"I'm glad you're safe." His words warmed her.

And yet, she was excited to be where she was. Which gave her a huge case of the guilts.

She told him to get some rest. He wished her good luck the next day.

And disconnected the call.

Pierce was pulling away from her. She could feel it. Ever since she'd mentioned adoption, ever since his nightmare…

Getting into bed, Eliza willed herself to sleep. Willed herself to allow herself a win the next day. She loved her life. Loved Shelby Island. Loved the inn. And loved Pierce.

Truly and desperately.

How could she possibly need, or even want, more than she had? She'd long ago accepted that she'd never raise a child.

Never be a mother.

But being a chef worthy of a win on a nationally syndicated reality TV show? She wanted it. More, she needed it. Needed a reason to feel proud of herself. Needed to know she had a personal self. She needed it so badly she couldn't make herself quit and go home where she belonged. And hoped that she wasn't jinxing all of the good in her life by clinging to the chance to prove something to herself.

Hoped that she wasn't being selfish.

And knew that she was. She wasn't calling the agency to tell them to release her contact information to her son. She would. Just not yet. She wasn't telling Pierce he'd fathered a son.

And for the next four or five weekends, she was leaving Pierce, their home, her guests, in pursuit of a dream.

PIERCE WORKED A security detail on Saturday—having put in for the extra work when he knew Eliza would be gone. And then, instead of heading home, or out to fish, which was what he'd told Eliza he thought he'd do, he went downtown to Charleston police headquarters and knocked on the door of the shrink on duty.

A woman he'd seen in the past. But hadn't visited in more than a year.

They chatted. But only long enough for him to report his recent nightmare—to follow protocol. He wasn't going to put other lives at risk.

Long enough for her to shrug and tell him that she wished more of the officers she saw were as healthily aware of their mental states as Pierce was. Doing what they did on the streets, seeing what they saw, it came with a price.

Pierce had already been paying the price before he'd become a civilian cop. He figured he was a good fit for the job because it couldn't take his soul like it did a lot of guys'. He'd already lost his.

But he was going to make certain that no one else paid his price with him. For him. Or because of him.

THE FIRST THING Eliza noticed when she entered her on-set kitchen Saturday just before noon—about the time Pierce would be enjoying his midafternoon fishing at home—was that the dried porcini mushrooms she'd ordered for the beef fillet dish she was preparing were nowhere to be found.

Taping didn't start for half an hour. She didn't panic. Or even worry. She just set out to find her mushrooms. When they didn't turn up in any of the group storage cupboards, she started asking other contestants to check their kitchens.

The mushrooms didn't turn up. But another contestant who needed them did. Grace Hargraves, the eighty-one-year-old contestant from Utah who'd rented a condominium in Palm Desert for the duration of the show.

"There are cans of mushroom soup in the general supply closet," Eliza told her. "We can rinse the soup through strainers and at least get bits and pieces of mushrooms for flavoring." Her mind raced with other ideas.

The crumpled look on Grace's wrinkled face looked more lost than determined. "The porcinis were my secret ingredient," she said. Her kitchen, in the same pod of four as Eliza's, was two down from her. Beach Boy was stationed between them and hadn't yet made it to the stage.

Various techies, from lighting and sound to camera assistants, were busily preparing for the taping. Other than for the final show, *Family Secrets* had no live studio audience. One family member or guest, with previous approval, could sit in the audience or watch from the monitors in the green room.

So far, on their side of the stage, it was just Eliza and Grace. And various young men and women scurrying around without even appearing to see either one of them.

Eliza called out to the young man who was closest to them. Though he probably had something important to do, he seemed least rushed as he appeared in her peripheral vision, hovering on the edge of the stage.

Daniel Trevino, his name badge read as he approached them. Eliza quickly apprised the blue-eyed blond of the situation, with Grace piping in, her worried tone leaving no doubt as to her angst. Saying he was new to the show but would go find someone who would know what to do, Daniel hurried off.

Ten minutes before they were due to start taping, the other contestants were called to take their positions on stage. They all had mic checks. And Natasha Stevens, the show's host, stopped by to speak with Grace and Eliza. She'd sent Daniel, a recently hired high school student, to the closest grocer for more porcinis.

"They have to be soaked," Grace said, her voice sounding a lot stronger than she looked at the moment. "Half an hour. They have to soak for half an hour."

*In room-temperature water,* Eliza said to herself. General instructions called for hot-water soaking, but she'd discovered that room temperature left far more flavor in the mush-rooms.

"I know." Natasha was nodding.

"I've got my stroganoff timed down to the minute. If I don't start soaking when you say go, I won't finish in time."

Eliza watched the exchange, plan B already firmly in place. She'd strain the soup. Still had the eight ounces of mixed mushrooms she'd ordered. And would add more whip-ping cream sauce to the finished medallions to make up for the lack of mushroom. Her se-cret ingredient was the sea salt crusting the outside of the steak, anyway…

"The best I can do at this point is to assure both of you that the judges will be made aware of what happened here." Natasha, gorgeous as usual with her long auburn curls flowing over her tight black tunic dress, did not look happy. "My shoppers each signed off on their orders…" There were two of them, one for each pod, and then in preparation for the day's show, each checked off the other's lists, as well. "And Angela checked your kitchens as well, first thing this morning." Angela had been Natasha's stage manager from her very first show several years before.

Grace nodded. And was shaking her head, her shoulders hunched, as she made her way back to her kitchen. Being on a cooking show was Grace's lifelong dream, the older woman had told Eliza when they'd run into each other, literally, in the green room the week before. Eliza could relate. She wanted this win so badly she could hardly focus on anything else at the moment.

With permission from Natasha, Eliza started straining cans of mushroom soup. It was a poor substitute for the ingredient that should have been provided. Neither her dish nor Grace's would be as good with the cheap substitution, but she strained enough for both of them.

And was nearly sick with relief when, just before Natasha gave them the command to start, Daniel showed up with their porcinis. The young man might look like a stereotypical California surfer dude, but he'd come through in a pinch.

Eliza hoped that Natasha rewarded him accordingly.

PIERCE WATCHED THE show while propped up on his and Eliza's pillows in their bedroom. Margie and the five other rooms' worth of guests they had with them that weekend were all huddled around the TV in the entertainment room at the back of the inn. Margie had asked him to join them, but understood when he shook his head. She was as close to a sister as any woman Pierce had ever known. And truly didn't seem to mind covering for him when he needed solitude in a home almost constantly filled with guests.

She filled a plate for him of assorted homemade cookies and even had his glass of iced lemon water already prepared when he came in from vacuuming the parlor after the evening's social hour—an event that had taken place an hour earlier that night in deference to the timing of the West Coast show.

Pierce already knew the outcome. Eliza had called him before she'd boarded the shuttle headed back to the hotel. Margie and the others didn't know that, though.

He watched with the diligence of an officer on a stakeout. Noticed every aspect of every contestant as the camera panned across them in their kitchens, studied character giveaways when one or the other was on close-up. Listened to their tones of voice when clips from the previous weekend's introduction session were dubbed into the current show.

On a commercial, he got up to refill his water.

And was right back in place, intent, when the show returned to the airwaves. He caught defensive glances. Worried frowns. A toe that tapped almost constantly.

And his wife—looking more desirable than he'd ever seen her as she talked about her ultimate dream of achieving national recognition as a professional, award-winning chef. A dream she hadn't even dared let herself think could ever be a reality. He'd helped her choose the black leggings and short plaid flannel dress with the wide black belt at the waist. He hated the shoes she'd purchased to go with it—platform sandals that put her a good four inches off the ground. But had to admit that they made her calves look good. Darn good.

Taking a bathroom break during the next commercial, Pierce ran cold water over his face. Avoided the mirror that covered the wall in front of their sinks. And thought about opening a bottle of wine. He didn't, of course. He and Eliza rarely drank, and if he opened a bottle just for himself, the rest would go to waste.

It felt good to think about it, though. To know he could if he needed to.

And when the last ten minutes hit, he was back in place, watching everything unfold. In spite of knowing what was coming, he stopped breathing while the second runner-up was called. As though Eliza could have made a mistake. Or the show had been retaped.

No, she wasn't called. The contestant was Grandma Grace with her porcini-and-beef stroganoff. The fiery-haired hostess talked some more. About judging standards, giving the credentials of that week's judges, including the ten-year-old girl who was the daughter of a local restaurant owner. One of the *Family Secret* trademarks, Pierce had learned, was that every single competition included one juvenile judge. The show was based on secret family recipes. Natasha's take, as she explained before she announced the first runner-up, was that if the kids didn't like it, it wasn't a family recipe.

The trick was to have recipes that stood out enough to impress food critics and children alike.

Hand to his chin, Pierce watched as Luigi

Procopio, owner of the Idaho Culinary Institute, won first runner-up for his cheese-stuffed, syrup-braised pork chops. He listened as the man blubbered about his surprise, and had to admit that the middle-aged chef seemed genuine in his shock.

Had to wonder, too, how Procopio had come to own an institute dedicated to cooking if his own abilities took him by such surprise. Wondered if the man's students knew he had such little faith in his abilities.

At least Pierce did what he knew he was good at...

He'd have gone on wondering about anything he could if his gaze hadn't been glued on the dark-haired, dark-eyed woman standing between two of her fellow contestants in the line left of those who hadn't yet been called. In the line of those who were hoping their name would be the next one.

The tension in Eliza's shoulders might not have been noticeable to most of the show's viewers, but Pierce saw it. The lines around her lips as they tightened when Natasha said that the time had come to announce the winner for week one of the current contest on *Family Secrets*.

Eliza's parents were watching. Pierce had

called them himself to remind them. She'd be hurt if they watched it after it aired.

The call had been brief. But cordial.

Natasha talked about the show's four main competitions. About the final round that would take place during the fifth week, assuming one contestant didn't win all four main competitions. She talked about the national distribution of one recipe from the overall winner—whether it was in frozen form, or some other packaged rendition.

Afraid Eliza might turn blue right there on the stage, Pierce sat up. It wasn't the first time he'd drawn on his wife's tension, taken it upon himself.

But it was the first time he'd done so after the fact.

Pausing at the microphone, Natasha glanced over the line of hopeful-looking contestants under the bright lights above the stage. And then she held up a card. Opened it.

Knowing his expression was grim, Pierce waited while the host looked at the card and said...

"Eliza Westin."

## CHAPTER EIGHT

PIERCE WAS WAITING for Eliza as she came into the portion of the terminal open to the public. Instead of standing back against the wall as usual, he left his position to meet her right in front of everyone, picking her up off her feet as he hugged her.

She didn't see the roses he'd brought with him until he put her down, barely able to see them then through the tears in her eyes.

She'd celebrated a little bit the night before. With the twins from New Orleans. Only a couple of years older than her, they were fascinating. As was their relationship with each other—best friends from the womb.

Their independence and the joy that seemed to bubble out of them.

And she'd come home with a bigger weight on her shoulders than she'd taken with her when she'd left.

Pierce had been properly excited for her when she'd called him to tell him she'd won.

And again when he'd called her after he'd watched her win. While he had her on the line he'd headed into the entertainment room with an inn full of guests and Margie, and they'd all congratulated her.

He'd been in a good mood when she'd called him that morning to let him know she was at her gate. And still, her spirits had plummeted as the plane had descended into Charleston.

Which made no sense at all.

She'd give up the win, the show, even being a chef, if it meant losing Pierce again. She knew that hands down.

So why wasn't she as happy about her win at home as she'd been when she'd still been in California?

Eliza had no answers and, over the next week, wouldn't let herself dwell on anything but the inn, their guests and Pierce. She prepared her special cobbler, made with maple syrup, apple juice and cherries, among other things, for Pierce one night—a trial one for the dessert competition in California on Saturday.

And she thought constantly about ways she might broach the subject of their son with Pierce. She couldn't not do so. The boy had made an inquiry. Chances were he'd merely been curious. But there was also a chance that he needed them.

Regardless, Eliza couldn't pass up the chance to be in the presence of her son. To look him in the eye. To know what he looked like. To see the young man he'd grown up to be...

Every morning she told herself she'd talk to Pierce that night. Every evening she had the distinct impression she should put off doing so. Pierce wasn't having nightmares or exhibiting any other signs that he was struggling any more than usual with PTSD issues. If anything, he seemed more social with the guests. But he also seemed...distant.

He kissed her good-night, but other than her first night home, he hadn't pulled her body to his all week. He'd rolled over and gone to sleep.

Or pretended to do so.

And he hadn't called as often during the day, either.

"What's wrong?" she finally asked him Thursday evening as they sat at their little table in the private eat-in kitchen they rarely used. Because she was in the big kitchen during the day, she generally prepared and plated their meals there, to carry them into the dining room in their quarters.

That night she'd made breakfast for dinner since they'd missed breakfast the past Sunday due to her absence. And would be missing the next four, too. Unless she happened to win all four competitions. Then there would be no need for a fifth, champion round. She would just be it.

She wasn't going to think about that, though. Not then, at any rate. "You've been different this week," she said to Pierce when he answered her question with silence.

He looked at her. Straight in the eye. An acknowledgment that she was right. And continued to eat his omelet, his fork in one hand, a piece of sweet toast in the other.

"You're making me nervous," she said. He'd asked her always to be honest with him. Doing so now seemed more important than ever.

He chewed. Watched her. Then shook his head and, putting down his toast, took a hold of her hand as he said, "I love you, Eliza. I always have your back. You never, ever need to be nervous around me." He was looking her right in the eye.

And just like that, her worry dissipated.

Her heart opened. And filled, like it always did when she let Pierce inside. Like it always had. Since she was barely into her teens.

PIERCE KNEW WHAT he had to do. He'd been getting himself ready all week. Preparing for the internal battle that he was determined to win. He wouldn't let his own need weigh Eliza down. He was not going to be the spouse her father had projected he'd be all those years ago—the one who held her back.

He'd known going into the marriage that there would most likely come a time when Eliza would be happier without him than with him. He'd hoped not. He'd have prayed not if he'd thought anyone would have heard him.

Putting down his fork, he sat back. She would leave again the next morning. His time was up.

"I've been thinking about what you wanted to talk about last week," he said. A slow start. He had to keep this to the point. "Kids," he said to that end.

She raised one eyebrow, and the hope that spread across her face was another nail in the coffin he'd been lying in for years.

"You're thirty-three," he said next. And hated the second stumble. She knew how old they both were. Though the thirty-five years hanging on him left him feeling like an old man. "You have a right to children, Eliza," he said. Finally. On track. "And in some ways, this is even more important— they have a right to you."

The rest of his food sat untouched. No longer hungry, he pushed the plate away.

Her eyes widened. She wasn't eating, either.

"I'm not going to stand in your way."

She smiled. Then, cocking her head in the way she did when she was trying to understand something, she said, "Wait a minute."

He waited.

"Are you telling me that, at some point in the future, you'd maybe be open to considering adopting a child?"

"Absolutely not." He spoke before thinking. His response would have been the same if he had thought, just more gentle.

The light in her eyes died out. "Are you telling me you're leaving me?"

"Absolutely not." Another gut response. And he wasn't. "I'm not going to leave you, Liza. You have to know that by now."

"Then what…"

"I just want you to know that if…or when…

you're ready to move on, I won't stand in your way." His throat tightened in a sensation he didn't recognize. And couldn't abide.

By God, was he going to…

No. He was fine. Any tears Pierce might have had, or shed, had long since gone into dry rot.

"You're giving me permission to leave you," she said.

He nodded.

Whatever he'd been expecting, it hadn't been Eliza stabbing a piece of omelet with her fork and putting it, as delicately as ever, in her mouth.

She chewed. Swallowed. Took a bite of toast.

"You haven't finished your dinner," she said, pointing at his plate with her extended pinky finger.

So…she was…calm. Completely. Because she'd been thinking along the same lines? Was already aware that she needed to move on?

Because of that *ultimate dream* of hers to *achieve national recognition as a professional, award-winning chef.*

Coupled with the fact that he hadn't even been able to handle a mention of children without having a flippin' nightmare.

To say he wasn't hungry would sound truculent. Childish. So Pierce pulled his plate back in front of him and ate.

ELIZA DIDN'T KNOW whether to smile or cry. So she ate.

She and Pierce were quite a pair. Mucked up and so in love, too. That he'd offer to stand by while she walked away from him was not a shock to her.

Of course he would. Pierce would no more hold her back than he'd stick a gun to her head.

He also didn't want her staying with him out of guilt. Or duty. She knew that, too.

What she didn't know was how to give them both what they wanted.

What they needed.

She knew one thing, though. "I am not going to walk away," she told him as she finished the last bite of food and set her fork down in the middle of the empty plate. "There is nothing this life could offer me that would be worth losing you over."

"Eliza, I won't have you…"

Shaking her head, she put a finger to his lips. "You didn't live inside me for those years without you, Pierce. You don't know how half-alive I felt. But I remember every day. Every time something good happened and I'd think about how much better it would have been if you were there to share it. And when bad things happened and I'd wish for your arms around me. Every time I saw a couple. Or went on a date and couldn't find a way around you. All of them, Pierce. They taught me all I ever need to know where you're concerned. I told you when I was fifteen that you were the love of my life. I was a kid, Pierce. One who maybe shouldn't have been able to know something like that, but I did. And I do."

The words were driven from her. Pure truth.

A truth that was at odds with the circumstances their lives had dealt them. Circumstances that were looming, escalating, moving in. There was a chasm between what he could handle and what she had to handle. She couldn't guarantee they wouldn't fall into it. She just knew that she wouldn't be the one to walk away.

He gave her a slow nod, never breaking eye contact, as she leaned over to kiss him.

# CHAPTER NINE

ON FRIDAY EVENING, Pierce was sitting at the antique leather-topped desk Eliza's grandmother had set up in the foyer of the inn to use for check-ins. They had one more guest due and Margie was busy in the kitchen, putting food on silver trays for social hour.

Picking up a brochure from the Plexiglas holder gracing one corner of the desk, he read about things to do in Charleston.

And thought about his wife with hours to kill in California. She'd taken the earlier flight again that week because she'd reached her destination so late the week before.

He hadn't asked her what she was going to do to fill the extra time. She'd tell him if she wanted him to know.

The bar in the parlor was already set, wine open—one red, one white—bottled water on ice, homemade sweet tea in the pitcher. Unsweetened tea and coffee packets were stocked by the single-serving coffeemaker.

Four rooms were filled that night. All six on Saturday. There'd be much to do. And there he sat. Waiting to deliver a key. They had three new check-ins that day. Two were already upstairs. One was late.

The inn's phone's ringing startled him. He didn't usually man the desk. Or take reservations. All thoughts of getting it right fled when he recognized that area code on the caller display. California.

He grabbed the receiver so quickly he fumbled it. "Hello?"

Eliza was in trouble. If not, she'd have been calling his cell.

"Rose Harbor," he said, using the proper salutation when there was no response to his urgent greeting.

His words were followed by a very distinct click. Someone had been on the line. And then hung up.

*Why?*

ELIZA DROVE TO Anaheim again that Friday afternoon. Instead of waiting outside to watch the comings and goings, she parked, walked inside immediately and asked to see Mrs. Carpenter.

She was told to have a seat in the empty

waiting room but didn't have to wait long. Mrs. Carpenter came to get her herself. Showed her back to the same office they'd been in two weeks before.

"It's good to see you." The woman's soft tones were as Eliza had remembered. And something that had been doing somersaults inside her for more than a week calmed.

Eliza nodded. Wondering if the woman would feel the same after she heard what Eliza had come to tell her.

"Has he been here?" were the first words that actually came out of her mouth. And she was appalled.

"I can't tell you that."

"He has, hasn't he?"

"I can't tell you that." The woman's bland but kind expression didn't change. Neither did her posture. There wasn't even a twitch at the side of her mouth.

Eliza needed to know.

But finding out was not why she'd come.

"My husband is his father."

That wasn't why she'd come, either.

Mrs. Carpenter, as professionally turned out as she'd been the first time they'd met, in a blue suit instead of gray this time, folded hands with manicured and polished nails on top of her desk.

What a mess her life had become.

"He suffers from PTSD," she said next.

The counselor's perfectly shaped eyebrows drew together. "He doesn't know he has a son, does he?"

Eliza's eyes filled with tears as she shook her head.

THE FIRST THING Pierce did, after hitting the automatic callback key only to have the number ring incessantly without going to voice mail, was boot up the computer Eliza used for check-ins and connect to the internet. Within seconds he was staring at a reverse phone lookup site. He typed the number he'd read on caller ID. And tapped his fingers while he waited.

He read the results that popped up, his heart pounding.

The call had come from a landline in Palm Desert. A private landline.

That's when he did what he should have done to begin with. He dialed Eliza's cell.

She picked up on the second ring.

"Pierce? Is everything okay?" They'd just talked a couple of hours before. And had planned to speak again when she was in her room for the night.

"That's what I want to know," he said, barking a little more harshly than he might otherwise have done. "We just got a call on the Rose Harbor line from Palm Desert. We got disconnected and they didn't call back. I thought it was the hospital. Where are you? Are you okay?"

What kind of cop was he? Babbling and exploding with questions, rather than calmly waiting for his wife to reassure him.

But…

He could let her walk away. He couldn't bear it if she was taken from him…

Knowing that it was no less than he deserved.

"I'm fine, Pierce!" she said, a note to her voice he didn't recognize. Or rather, the one he recognized from her time in Palm Desert. Being there, being a part of something so much bigger than Shelby Island, was doing something for her.

Something he couldn't do.

"I told you I was renting a car again…"

She had.

"So you're just out exploring?"

"Yep."

Sounded like whatever she was seeing made her happy. And whatever it was, she wasn't sharing it with him.

"I won't keep you, then. I just needed to know you're okay."

"I'm fine. And sorry you were worried. The call, do you think maybe it was someone here locally who's a fan of *Family Secrets*? The show has a ton of fans here. There's *Family Secrets* memorabilia in pretty much every store. Maybe someone saw me win last week and wants to book a room at Rose Harbor."

Maybe. And they'd hung up because…

Pierce got a hold of himself.

She was right. He knew she was. And hated how insecure he felt. "They got any extra-large *Family Secrets* T-shirts in those stores?" He heard himself ask. And felt like a high school teenager who knew he'd never be good enough for her.

"Of course. You want one?"

He didn't wear T-shirts, only undershirts. "I do," he told her. He'd wear it, too. Because his wife was a *Family Secrets* winner.

And he loved her to distraction.

"I JUST LIED to my husband." Eliza felt the room closing in on her, the world closing in on her, as she faced Mrs. Carpenter across her desk. "I told him I was out exploring."

"Telling him you're sitting in an adoption agency office, while he's in South Carolina and you're here, would have been the better option?"

Of course not. Nor the kinder option.

"And not that I condone either lying or justifying. But in a way, you *are* out exploring. You're exploring your options, as opposed to the scenery, as he's probably thinking."

"As I led him to think by not saying different."

But the older woman was right. It would have been cruel to tell Pierce the truth while she was so far away.

And he was going to be alone in their bed that night. The thought of him suffering through another nightmare made her shudder.

She'd promised him—and herself—that she'd do all she could to make certain that never happened.

She'd never thought there'd come a day when she'd actually be the cause of one.

But then, she'd never allowed herself to think, or even hope, that she'd ever have occasion to tell him about their son, either.

"Has he been here?" The question erupted out of her one more time.

"I can't tell you that." The compassion in the other woman's expression hadn't grown. Or lessened.

"I need to ask you to hold off a little bit longer in giving him my current information," she said next. She could have called with the news. She'd wanted to look Mrs. Carpenter in the eye. To make certain that the other woman understood that it wasn't a question of if she'd release the information. It was merely a question of when.

"You never have to release it." The counselor leaned forward, her gaze direct.

Eliza stood. "Yes," she said, nodding. "I do."

She turned, intending to leave.

"Is he seeing a mental health professional?"

Eliza froze at the question directed at her back. She thought about continuing out the door, back to the hotel. Joining the others for happy hour. Focusing on the reason that had paid for her trip to California. Her appearance on *Family Secrets*.

She was already guaranteed a spot in the final round. Had already crossed all but the last hurdle to proving to herself that she could win.

Eliza turned back.

"My husband?" she asked.

Mrs. Carpenter nodded, and Eliza sat. "Yes."

"Do you know the source of his disorder?"

Pierce wasn't *disordered*. He'd served his country. Had seen things no human being should see. "He served two tours in the Middle East. Experienced combat while he was there."

And regardless of what he thought, what anyone thought, that fact made him better father material. Not worse.

"My husband is the most honestly aware person I've ever known," she said, flooding with love for Pierce, even then. "And the most accountable, too."

"I'm assuming, since he doesn't know about your son, he doesn't know you were ever pregnant?"

"I was days before my sixteenth birthday when Pierce left for Iraq. He was eighteen. Our son was conceived the night before he left. I didn't hear from him…"

For all those months. Had feared he was dead. Until her father had made inquiries and confirmed that he was not.

"I know now that that last night Pierce and I were together, my father had seen him dropping me off. He followed him. And warned him to stay away from me. Pierce was eighteen. I was underage. He could have been arrested for statutory rape. My father threatened him with charges if he didn't leave and never contact me again." She hadn't known that until Pierce had come back into her life.

It was the one thing she still held against her father. Not that he'd felt it his duty to protect his daughter, however erroneously. But because, even after he'd known about the baby, he hadn't told her why she'd never heard from Pierce.

"Pierce was injured in a fight with some insurgents one night…" She'd never told anyone. Not even her parents. "Physically, he recovered fully, except…he's sterile," she finally said. Permanently. Irrevocably.

There were some problems love just couldn't solve.

PIERCE WAITED FOR Eliza to call him Friday night. He was not going to let paranoia poison their relationship. Nor was he going to take away any of her personal freedoms. At the same time, as her husband, he had a right to know her business.

Firmly prepared for her call, he sat in their

dark bedroom, his cookies and iced lemon water on the nightstand beside him, as he waited for his phone to ring.

Picked up on the first jingle when it did.

"Ah, Pierce, it's good to hear your voice. I miss you so much."

*Pierce.* Not *babe.*

But she was missing him...

The thought threw him into a bit of a tailspin. He'd been picturing her having the time of her life. Forgetting him for a few hours.

Not missing him.

"I miss you, too." Not something he'd ordinarily say, either. Things were changing. They were changing.

"I drove out in the desert today. I know you had enough of it in the Middle East, but here, Pierce, it's...so vast. Incredibly beautiful. I felt such peace. And the mountains, they aren't like anything we see back home. Every range is different. Different color. Different rocks. Different vegetation. It's like, every few feet, anything is possible."

She'd spent her day driving in the desert. She'd told him. He hadn't had to ask.

Pierce settled back against the pillows, his head resting in the softness, letting down feathers cradle him.

"How's the weather?" he asked.

"Beautiful. In the eighties today. And the sky…it's so pristine. And blue. No clouds…"

She'd taken in the weather. Not taken in a new life without him.

"It gave me a lot of time to think, babe."

*Here it comes.* He didn't bother lifting up. Their pillows could take the blow with him.

"I just… I love you, Pierce. More than I think you'll ever know. I just want you to know that. To believe it."

He did believe it.

"I want you to let my love bring you real joy…"

She wanted it, so he wanted it for her.

Pierce just didn't know how to tell her that he'd left any possibility of him knowing real joy in a tiny village in the middle of godforsaken territory in the Middle East. His capacity for joy had died right along with the eight-year-old boy he'd shot.

Point blank.

## CHAPTER TEN

ELIZA MADE IT a point to be early on the set the next morning. All of the contestants arrived together in the van—minus Grace, who rode with the friend who was staying with her at the condo she'd rented. They all settled into the green room, some studying the recipes they weren't allowed to take on stage with them, mental rehearsal. Some chatting and having coffee. There were hair stylists and makeup artists there to assist. Kaylee Newcomb, the young blonde who'd auditioned for the show as a way to break into show business, was availing herself of their services. Surprisingly, Jason Wright, the dark-haired young man with a popular fast food stand on the beach in Florida, was waiting in line behind Kaylee. As the most laid-back member of their cast, Jason didn't seem the type to submit to someone putting goo all over his face.

Eliza was curious about the process, about

how she'd look if she let the professionals go to work on her, didn't want to know badly enough to stick around.

She wanted to check her kitchen. To make certain that everything was in place. Natasha had assured them, after the mushroom disappearance and near-disaster the previous week, that there'd be an extra preshow check of all kitchens for the duration of their competition. She needed this win.

Especially with everything else going on, with Pierce, her son…if she didn't win this show, if she didn't prove to herself that she could be the best at something, the life would be squeezed out of her.

It wasn't like she needed the win to change the circumstances of her life. She loved Rose Harbor. Wouldn't give it up even if she didn't need it to make a living. She loved Pierce and wanted no part of a life without him.

Yet the idea of being a winning chef…it changed things inside her. Healed things inside her.

And maybe that was the answer she'd been seeking. She needed this to complete something inside her—not to change her external circumstances. She'd be better for Rose Harbor, better for Pierce and her marriage, if she could come home with a prestigious title she'd won by her own talent, hard work and diligence.

Amid the flurry of preshow techie activity, another one of the local high school drama class interns was mopping the kitchens when Eliza entered the stage. Camille, she thought her name was.

Being the proprietress of a bed-and-breakfast made Eliza conscious of everyone around her. Getting to know them. It made her great with names.

She'd met Camille the first week of taping. The girl had been filling the refrigerator in the green room with drinks. She'd asked if there was any brand in particular that Eliza liked. She could make sure that some would be there each week.

Later, Eliza had heard Camille asking Jason what types of snacks he liked. He'd said that he was fond of a certain kind of trail mix, and both of the previous two weeks it had been there. Eliza assumed she'd done the same for the other six contestants, as well.

Natasha ran a great show. Right down to the smallest details of comfort food in the green room.

And Camille was finished mopping. Ten

minutes until call. Fifteen minutes before show time. The timeline was closer than she'd have expected, but Natasha didn't want her contestants to have to stand around in their kitchens for a long period before go time. It was like she really, truly wanted every one of them to have the best chance to succeed. She seemed really to care about her contestants, not just about the show and the money.

Other than checking supplies, they weren't allowed to touch a thing until the clock started ticking. Anyone caught getting a head start was automatically disqualified.

In her kitchen, Eliza went down her list, relieved to see that everything was where it should have been. Grace had come on stage right behind her and gave Eliza the thumbs-up, so her ingredients must have been complete, as well. A couple of other contestants trickled in. Luigi. The twins. And then, at call, the rest arrived and took their places.

Eliza wasn't as concerned about time that week. Their subject was dessert, and her cobbler didn't require the full fifty minutes they were allotted for preparation. She'd need half an hour, tops, so she took her time. Reveled being in her on-set kitchen. Soaked up the whole television experience. Having a win under her belt helped ease the tension, too, though she still wanted to win this week's competition. If she took all four wins, she wouldn't have to make a sixth trip to Palm Desert for the final round. There would be no final round.

She'd be the winning contestant...

Aware that Saturday of the buzz around her as her fellow contestants moved about their kitchens, as measuring spoons, pans, bowls and mixers clattered, as oven doors, and refrigerator doors opened and closed, as faucets were turned on and off, Eliza smiled to herself. Measured apple juice, maple syrup and cherries, mixed them in a glass bowl and set them aside.

She had to tend to the base, which would be baked. Flour and sugar went in the sifter. Next, baking soda, water and egg would be put in a bowl for whisking. Most people put the baking soda in with the dry ingredients. Eliza's grandma had taught her to put it in with the wet. Said it gave the finished result a better texture.

The lights were bright. Maybe her tapered white blouse had not been the best choice since it might start to show sweat stains. She just loved how it looked with her dark hair.

Thought the contrast drew attention to her eyes. Which, in her opinion, were her best feature.

Wiping her hand along the side of her navy pants—before she thought about the flour mark that would leave—she measured baking soda and tipped it into the bowl with a silent admonishment to stop being so vain. Was Kaylee's whole star-struck mentality getting to her? Eliza didn't even want to be a television star. She wanted to be respected for the talent she loved—cooking.

Bottled water in hand—the kind she always used at home—she measured the tablespoons needed and with her other hand started to whisk the soda briskly so that when the water hit, it didn't form globs. The egg would go in last, cracked on the side of the bowl with one hand while she continued to whisk—just as her grandmother had taught her.

But first, whisk. Pour water and…

It wasn't so much that the mixture in her bowl did anything alarming. It just grew when it wasn't supposed to.

"What…" Eliza's half-formed utterance drew the attention of the other chefs in her pod. The camera happened to be on her as well, so she caught Natasha's attention.

"Cut!" Eliza wasn't sure who called the command. Natasha and other show workers gathered around Eliza's kitchen.

She was busy smelling the mixture in her bowl. She'd recognized the visual surprise seconds after it had happened. From a high school science class.

Natasha and a security guard gathered on either side of Eliza. Her entire body flashed hot. And then cold.

How could she have made such an incredibly stupid mistake? On national television?

"It doesn't really smell strong enough, but I think I put vinegar in with the baking soda," she said, shaking her head. What idiot couldn't tell the difference between a bottle of vinegar and bottled water? She'd been so sure. Floating on confidence and thinking about her looks.

Well, didn't she just look great now?

No real harm had been done. The mixture in her bowl looked normal enough. An instruction went out over the microphone for all other contestants to continue cooking.

Natasha reached around Eliza for the bottle of vinegar she'd mistaken for water.

"Something's been added to this water," she said, her voice harsher than Eliza had ever heard. Grandma Grace came over, saying that her pie was in the oven, and looked at the bottle. Jason glanced up from the dough he was rolling.

"Why would someone add something to her water?" Grace asked, frowning.

"I apologize, Mrs. Westin," Natasha said. "We *will* get to the bottom of this. First, though, will you be able to complete your recipe on time?"

She'd have to start over, of course, with the wet ingredient bowl, but she'd only just started with it.

She'd be disqualified if she couldn't. It was in the contract they'd all been required to sign. If for any reason a contestant couldn't complete a menu item, whether it be a fault of her own or for any other cause, the contestant would be automatically disqualified from that day's competition and could not hold *Family Secrets*, Natasha Stevens or any of the show's personnel liable.

"I can finish," she said, still unsure what had just happened. She'd thought the mistake had been hers.

And it hadn't been?

She smelled her bottle of water as Natasha had done. The smell of vinegar was slight.

There couldn't have been much of the liquid in there at all. But vinegar didn't belong in her recipe…

And she knew it would give it just enough of an off flavor to cause a loss.

Still, she'd had extra time, and it would only take a few seconds to start this part over.

Cameras were told to roll. They were back on air. With Natasha still in Eliza's kitchen. The host explained the mishap as a mistake. Didn't say whose mistake, nor did she explain further. She talked for a moment about kitchen safety. And then, on air, asked Eliza if she thought she could continue the day's competition.

With a smile on her face that was completely forced, Eliza assured her that she absolutely could. And then words just kept coming out of her mouth. "Thanks to my grandmother," she said, her smile becoming more genuine as Natasha's camera stayed on her. "One of the first cooking secrets I learned from her was always to prepare items in parts. That way, if something goes wrong, only one part is wasted…"

Natasha moved to other kitchens, spoke with other contestants, asking them questions about what they were preparing. About their techniques. Asking for hints and secrets that their viewers could use at home.

Eliza whisked water and baking soda. Added egg. She poured the fruit and syrup mixture and baked her cobbler.

All the while wondering who among them was trying to sabotage her.

And why.

THE MOST LIKELY culprit was one of the other contestants. Pierce had the thought as soon as he heard about what had happened. Eliza had called him as soon as the taping was done. As she had the week before.

He'd be seeing it on television later, and she didn't want him to be caught off guard.

"Are you okay?" was the first thing he asked her.

"I'm fine. Really, I think I did okay. Everyone including Natasha says I made a great recovery…"

She didn't sound okay. She was excited. But a bit…off, too.

"Was anyone else affected?" He had his cop hat on. It was the best way to keep himself in line.

"No."

"That's two weeks of competitions, and

twice that your kitchen has been tampered with."

"I know."

"I don't like it."

"I don't, either."

"What are they doing about it?"

"Natasha had the security guard take the bottle before cameras rolled again to see if they can get any prints. They turned it over to police. They're going to check what's in the bottle just to be sure it's nothing serious or harmful, but I'm sure it's vinegar. And if it is and they don't get any identifiable prints from it, they aren't going to open an investigation. She doesn't want the negative publicity for the show and it's not like any of this is dangerous, or putting lives at risk. Still, she seems really determined to get to the bottom of it. It's cheating and whoever it is will be disqualified. She's calling in an extra security detail."

He didn't disagree with the assessment. Or the action taken. He still didn't like it.

"Do you think I should pull out of the competition?"

Here was his chance. If he told her she was in danger, would she come home for good? "I do not think you should pull out of the competition." He needed to focus on finding out who was trying to hurt her chances in the competition. "The only threat has been to your chances of winning. Not to you personally."

Before she left to get on the shuttle back to the hotel, he asked her more about her fellow contestants. And that night, instead of sitting alone in his room to watch the show, he watched it from his precinct in Charleston with a computer on his lap, doing official database searches during commercial breaks.

He was back home when Eliza called to tell him that she was in her room for the night. By then he knew everything police could know about every one of the seven contestants who'd shared the stage with his wife that day.

"Jason Wright has two priors," he told her as soon as he'd picked up. "One for possession and one for assault. He got off light on the possession. It was a first offense. And charges were eventually dropped on the assault case. He made restitution, though. One thousand dollars."

The twenty-eight-year-old had the kitchen right next to Eliza. Pierce liked him best for having done this.

"The twins aren't in any criminal database.

I did find, though, that they were put in the foster system when they were twelve."

"Do you know why?"

"Not a clue. The only other person who came up, believe it or not, is Grace Hargraves."

"Grace?" Eliza's shock made it all the way home from California.

"Her daughter took out a harassment order on her forty years ago."

"Her daughter? I didn't know she had a daughter. Does it say what happened?"

"The complaint read that Grace had written to the daughter at home, asking for contact. There were some other things, times she'd tried to see her or left a note on her car, over a series of a couple of years, but that was the basis of it."

"You can get a harassment order for that?"

"Depends on the circumstances, but generally, the served party appears and gives her side, and the judge then decides if the order was warranted."

"But you can't see that part?"

"Grace didn't ever appear in court. She just let it ride."

"I'm guessing she couldn't bear to face her daughter in a court of law. What mother would put her child through taking her own parent to court over something like that? No matter who was right or wrong, and what was to be gained. It sounds like Grace just wanted to see her daughter. But if the woman didn't want to be seen so badly that she'd file against her own mother, then no matter whether there was an order or not, Grace wasn't going to get to see her. Who knows? Maybe Grace *was* harassing her. Parents need to see their kids, you know?"

They were back to the kid thing. It kept coming back to the kid thing. It wasn't going to go away.

## CHAPTER ELEVEN

PIERCE WAS TRYING to figure out how to deal with "the kid thing," which was starting to form what felt like a canyon between them, when Eliza said, "Natasha instated a new set of stage rules."

Pierce wondered if she'd changed the subject on purpose.

"None of us are allowed in our kitchens until five minutes before the show starts. And she's limited the number of staff who have access to them. She's also going to check each one of them over herself, inspect all of our ingredients, right before call," she continued.

Natasha Stevens's decisions seemed to be sound. He wasn't worried about Eliza's safety on the set, or as part of *Family Secrets*.

He still wished life wasn't unfolding this way.

"It's odd how you were singled out," he said, thinking aloud, consciously allowing himself to be distracted from the bigger problem between them. If the sabotage had happened that day only, he'd understand. Eliza had been the previous week's winner. She was the standout.

But what about the week before? With the mushrooms?

"It's not like you own a famous restaurant, or a culinary school," he continued. "How would anyone have known that you were the one to beat before you'd ever competed?"

"You think maybe one of the contestants could have come to Rose Harbor? Or knows someone who has? Someone who's tasted my cooking?"

A far-fetched possibility—but one he'd pursue. "I was thinking more that last week was an accident. A mistake. And that this week was the only sabotage. Because you won last week."

"If that's the case, then Grace's kitchen will be in danger next week." Eliza sounded more like herself as they talked things through. Calmly. Cerebrally. On the same team. And he started to relax.

He and Eliza were a team.

And Eliza's mishap had been neither physically dangerous nor personal. "With the new measures in place, I doubt there'll be any kitchen in danger next week," he said. He'd done well. Handled the sabotage situation. And acknowledged that he and Eliza were going to have to face the fact that she was suddenly interested in children.

He'd done both and come through on the other side calmly and rationally when his first instinct had been to jump on a plane and get to Eliza before any further harm could befall her. And pretend that the whole kid thing was just going to fade away. Be brushed under a rug and never seen again.

"You should have seen Grace today after the show, Pierce. She was so excited and did this little jig. She would have fallen, too, but that kid Daniel who went and got our mushrooms, he was right there, stepped in and managed to catch her in time. He took her into a two-step like the whole thing had been planned, and she laughed out loud..."

That was his Eliza. Taking as much pleasure for others as she did for herself. Willing to listen to her all night if she wanted to sit up and chat with him, Pierce lay in the dark and wondered how he'd ever gotten to be so lucky.

Thankful that Eliza had married him. That he had moments like these.

Determined to store every last second so that if and when the time came that it was over, he'd always have the memories.

It was memories of Eliza, of the sweet love she'd shown him that last night they were together, that had kept him alive in the Middle East. And had kept him sane all of the years since.

Knowing that those same memories would see him through the rest of his days gave him the confidence to believe that if she'd be better off without him, he really would let her go.

Her voice growing soft with fatigue, she'd started talking about the morning. The time the shuttle would be picking her up. Her flight.

And then it was time to say good-night. He didn't want to. But they both needed to rest. He had guests to see to on her behalf in the morning. Dishes to do after Margie served breakfast. Eliza's assistant had insisted on cleaning the rooms, but he'd managed to get her to agree that he'd do all of the vacuuming...

"Night, Pierce. I love you."

"Night. And Eliza? Congratulations again on your first runner-up award today."

She'd barely mentioned the near-win when she'd called him earlier.

So Eliza.

Always thinking of herself last.

*THE PHONE CALL!*

Eliza had no idea why she woke from a sound sleep Monday night beside her husband with those words clearly in her mind. Couldn't remember what she'd been dreaming. Even if she'd been dreaming.

But as she lay there, willing her heart rate to slow and her body to relax, her mind raced. So much had been going on...so many things grabbing her focus. Her worry. Her heart.

She'd forgotten all about the phone call that had come in on Rose Harbor's line on Friday. She'd been with Mrs. Carpenter when Pierce's call had come in. He'd been concerned that she was all right.

She'd been all over herself hoping that she didn't give him any cause to figure out that she was keeping a huge secret. Just until she could figure out how to tell him in such a way that wouldn't obliterate him. Their marriage. And any chance they had of ever being a family.

A family?

In the dark of the night, the question refused to be unanswered. Was she really hoping that someday she and Pierce and their son would be a family?

That the boy she'd given away would be a part of them? Even if from a distance?

She couldn't be. Couldn't be so stupid as to pin her happiness on something so nebulous. On something so completely out of her control.

The phone call. She'd been so busy dealing with everything else, she'd let the phone call slide into the ether.

Then, last night, they hadn't made it back from the airport until after social hour. She'd been tired. So had he. He'd been so happy to see her—and she him—she'd closed her mind to anything but an evening together, just the two of them.

The phone call.

Shivering, Eliza couldn't push it away anymore. Her son had been given seventeen-year-old contact information for her. She and her grandmother hadn't lived at Rose Harbor yet then. But Grandma had worked there. There could have been some mention of the place.

The adoption agency was closer to Anaheim than Palm Desert. But the distance was almost the same from Charleston to Shelby Island. Area codes covered distances—maybe halfway between?

What if?

Oh, God.

What if that call had been their son?

Pierce hadn't said any more about the call. Or mentioned any others. Other than making certain that she was all right, he hadn't seemed concerned about it at all.

But she was, all of a sudden. And scared, too.

*What if?*

She couldn't let Pierce find out that way.

Would the boy call back? Had he given up? Had it even been him at all?

If only she could contact him. Talk to him. If only she knew what he wanted, if he needed anything. If only she could know what she was opening Pierce up to.

If-onlys and what-ifs weren't going to help her.

With her stomach knotted to the point of pain, she lay there and willed daylight to arrive. To infiltrate the confusion and fear. Eventually her mind moved to cooking. First to Grace and her little victory dance. The memory brought a smile. Her mental journey moved from there to the upcoming week. Finally landing on the recipe she'd submitted for the vegetable main dish competition. It wasn't a category that had appeared on any of the previous shows she'd seen. Still, she'd been making vegan dishes for a long time to satisfy her diverse clientele. She also had a child judge to please—and for most children, vegetables were the hardest sell.

Thinking about the frying batter she'd perfected over the years, and the onions and green beans and cauliflower and broccoli kids had consumed like they were french fries, she hoped her basket of fried vegetables would please the judges. With the sauces she served to complement them, they were filling enough for a main dish.

Too filling for anything but, many guests had told her over the years.

And the secret to her recipe? Other than the type of ale and the sea salt, the secret was the ice cube. She dropped it into the batter just before rolling her vegetables in it. The cold kept the batter crisp when it cooked.

And that was something she'd discovered all by herself.

Pierce groaned.

Eliza was back to the present in a flash. The peaceful lethargy into which she'd fallen vanished as if it had never been.

She waited.

Nothing happened.

Pierce's breathing was normal. His body appeared relaxed.

She had to quit worrying.

And get her life in order before it exploded on her.

## CHAPTER TWELVE

ON TUESDAY OF the week after the second sabotage, everything changed again. Eliza was in the middle of checking in a young couple who were brand new to the inn. To South Carolina beaches. They'd been together for a couple of years, and that week, there at Rose Harbor, the man planned to propose to his girlfriend. He'd called ahead to make the arrangements with Eliza. She was delivering a plate of homemade chocolate chip cookies to their room on Thursday night while they were eating at one of the popular restaurants down by the beach. One of the cookies would have a diamond ring in it.

She didn't even have the ring in her possession yet when her cell rang. She glanced at the screen, as she always did with a husband in law enforcement—as she supposed most police spouses did when their partners were at work—more to reassure themselves than because they expected anything to be wrong.

The incoming call had a Charleston exchange.

"Just a minute. I have to take this," she said, motioning for Margie to finish the check-in. She'd get the ring later.

Moving toward the back of the house, she pushed the button on her phone to answer the call. "Hello?"

Their bank's main branch was in Charleston. Her dentist's office was, as well. There was no reason for her to be alarmed. And yet...

"Mrs. Westin? This is Captain Montoya..." Pierce's boss.

Eliza slid down to the floor.

And prayed.

THE EVENING NEWS made Pierce out to be a hero. Sitting in the hospital emergency room in Charleston, Eliza overheard Tracy, a female officer who'd ridden with Pierce on several occasions, telling another officer that "Westin had a death wish."

While out driving, her husband had seen a group of teenagers beating up a younger boy in an alley. He'd immediately radioed for backup but hadn't waited for a response before heading right into the fray.

From what little she'd been told, his presence hadn't immediately stopped the fight, but he'd used his body to shield the boy from any more blows. And all four teenagers were in custody.

By all accounts, he'd saved the boy's life.

No one knew, or weren't sharing, what the fight was about. Or even if it was gang-related, though there were suppositions that it was. Pierce worked a tough beat.

At his request.

But that didn't mean that he had a death wish. Did it?

He was still alive.

Even if he had the wish, he hadn't gotten it.

But she knew he didn't. And other people shouldn't be saying he did.

Waiting was the hardest part. Waiting for Pierce to come home and claim her. Waiting for their baby to be born. Waiting for test results when they'd thought her mother had had a heart attack, but it had turned out to be indigestion.

Pierce was alive. In with the medical team.

He'd been conscious, and bloody, when they'd brought him in.

She was waiting to hear the extent of his injuries.

"He's going to be fine." Jamison, an officer

who was a year or two younger than Pierce and was closest to him of anyone in the department, sat down beside her. Eliza had met him on several occasions. He took her hand, and she let him hold it.

One by one they were all arriving. Beat cops. Detectives. As they finished their shifts. Or before they started them. The men in blue took care of their own.

And the family of their own, too. She'd already talked to the head of the officers' spouses' group. Would have all the support she needed.

What she needed now was to take Pierce and go home to Shelby Island. *Family Secrets*, adoption agencies, possibilities all faded into nothing if Pierce wasn't there with her.

All of her fear from the night before came back in an inferno that threatened to consume her.

"Do you think Pierce has a death wish?" she asked Jamison.

He couldn't die. He didn't even know yet that he'd fathered a child. A boy.

A son.

If he had a death wish, would knowing about the boy save him? Or push him over the edge?

"I don't know about that," the officer said. "But I'm guessing if he did, he'd be gone already."

The words settled her. In the moment.

And she waited.

As soon as Pierce heard that Eliza was in the waiting room, he knew he was going to be fine. Made no sense. She'd be there if he was on his deathbed, too. But knowing she was there…he didn't feel like death.

Neither did he feel so hot.

"Can you feel that?" The doctor moved Pierce's left arm.

"Yes, I can." *Thank God.* He could feel everything. Every muscle he owned had an ache in it. But so far, as far as he'd heard, there was nothing seriously wrong with him.

He had stitches above his right eye. He hadn't seen them yet, but by the feel of things, he wasn't going to be his usual handsome self when his wife walked in that door.

At least nothing was broken.

His left wrist was sprained. He had various lacerations. Another cut on his left shoulder that was being stitched. A stiff neck. A multitude of bruises. But as soon as the tests came back saying there was no internal damage, he was out of there.

No matter what anyone said.

He'd been hurt before. Much worse and with less medical attention.

He knew he'd heal better at home in bed with Eliza. He had only three more nights before she left again.

THAT FIRST NIGHT, Eliza focused solely on Pierce's immediate needs. He could walk, albeit painfully. He could sit up. He could feed himself.

"You're lucky both the sprained wrist and stitched shoulder are on the same side," she told him as she brought him his iced lemon water and cookies just before bedtime. He'd insisted on sitting on a chair in their room when he'd first come home, shortly after social hour. But ten minutes of that and he'd been in the bed.

Her man was strong. And stubborn. But he wasn't stupid.

"Twice lucky because it's the left side and I'm right-handed," he said, raising the glass of water gingerly to his assaulted lips as he took the antibiotic she'd just handed him.

He'd refused all pain medication. Not that that surprised her any.

Still, the doctor had given her something to help him sleep. If he had a rough night, she intended to use every ounce of power at her command to see that he at least took the sleep aid.

"No." He looked at her from his one good eye. The other was swollen shut. To match his bottom lip. "Thrice lucky," he told her.

"How's that?"

"Because you're here."

The line was corny. And nothing Pierce would normally say. It could be drugs talking from whatever was left of what they'd put in his IV earlier in the day.

The look in his eye told her what his words wouldn't say.

He loved her. He needed her.

But he didn't believe she'd always be there.

By Thursday morning, Pierce was going nuts. He couldn't stand the inactivity. The only thing keeping him cordial was the fact that Eliza was so sweet in her dedication to him. He couldn't so much as turn his head without her checking to see if he needed something.

He needed to get back to work. Even if he was just kept busy in the file room.

He was out on the porch, attempting to tighten the screws on a screen that had blown lose, when Eliza found him.

"What are you doing?"

"The rattling was bothering me," he said, ratchet wrench in hand.

He gave her credit for leaving him to it.

But he could tell, when she found him in the entertainment room just after ten, throwing darts with far more force than necessary, his wrapped left wrist hanging limp at his side, that she had something on her mind.

"We need to talk."

She stood there facing him, arms crossed.

"I'm waiting for it to be late enough in Palm Desert, and then I'm calling Natasha to cancel my appearance on the show. At least for this week. If I can miss one week and still compete, I'll consider doing so, but..."

Cursing his nervous energy, he said, "You are not canceling your appearance." He'd check himself into a hospital before he let that happen.

"I'm not leaving you alone like this."

"Margie will be here." She had come in on Tuesday, when Eliza had had to leave the inn to be with him in Charleston, but she'd had Wednesday and Thursday off. And he could vacuum. He could be of some assistance.

"Pierce."

"I'm not budging on this one, Eliza. You go or I find a convalescent center that will take me."

Her jaw tightened. She looked like she might cry. He didn't want to be harsh with her. He just knew that she had to do this. Had to have the chance.

He might not understand why it was so important, might not want her gone, but he knew his wife well enough to know that whatever was happening had to happen.

"Fine," she said. "I don't like it, don't like how you just cop your attitude and it's your way or the highway, but...you're probably right. You'll be fine."

Of course he would.

"And...I don't cop an attitude." He didn't quite mimic her, but he came close. He wanted to tell her to go. Leave him and his nasty mood. But was afraid that she'd take that as more of him demanding his way.

Why couldn't the woman see that he lived to serve her? To give her whatever happiness he could give her? He needed her, but he would not let his need suck the life out of her.

In his whole life, Eliza was the one bright spot that wasn't of his own making. He'd never known his mother. And while his old man had been congenial, when he'd been conscious, he sure hadn't been a positive influence...

"Yes, you do cop an attitude," she said, standing her ground in such an uncharacteristic way, he figured he wasn't the only one suffering from having him in invalid mode. "This is just like eighteen years ago, Pierce. I begged you not to join the army. But you wouldn't listen. You were so sure it was the best thing for both of us. That you'd get your career training, be back for me..."

What?

He knew why he'd joined up. He was never going to amount to anything but the son of the town drunk if he'd stayed. The army had been his only chance at real training, at having a career instead of just a job. And she knew why he hadn't been in touch, too. Her old man would have had him in jail.

They'd been through all of that. Had put it to bed. Hadn't talked about it, in accusing terms, since before they got married. Why was she bringing this up now? What was she doing?

With an instant mental slowdown, Pierce watched her. What had he missed?

"I did come back for you." They were the only words that occurred to him that he could actually say.

And knew, when her face tightened, that they weren't the right ones.

"Eventually," he added. Which didn't make things any better.

"We need to talk about kids, Pierce."

She could have slapped him. That would have been kinder.

"Or rather, we need to talk about why you risked your life, why you let yourself get nearly pummeled to death, rather than wait for backup as protocol dictated…"

He'd wondered what she'd heard when she'd been in the waiting room with his fellow officers the day he'd been injured.

Jamison had said something about her asking him if he thought Pierce had a death wish.

If Pierce had been in top form, he'd already have had this one on the books. He'd forgotten, until that moment, that his sometime partner had given him the heads-up when he'd stopped in briefly to speak with him the day of his attack while Eliza had been signing papers to get him released to her care.

"The kid didn't have time for me to wait," he said now. "I was the only one there, the only one who could assess the situation, and I knew that if I didn't act, that boy was going to be dead."

As it was, the kid was hospitalized, in serious condition. He was conscious, though. And coherent.

"There were other things you could have done. From what I heard, you just barreled yourself right into the fray. You didn't even pull your stun gun. You could just as easily have been dead, too, Pierce. Which wouldn't have helped the kid any. You saw a kid in trouble and you threw your training to the curb."

"I knew what I had to do. A stun gun would have stopped one of them while another landed the death blow. No one was going to listen to me, or care. And the seconds I spent trying could have cost the kid his life."

"You don't know that for sure."

"So you'd rather I save my own hide than take a chance to help someone else?"

Her hands dropped to her sides. She shook

her head. "I just…you've got this thing with kids," she said. "You marry a woman to save her kid, living with him gives you nightmares and you divorce her because you can't help him. Me talking to you about kids gives you nightmares. Yet you risk your life, and your career, to save a kid. I don't understand. And I think I need to."

He'd known the time was coming.

He wasn't ready.

He had to tell her something. Part of it, at least. He had to break the pact.

And something wasn't right. His injuries weren't the only thing bothering her. His actions on Tuesday weren't all of it. She wasn't meeting his gaze.

"What's going on?"

"I don't know! That's what I'm asking you!" She might not be letting tears fall, but they were in her voice.

He thought about what Jamison had said.

"You think I have a death wish."

"No!" She shook her head. Hugged herself. "Well, when I heard someone say that, I wondered, but…" Her gaze cleared, and she stared at him. "Do you?"

"No. I do not." He had no trouble meeting her head-on with that one. "I've got work to

do. And… I want every single second I can
have with you."

"I want that, too," she whispered.

They weren't dealing with the issues. But
he went to her. Took her in his arms. And
held on.

Pretending that they'd solved everything.

# CHAPTER THIRTEEN

ELIZA'S BAG WAS packed before social hour Thursday night. She'd iron the navy dress pants when she got there. And hang the tweed jacket with navy leather pockets to steam in the hotel bathroom.

In the kitchen, making dinner for herself and Pierce while Margie put out the social hour fare, she timed her movements. The fried vegetables would please him. And serve as her only practice run for the third of the four *Family Secrets* competitions.

Now that they had two winners—Grace and her—there would be a final round. Another week she'd have to be away from home.

She wanted to be upset by that. Put out.

But she wasn't.

She was excited to have confirmation of a fifth show.

This was her last night with Pierce before she was once again in California. She'd been debating all week about going. And all afternoon about whether or not she'd try to see Mrs. Carpenter again.

The woman knew now why and when she'd be in town. Had said she was going to watch the show.

The adoption counselor was the only person in the world who knew all sides of Eliza's story.

After dropping an ice cube in her mixture of flour, ale, cornstarch and sea salt, Eliza started to roll the vegetables in the batter and place them on a tray in assembly line fashion. She had fifty minutes to make these and the sauces for dipping, too. The clock was ticking.

A lot of clocks were ticking. She was thirty-three. If she was ever going to be a mother...

No. Wait. That one wasn't even on the list.

And she couldn't afford to put it there, either. Not with everything else already in front of it.

Her clock with Pierce was definitely ticking. She had to tell him about the baby. What if, while she was gone, the Palm Desert caller rang back? What if it *was* their son?

Drop. Roll. Place.

For all she knew, the boy's clock was ticking, too. If, God forbid, he was in trouble. But even if he wasn't, he was young. Barely seventeen. If she didn't make herself accessible soon, he might just give up.

And then she'd never know him.

She wanted to tell Pierce about the boy at dinner. But then chickened out and invited Margie to join them for the test run. Eliza had the meal plated in just under fifty minutes. But was it as good as usual?

"Delicious," Margie said, licking her fingers as she helped herself to more.

"You're going to win," Pierce told her. She couldn't tell if he was happy about that or not. His wrist was hurting him.

And he wouldn't take anything to ease his pain…

She couldn't tell because they weren't in tune with each other. She wanted to pretend otherwise. But couldn't.

He insisted on vacuuming the parlor after social hour, even though she assured him quite sincerely that she was happy to do so.

Because he had, she had the kitchen cleaned and breakfast prepped and ready to go by the time the front room was set. Half an hour earlier than usual.

"Let's go sit," Pierce said, taking her hand

as he headed out to their private rose garden. When he started toward the gazebo, she wanted to hope he'd planned a romantic tryst to calm her heart and send her off with a good memory to replace the bad they'd added to their repertoire that week.

She wanted to concentrate on their love so it would keep her focused and strong as she faced the world, and her problems, alone.

But dread was heavy on her heart.

They'd furnished the gazebo with padded wicker furniture. A love seat and two rockers, a glass-topped wicker coffee table in the center.

She wanted to rock.

But when he chose the love seat, she settled beside him. Even now, fearing the worst, she was awash in love for him. This man. Her Pierce.

She'd never wanted another man like she wanted him. Never trusted one like she trusted him.

In all of the dates she'd been on in college and afterward, her heart had never felt the flutter, her insides had never rushed with butterflies, like they did when she was with Pierce.

"We need to talk."

His words were a death knell.

She couldn't let this die. Not without fighting for a chance. As easy as it might seem to be to just sit back and accept what was and move forward, to let others convince her what was right and best, she couldn't do that anymore.

Not again.

"Yes, we do," she told him.

*Now's not the time. It's not fair to him. You're leaving in the morning. He's injured.*

"I have something to tell you." She blurted the words before they could be stifled. Now she was on the front line without a shield.

He studied her. "Okay."

She couldn't let him cop his attitude on her one last time. Couldn't let him decide that she'd be better off without him. Which was what she'd expected to hear if she'd let him go first.

"I have a secret, Pierce. A big one." Clasping her hands together in her lap, she squeezed. Swallowed. In spite of all of the hours she'd spent thinking about this moment, preparing for it, she didn't know what to say.

Her heart pounded while her lungs tightened around the air she couldn't seem to get enough of.

"But before I tell you, I need you to promise me that you won't shut me out. That you won't just go away and refuse to discuss it."

"I'd never do that."

"You have no idea what you'll do. You don't know the secret."

"I know you. And I know how completely I love you."

If only life were that easy. That clean.

She knew him, too. Knew how much she loved him. And yet she'd bet Rose Harbor that he'd been about to tell her he was walking away.

So maybe it would be kinder to leave him to his ignorance and let him go. Why hurt him with what he could have had, when there was a chance they'd never even hear from the boy again?

*What if he calls again when I'm gone?*

She'd stay home. Pierce was injured. And the problems between them had grown too big to ignore. She was needed there.

To save her marriage.

"You don't know me as well as you think you do." She was selfish. And weak. She should never have let her parents talk her into giving away the child she and Pierce had made from their love.

Should never have complicated the mistake by letting them talk her into believing that it would be for the best if she never mentioned the baby again. If she acted as though that nine months, that one incredible morning and horrible, horrible afternoon, had never happened.

"What's going on, Eliza?" He didn't sound angry. Or fierce. Not commanding, or even defensive. He sounded loving. And concerned.

She couldn't do this to him.

"Nothing. I just… I want to stay home. With you. I want to drop out of the show."

No, she didn't. At all. It was the last thing she wanted to do. And yet…she did.

How could it feel as though she needed both things?

Eliza wasn't even sure she knew who she was anymore.

"What's going on, Eliza?"

And still, she knew how much she loved Pierce. No matter what else changed, her love for him was constant.

She couldn't hurt him with the truth. Not Pierce…

"Have you met someone in California? Is that why you have this sudden urge to stay home? Did you sleep with someone else?" There was no accusation. Just a question.

"No!" She was pretty sure the look of horror on her face didn't even come close to matching what she felt inside. "How could you even think…suggest…"

He shrugged, his facial muscles somewhat more relaxed, but otherwise giving no indication how he was feeling.

Or what he was thinking.

"You love being on the show and suddenly don't want to go. And now you tell me that I don't know you like I think I do. There's been something different since the first time you were out there. Maybe even before. I'm not sure about that. As I've been trying to pinpoint the moment of change, I find that, prior to your first trip to California, I wasn't looking for anything different between us and was, as usual, pretty wrapped up in my own perspective. What is clear to me, though, is that since that first day you were out there, there's been something you aren't telling me."

"Why do you say that?"

He looked at her, raised his wrapped wrist and let it fall to his leg. "Honestly, I don't know. You tell me where you are, what you're doing, but not with your usual insights. It's more like a travel log than the Eliza flair I'm used to."

Her eyes flooded with tears. Something she'd decided from the very beginning was not going to happen. She had to be the strong one here. She was the one who knew the truth. Who'd made the choice. Who'd kept the secret.

Pierce was the injured party.

"I had a baby, Pierce." The words were pressed out of her by the emotion building inside. "I had a baby." Tears choked her. Engulfed her. She shook her head. Looked at him as though he'd have answers enough for both of them, while knowing it was far too late. "I had a baby." She wailed.

It was as though, once she'd let out the truth, she couldn't stop. She was going to sit there and confess as many times as she'd refused, over the years, to let the truth free.

"I had a baby... I..." she hiccupped. Choked for air. "I had a..." She couldn't breathe. "I hadda..."

Pierce's good arm came around her and, sobbing, Eliza collapsed against him.

## CHAPTER FOURTEEN

USED TO DEALING with traumatic situations, Pierce didn't feel much of anything at first.

Eliza was crying. Comforting her was what he did. Anytime he could.

*I had a baby. I had a baby. I had a baby.*

Was she out of her mind?

She'd gone to California for the first time in her life less than a month ago. She couldn't have given birth there.

She was crying so hard she was struggling for breath. He rubbed her back. Kissed the top of her head. Had to calm her down first.

At the moment, he wouldn't be able to get through to her, and she wouldn't be able to communicate with him even if he did.

A cop looking for answers, he had scenarios running through his mind. Had she arranged to adopt a child behind his back? In California? She'd tried to talk to him about adoption right after her first trip out. Had she had a kid lined up and had to back out because of him?

He didn't know a lot about the process, but he knew enough to know that even private adoptions took time. Background checks. He knew because sometimes law enforcement was called if there was a questionable report. He'd taken such a call once. He'd been on desk duty...

Eliza sniffled hard and, searching for anything that could double as a tissue, Pierce grabbed the linen doily from beneath the flower arrangement on the coffee table and wiped at her face. Like a child, she let him.

He could feel the change come over her, a ripple running up her backbone. She straightened.

"I'm so sorry," she said, shaking her head. "I...had no right to..."

Whatever else Pierce knew, he was sure of this. "You always have the right to feel your feelings, Eliza. They got the better of you for a reason." What he needed to know was why.

And he needed to know soon.

Before she left town again.

He'd been planning for a rough night. Had already planned to take one of the sleeping pills the doctor had given him the other night before he left the hospital. To protect Eliza from any residual nighttime horror he might put them both through after he told her what he'd brought her out there to tell her.

He still hadn't been sure exactly what that would be.

Not the whole thing, for sure. He couldn't break the pact without talking to someone first. Either a counselor or the other three men in his unit who were keeping it with him.

Men he hadn't spoken to since he got out.

He had no idea where they were, what they'd done with their lives. Wasn't even sure they were alive.

But he'd thought about looking them up. On Facebook first.

Using the police database to search for possible priors on people who had reason to sabotage his wife, while out of his jurisdiction, hadn't been completely against policy.

Using it for his own personal needs…was.

He didn't like it at all when she pulled away from him completely, sat up and turned to face him.

Until that moment, while he'd been worried about her, he hadn't been afraid for…them. At least, not due to whatever she had to tell him. Not since she'd assured him there was no one else.

"What's going on, Liza?" He didn't use the pet name much anymore. And had used it twice recently. It had been all he'd called her when they'd been in high school. It was like he had to pull her back to him in any way he could. The thought disgusted him.

Disappointed him. He wasn't that kind of guy.

"I already told you. I had a baby." Her eyes teared up again as she looked at him, but they were strong and steady, too.

She seemed completely lucid. Didn't repeat herself this time.

He shook his head. "I don't understand what you're telling me."

"I had a baby, Pierce." She said the words slowly. Distinctly.

"I know what you said. I don't understand what you mean. When? When did you have this baby?"

He'd been back in her life for seven, almost eight years. Had seen her almost every day of that time…

"Seventeen years ago." She was frowning. Looking confused.

He waited for cold, harsh reality to take root.

"Seventeen years ago." He repeated the words. His heart in deep chill. Deep, deep chill. Lifting his injured hand, he let it fall to his lap. Felt a twinge of pain. And wondered that he could feel anything at all.

"You had a baby a year after I left?" She'd found someone else that soon? What had all that been about her never finding anyone to replace him? About never having fallen in love again?

About…

"Nine months after you left."

The distinction seemed really important to her.

And then he knew.

It had taken him a while. Too long, probably.

"You had my baby."

Eliza had had his baby. *His baby.*

*Oh, God. Take me now. This instant.*

He'd left her…barely out of childhood…to deal with that all alone…

He stared at her, fire ripping through him, thawing the chill, burning him with searing hopelessness. "You had my baby?"

She nodded, looking frightened.

Her fear confused him. "Why didn't you tell me?"

"You didn't come back."

Her words echoed the ones she'd said the other night. *You didn't come back*. Suffused with more input than he could process, Pierce stared at her.

"When I did come back. Why didn't you tell me then?"

The truth occurred to him. She'd lost the baby.

He hadn't given her a chance to let him know that. No wonder she was struggling. She wanted a family. With him. The family she'd lost...

"Because I'd let myself believe that it was best...afterward...if I started a new life without carrying around what I couldn't change. My father insisted, as part of his agreement to let me live with Grandma, that I not tell anyone."

*Her father*. Pierce wasn't much for hate. Especially involving a family member. But he was close in that moment to hating Jonathan Maxwell. Eliza's dad had too much to answer for.

If not for him, Pierce would have been back. He would have known.

He might not have been able to prevent

what happened to the baby, but at least he'd have known. And been there to help Eliza...

The intensity in her tears was fully understandable to him. By God, she'd carried around that grief for *seventeen* years?

What kind of animal asked his daughter to keep something like that buried deep inside?

To him, in his case, the whole thing made sense. He'd broken the law—a legal adult, he'd made love to someone who was, by law, underage. Never mind that Eliza would have been sixteen in less than a week. But the truth was, he'd known at the time that it was wrong. Too soon.

He'd just been so afraid to go. Afraid he wouldn't make it back. Afraid that she wouldn't wait for him. He'd needed the memory of her to keep him alive.

He'd been just what her father had called him. A self-serving punk.

And after what he'd done in the Middle East, killing that boy, he didn't deserve to know the joy of having a child of his own.

But Eliza...

Her only sin had been to love him too much.

"I'm not proud of what I did, Pierce. I know now that it was wrong. Completely, horribly wrong to deny the existence of our child to the point of pretending like it never happened…"

He wanted to take away her pain. Feared that he was many years too late.

"My father was right," she said now, a hint of bitterness in the sharp chuckle that escaped her. "I'd have been branded if I'd gone to my new school here in the South as the girl who'd been pregnant. It was much easier to pretend it had never happened, because losing him had just about killed me and…"

Him. *Him?*

His insides started to tremble.

"It was a boy?" He didn't recognize his own voice. Felt like he was choking, but didn't even cough.

A boy for a boy. It made sense to him. He deserved that.

But did she?

Surely no fate would require her to pay that ultimate price for having picked him to love. Even Pierce, in his most maudlin state, couldn't make that one work.

She nodded. Teared up again as she looked at him. "I'm told he had a head full of hair. And blue eyes. But babies are often born with blue eyes and then they change…" Her lips turned, like she was trying to smile through her tears. They turned downward instead as her chin puckered.

How could she have kept this inside her all these years?

How could he not have known?

One thing was for certain. Eliza was much stronger than he'd ever known. Stronger than she gave herself credit for.

When she was calm again, he asked, "What happened?"

Best to get it all out now. He didn't want her to have to go through this again.

"What do you mean, what happened?"

"With the baby. You said losing him just about killed you. Did you hemorrhage? How far along were you?" *Where is he buried? What did you name him?*

A look of inexplicable horror crossed her face, and Pierce cursed himself for pushing her too far. How could he possibly know what was best?

"The baby didn't die, Pierce."

It took a few seconds for her words to register. He heard them again. In his mind. And then again. An echo that he had to resist.

And couldn't deny.

Her horror had entered him. Taken him over.

"Are you telling me that we have a son?

Out there?" He welcomed the sharp pain that shot up his arm and through his shoulder and beyond as he flung his bad hand toward the yard.

"He's alive. Yes." The three words changed everything. Everything.

Now nothing made sense. Jumping up, he left the gazebo. Needed air. Space.

"I'm going for a walk," he said, not even sure she heard him. He didn't give her a chance to reply.

He just strode off and left her all alone.

Again.

## CHAPTER FIFTEEN

IF IT HADN'T been so late, Eliza would have called Natasha Stevens. Not that it was all that late in California. But it was after business hours. And her conversation with the other woman, while horribly personal to Eliza, was really just business.

She thought about phoning anyway and leaving a message. But didn't think quitting the show was something she should do over voice mail.

Probably best to give herself some hours to collect herself before telling anyone anything. And to find out exactly what she'd be telling them.

Had Pierce left her or just gone for a walk like he'd said?

Would he be coming back?

Margie had long since left. And Eliza had made it a point never to go out into the public areas of the house after social hour. If she went out, her guests would think she was accessible. *You have to set boundaries*, Grandma had said.

She hadn't been talking only about the rules of being a healthy innkeeper.

Eliza paced the backyard for a while—the walled-in part that was private for Pierce and her, not minding at all that the air had grown too chilly to be out without a sweater. She welcomed the cold on her overheated skin.

When she started to get headachy, she figured she was probably a bit dehydrated from all the crying and went in to get a bottle of water.

Being practical helped.

Brought her back to reality.

And the reality was, she was going to be just fine.

She was always just fine.

What other choice was there?

She was alive. So she would live. She breathed, so she would take breaths. Simple really. A truth she'd learned a long time ago.

Glancing out the window, she hoped she'd see Pierce on the front porch. He wasn't there.

She didn't blame him. Keeping the existence of a son from a sterile man had been wrong. Terribly wrong.

But it wasn't like Pierce could have seen the boy. Or had any part in his life.

She hadn't named Pierce on the birth certificate. Again, with advice from her father, advocated for by her mother. She couldn't give the baby up for adoption without Pierce's signature if she named him as the father, they'd said. And since he hadn't contacted her, how was she going to get his signature?

They'd told her to grow up. Look at life realistically. An older high school boy had had his way with her his last night in town, and then he'd gone off to see the world, leaving her to bear the consequences alone.

She'd tried to believe them. Might have for a while. It was so hard to remember exactly what she'd thought during those frightening months. What she'd known for certain was that at sixteen, with no one to help her, she'd never have been able to give that baby a good life.

He'd have ended up like Pierce, only worse, living in a trailer, if they were lucky, with a mom who didn't have it together enough to provide for him, let alone give him fair chances.

It's the last thing Pierce would have wanted.

*Pierce would have wanted...*

What did Pierce want now? She paced another ten minutes. Through their private quarters. Out to their porch. And then down the steps to the walk. She stood in the front yard, looking up and down the street. A few late strollers were about. Balmy weather in March was a welcome respite from the winter's cold. There were lights on down at the beach, restaurants and bars still open.

Was Pierce there? Making plans?

Eliza wasn't sure when she started to get mad. But when the anger built, it didn't seem to stop.

How dare he walk out on her again.

And if he thought she was just going to sit and take it...again...he was...

She didn't really plan to walk down to the beach. Her feet just kept moving. One in front of the other, until she was a block away from home. She hadn't locked the door. Wasn't completely sure she'd shut it all the way.

But she kept walking. To the sand. And beyond. She wasn't sure what she thought she was going to do. Couldn't seem to find coherent thoughts enough to string together. She walked.

Until she saw him. Standing down by the

ocean, hands in his pockets, the bandage bulging around his left wrist. Looking out to sea.

PIERCE DIDN'T QUESTION how Eliza came to be standing next to him. Nor did he look at her.

"Where is he?"

"That's the million-dollar question." Not an Eliza-type answer.

Pierce wasn't sure what to say to her. He felt like he didn't know her. And yet...loved her more than ever.

"I gave him up for adoption."

He'd figured that much out. Even before the ocean air had cleared his head.

"Here? In Shelby Island?"

"In Charleston."

"So he could be living close?" The intensity in his tone scared him. He could only imagine what it was doing to her.

What did she want? Had she ever even looked for the boy after she and Pierce had gotten back together?

Would she want to see him?

Or would it hurt too much? "He's not."

That made him mad. But the anger burned itself out before it was even fully ignited.

During his walk to the beach, two things became clear. He had no right to be angry.

And he didn't blame Eliza for her choices. They'd both been manipulated by her father. And even he had probably acted for the right reasons. Wrong actions. No way Pierce could ever condone the way the man had played God with his and Eliza's lives. But he was almost able to see that, as a father, Jonathan Maxwell had probably thought he was protecting his daughter's future. Doing what was best for her in the long run.

And…wait…

"How do you know he's not close if you don't know where he is?"

"The agency I used was here. Well, in Charleston…"

She paused, and his mind took a couple of steps back. "That's what you meant when you said your father agreed to let you live with your grandmother. He let you come here to have the baby instead of going back where everyone knew us…"

"No."

The wind blew her hair, and he wanted to wrap an arm around her. She should have grabbed a sweater before coming to join him.

"My father insisted that I come here to

have the baby, as soon as I knew I was pregnant, before I started to show. He didn't want anyone to know."

But…

"What about your junior year? You had to attend school. So the kids in your school here knew…" The realization brought a hint of relief.

"Grandma homeschooled me. She was a retired teacher."

He'd probably known that—the teacher part. When they were kids, Eliza had told him everything. From what she ate when they weren't together to what she wrote in her diary. They'd had no secrets.

Seemed forever ago. Another life.

He had to live in this one. Deal with this one. "So what did you mean when you said you made a deal with your father to stay with your grandmother?"

"After the baby was born…" The catch in her throat nearly undid him.

He was determined not to let that happen. If nothing else, he'd take this like a man.

"When I got pregnant, they sold the house and moved to Florida. I was supposed to follow them there. To finish high school there.

I didn't want to live with them again. Especially after all the pressure they put on me to give away the baby. I begged them to let me live with Grandma. And they did."

They weren't all bad. They loved her. And even then, their acquiescence had come at great cost to her. To live as though she'd never had a child? Pierce was piecing together a more complete picture.

The view was making him sick. And angry. And...

"I'm sorry." Sorrier than she'd ever know. Sorrier than he could ever tell her. So, so sorry. For so much.

In the past. And in the present, too. They weren't done yet.

"So, where is he?"

"I don't know, Pierce. What I do know is that he was adopted through a sister agency in Anaheim."

"He's in California?"

"I don't know that for sure. His adoptive parents lived there when they adopted him."

"What do you know about them?"

"Nothing."

He didn't want to hear any more.

Of any of it.

"I'm guessing your father knows?"

"I don't think so. We didn't vet them. We hired the agency to do so. I know there was an extensive, three-month background check on the receiving family. I know the couple was married and able to provide him with a good life."

Nervous again, Pierce looked out at the ocean. The tide was low, barely making a sound save for a soft rustle as water lapped gently at the sand, and it eased his pain just enough to keep him there. Made no sense, but he concentrated on the sound.

He said what he'd been trying not to think. "There's a connection between your trips to Palm Desert and your sudden need to speak with me about adoption."

"Yes."

"Tell me."

"I got a letter...just before Christmas... from the agency here in Charleston. It was forwarded from the address I'd lived at with Grandma, to Rose Harbor, as back then the inn was listed as her place of business..."

He wanted every detail. Wanted the space in between hearing and knowing...

Wanted to prolong finding out what he didn't want to know.

"He contacted the agency in California." The words, no matter how expected, were a shock to his system. "He wanted to know my contact information."

The boy, their boy, was looking for his mother? For Eliza?

This was huge. Huger than he'd ever imagined.

Or feared.

He'd killed a boy. Was not cut out to be a father. Most especially not to a boy.

Eliza loved him. But she'd leave him for her baby.

He had a son. He who could never father another child had a flesh-and-blood biological son.

She was telling him about the private adoption and all its stipulations. About visiting the agency. About not being able to obtain any information about their son. About being able to give the agency her current contact information, but holding off until she'd told him—Pierce—that he'd fathered a child.

The fact that she'd put him first humbled him. Moved him. Deeply.

And confused him, too. Why was he thinking of himself at a time like this?

But how could he not? What was he supposed to do with any of this? "You're going to give them the go-ahead tomorrow, right?" First and foremost, that had to happen.

The boy wouldn't be asking for information unless he had questions. Or needed something he thought Eliza could give him.

Could just be some biological history.

He had a son. With a head full of hair and blue eyes.

A son with a different adoptive father. A son Pierce couldn't hurt...

"I'm not going to Palm Desert, Pierce. There's no way I'm leaving now."

"There's no way you aren't," he told her. He wasn't her boss. He couldn't physically force her on that plane. Nor would he try. But he knew, deep down, she wanted to go.

He was on the verge of telling her that if she didn't go, he would leave her. He couldn't be responsible for her not following through with what she needed. But he stopped.

"I'm sorry. That was the wrong thing to say." Her *cop an attitude* phrase still stung.

"Thank you."

"Now." He turned her toward him, his hands resting on her shoulders. "Look at me."

She did. By the light of the moon. And she had never looked so beautiful to him. Tendrils of her hair were blowing lightly in the breeze. Her face was raw and open.

"Tell me that, in your heart of hearts, you don't want to go." *Heart of hearts.* Those were her words.

"I..."

"Eliza. We have to be honest with each other. We promised."

She nodded. "Part of me wants to go."

"And you'll give them the go-ahead regarding your contact information?"

"I think he might already have some of it," she said. A gust of cooler air swept off the ocean, and instead of cuddling up to him, Eliza hugged herself.

That hurt him. But he knew he couldn't let it.

She said, "I think that call last Friday, the unidentified one from Palm Desert..."

Had been from his son? He still had the number. Could call it back...

But he wouldn't.

"You think he's in Palm Desert?" Pierce asked.

"I don't know where he is. But… I was thinking…we should call back that number. You said you looked it up."

She knew he had the number.

And he had no reason not to give it to her.

"That's why you told me now, isn't it? Because you're afraid he might call again and I might answer?"

"I was going to tell you anyway, Pierce. I tried the first week after I met with the agency."

But she'd known about the letter for months.

About the boy for almost eighteen years.

He'd have bet his life that Eliza had no secrets from him. He'd truly believed that she couldn't. That the feelings she had for him were that pure. That she was that pure.

He was being unfair. He knew it.

And had never been more disillusioned.

Looking down at the top of his wife's head, he wanted to pull her close. To lose himself in her.

And saw a stranger. A mother.

Did he really even know her?

"I love you." He didn't blame her for needing to go. In some ways, he wanted her to do so.

Tears filled her eyes again. "I love you, too."

They gave each other everything they had.

Pierce thought it inevitable that it wouldn't be enough.

## CHAPTER SIXTEEN

IT WAS THREE hours earlier in Palm Desert. Not yet eight o'clock. She and Pierce had walked back together, separately. Until the last block, when he'd taken her hand.

She'd held on for dear life.

Pierce did not want to be a father. She got that. Even talking about being a father brought on his nightmares.

He'd tried.

Going to war changed people. It had most clearly changed him from a warm young man who poured out his heart to her, to an intensely private, mostly quiet man who still poured his heart into her.

War had damaged his body. And his psyche.

She loved him all the more for it.

And believed in him, too. They could get around this if he'd be willing to try.

"It's not like he's a boy," she said as they climbed the steps to their private entrance.

She was glad to see she'd closed the door. And was eager to get inside to her sweater.

And to the phone.

"I cannot be an example to someone who has biological reason to believe he is like me."

"He'd be like you were before you went into the army. What the army did to you… that wasn't biological."

He didn't say any more. But the firm expression on his face told her that her words hadn't swayed him.

Pierce didn't talk much about his time in the Middle East. Except to say that it was best for both of them if he didn't talk about it. Best if he didn't relive it.

As long as he continued to seek professional help when he was struggling, she was willing to abide by his edict.

Or she had been. Until their son had opened a door that she'd thought permanently closed.

Whatever had happened to Pierce, whatever he'd seen…they were going to have to deal with it. They'd already lost the chance to raise their only biological child. They couldn't lose the chance to have contact with him.

Or rather, she couldn't.

And if Pierce could…

"Let's try that number," she said as soon as they were inside, afraid she was poking him with a hot iron, but unable to stop.

They weren't going to make it if they couldn't deal with this situation.

"Please, Pierce. What if he calls back again when I'm gone?" She'd lunged for the inn's phone every time it had rung that week. And thought Pierce had probably noticed.

Without a word, he went to the internet, looked up his history and got the number. Jotting it on a scrap of paper, he handed it to her and headed toward the door.

"Aren't you going to do this with me? What if he answers? We need to do this together..." She was begging.

For their marriage.

They were on a downhill trajectory that they couldn't stop. But they could hold on to each other. And land together at the bottom.

Pierce went out back. She could see him heading toward the gazebo.

Picking up her cell, she considered taking the call outside to him. But she wasn't sure anymore.

Since she'd told him her secret, he'd been different.

Understandably so. The man had just discovered he had a son.

She'd been prepared for anger, but that's not how he'd reacted at all. He'd been understanding. Loving and kind. Like the Pierce she'd fallen in love with so many years before.

But unlike that young man, he wasn't sharing his feelings with her. Or his thoughts.

She looked at the number. At her cell phone. Put both down. Stood at the window in their small living room and looked out at Pierce.

She wasn't going to lose him.

Was she?

It was getting later in Palm Desert.

With shaking hands, Eliza picked up the phone. Dialed. Pushed Send.

Heard a click and almost dropped the phone.

Holding on with slippery fingers, she had no idea what to say.

*Hi, are you my son?*

*Hi, you don't know me, but I might have given birth to you...*

*Is that you? Are you my baby?*

"You have reached Palm Desert Television Studios. Our offices are..."

The studio.

It wasn't her son who'd called. It was someone from the studio. Why they hadn't called back, she didn't know. But didn't really care.

Sinking down to the floor, she put her head between her knees and started to shake in earnest. She'd wanted so badly for him to answer. For the waiting to be over.

Finally, even if only for a moment, to get to be a mother to the baby she'd borne.

*I got a call from this number, but there was no message...*

That's what she should have thought of to say. If she were rational, she would have thought of it.

For a moment there, she'd thought she was going to connect with her son. And for that moment, nothing else had mattered.

No one else had existed.

She'd left Pierce standing out in the dark alone, and reached out by herself to the son she'd given away. She'd made a choice.

Him over Pierce. The mother in her had won out over the wife.

And for what? She didn't even know if her son wanted to meet her. She knew for certain his father didn't want to meet him.

Which couldn't possibly be a good thing for the boy.

*Hi, I'm your mom. I'm so, so, so thrilled*

*finally to meet you. Oh, your father? Yes, I know where he is. I'm married to him, actually. No. No, he doesn't want anything to do with you. But it's not about you...*

It was quite possible, given the fact that they were dealing with a seventeen-year-old boy, that his request for contact had come out of a desire to know who his father was. He'd be at the age where he'd be defining himself as a man. And needed to know what kind of man he came from.

An athlete? Someone with a head for business? A bald banker with a paunch?

Raising her head, Eliza thought of Pierce out in their gazebo.

Was he worrying about what was happening in the house? Imagining her speaking with the son he wouldn't see?

Her heart ached for him. Yearned for him. She ached for all three of them.

What if Pierce had left again?

She jumped up. Reassured herself that he was still outside. Probably giving her enough time to finish her call.

Waiting for a sign from her that she was done?

She was losing it here. Hugging herself

around her shoulders, she knew she was in serious trouble.

What was she going to do?

Turn her back on Pierce? Unthinkable.

Ignore her son's plea? Impossible.

*Get a grip.*

For the first time since she'd left to go find Pierce, Eliza recognized herself.

Yes. She was going to get a grip. It's what she did. She'd pull it together. Act like the adult she was. She wasn't a kid anymore.

She'd made choices. Irrevocable choices.

She just had to find a way to live with them.

Somehow.

HE HEARD HER come outside. Could hear her steps in the grass as she crossed the yard toward him. He didn't look up. Didn't openly welcome her when she came into the gazebo and sat down in the rocker opposite the one he'd chosen.

He was glad she was there. Never in his life had there been a time when he hadn't been glad to have Eliza nearby. Didn't figure there'd ever be a time.

He also didn't figure he'd be at the inn much longer.

"It wasn't him."

He hated feeling the initial rush of relief that washed over him. The fact that he wasn't overjoyed to know he had a son, especially in light of the fact that he was incapable of fathering another, proved that he was somehow lacking in the emotional health category.

He'd known since the day he'd faced down an eight-year-old boy and pulled the trigger that there was something elementally wrong with him.

And he hated himself for the small thrill that escaped from someplace inside him when it hit him—again—that he had a son in the world.

"It was the studio." Eliza sounded different. Distant. Almost like she was speaking with one of her guests, except less nurturing. "I have no idea why they didn't call back, or why they were calling in the first place, but I suspect it might have been because I jumped in the town car that had been sent for the twins. Their flight was late and we were all there at the same time. I called to let the studio know, the driver said he'd let the other driver know, too, but lines of communication could easily have crossed with them."

He didn't mind listening to her talk.

"I'm going to go to the agency again tomorrow, Pierce. I intend to tell them to release my personal information. I'd like to add yours to the file, as well."

He could still hear the ocean in his mind. It was getting louder. It was one thing to think about having a son in the world, and entirely another to allow the boy to know who'd fathered him.

Seventeen was an impressionable, crazy, hormonal age. He would not risk having a young man look up to him, or in any way think that what he'd done was okay. He couldn't be that example...

A lesson learned during his second marriage. He knew why the nightmares had come. Because he'd taken on a responsibility he couldn't live up to. His life was not a good example for a young man to emulate.

"I'd need your permission, Pierce. In writing." If she knew that much, she must have already asked. She'd already been planning his involvement before he'd even known he was a father.

Again, he wondered who she was. And how she could have had so much going on without him knowing.

"Pierce?"

"No." He wasn't copping an attitude. He was, perhaps, saving a life. He'd be damned if any son of his looked up to him.

"That's it? No discussion?"

"That's it."

Her silence told him she was disappointed.

It was nothing compared to how she'd feel about him if she knew the truth. She deserved to know.

That moment was when Pierce hit his all-time low. Because he realized that he'd never had any intention of telling Eliza the truth. All the thought about the pact, about contacting his fellow pact holders—it had all been a way to buy himself time. To see how everything played out.

He couldn't tell her. Ever.

He'd rather lose her than have her know that he'd lost his soul.

There. The bald truth. Right in front of his face. The real reason he'd known that someday he'd have to give her up.

And that was *before* he'd known they had a son in the picture.

"Will you at least think about it?"

There was no kindness in letting her hope. "Thinking won't change my mind." Any more than regret could bring that young boy in the small desert town back to life.

The next move was up to her. Would she ask him to clear out while she was away? He wouldn't blame her. Should he offer to do so?

"But you do understand that I have to give him my information, right?"

"Of course. I wouldn't have that any other way." Another truth.

"So I have your support?"

"You always have my support, Liza. Always." That was a forever he could give her.

"Are you still planning to take me to the airport?" They'd discussed it earlier, when she'd been packing. His right arm was fine. The swelling over his eye was down. He could drive safely and easily. He just hadn't been sure she'd still want him to drive her.

And told himself not to get his hopes up because she did. "Of course."

"Can we go to bed now? We have to be up early."

He stood. Put his arm around his wife's waist, thankful that he'd have at least one more night beside her, and walked her inside.

## CHAPTER SEVENTEEN

ELIZA'S TRIP TO the adoption agency was quick. Mrs. Carpenter was out, and as always, the place was quiet that late on a Friday afternoon.

The receptionist was polite as she took Eliza's signed and dated written permission to release her information to her biological son in the event that he asked for it. It had even been notarized right there on the spot.

The middle-aged woman didn't ask about Pierce. Only Mrs. Carpenter knew that the boy's father was in the picture.

At least, Eliza hoped he still was. Though he'd held her close the entire night, he'd been more distant that morning than she'd ever known him to be. To the point of politeness when she'd called to let him know she'd made it to the hotel.

"Silence is the way Pierce handles his emotions," she reminded herself aloud as she turned her rental car back toward Palm

Desert. She'd originally thought she'd be no-good company for a cocktail gathering with her fellow contestants that evening, but was starting to think she'd go.

She needed to be out among people. Needed space to clear her perspective.

She needed to know that her husband would still be in residence when she returned to Rose Harbor on Sunday.

And she needed to stay busy so she didn't stare at her phone.

She'd give her right arm to hear from her son.

How could that be, knowing that if she did, she'd likely lose her husband?

The thought panicked her to the point that she slowed down, thinking she'd take the next exit, turn back to the agency and withdraw her permission. Her stomach fluttered as she worried that she wouldn't be in time. That the boy would already have her information.

And then she sped up past the exit. No matter what it cost her, she couldn't turn her back on the person who was alive because of choices she'd made. Period.

Her decision was made.

And it was final.

Pierce had no idea whether or not Eliza would call him when she got to her room Friday night. He wasn't sure about anything his wife might or might not do anymore. The hours that she'd been gone had been unkind to him.

He could see Eliza moving out to California. Getting into the television chef business. And becoming family to their son.

The Eliza he'd thought he'd known would never have left Rose Harbor. Or him. But that Eliza didn't exist, and he had to face that fact. The woman he'd married had gone through far more heartache at sixteen than he'd ever imagined. She'd made tough decisions.

Endured pain he'd never fully comprehend.

And then gone on to graduate from Harvard.

She'd made good decisions. Healthy, sound decisions. She'd made decisions that were best for others, and still managed to carve out a happy life for herself.

In all of that, he couldn't find the woman who needed him.

He waited for her call. Just in case.

And almost didn't answer when it came.

"Did you go?" He compromised with himself and picked up because he had to know whether or not the boy could possibly try to contact her at home while she was gone.

At least, that was what he went with.

"Yes."

"It's done?"

"Yes."

He wanted to be angry. To lash out. To storm out. In truth, he was glad.

She'd done the right thing.

"You ready for tomorrow?" he asked.

"Yes."

"You sound tired."

"I'm beat."

"You want me to let you go so you can rest?"

"No."

Pierce settled back against the pillows, taking a lot of comfort from that one word.

"I'm afraid you're not going to be there when I get back."

Comfort flew out the window.

"Do you want me to leave?"

"No! Did you hear what I just said? I'm afraid, Pierce. Scared to death. I don't want to come home and find you gone."

"You won't." This time.

But they both knew it might happen sometime in the near future.

"I love you."

"I love you, too."

"You haven't said anything about the fact

that I kept such a huge secret from you all these years."

"What's to say? You explained. I understand why you did it. I don't blame you." His jaw tensed as he spoke.

"I had your baby, Pierce."

"I know." What did she want from him?

"Are you angry with me?"

"For having the child? Of course not." He knew that wasn't what she meant. Was not proud of his prevarication. But there was so much about himself that he couldn't explain. If he got started, where would it lead?

"For giving him away," she said.

"Absolutely not." And then it occurred to him—idiot that he was, he'd been thinking of what she'd gone through, how it affected him, and hadn't thought at all about what she thought of it all. "And I hope you aren't angry with yourself, either," he said, on a roll now that he saw a small place where she might need him. "You have no reason to feel guilty, Liza. None. You were a kid. I was there for the conception and then I just left. You never heard from me again…"

"Because my father threatened you."

"You didn't know that. And even if you had, it shouldn't have made a difference. You had two years left of high school. No way to support a child. No support from me. What kind of life would the boy have had? You gave him parents, Liza. Family who loved and wanted him."

"I should have told you about him when you first got back in touch with me."

He wanted to agree. But selfishly, he was glad that she hadn't. He'd have had the same issues he was currently having. They'd have driven him away from her, and he'd never have known what it was like to live with her. Be married to her.

At the same time…

"I'm struggling a bit with the fact that you had such a life-changing event, and such an enormous secret, and I didn't have a clue." He was a cop. He was supposed to be trained to know when someone was lying. Hiding something.

"I had a lot of years to practice pretending it hadn't happened."

"But when you saw me again…the baby's father…"

He didn't have a right to pry. Especially when he couldn't reciprocate.

"I felt more at peace," she told him. "Like at least if we were together…"

She didn't finish the sentence. And Pierce didn't ask her to, leery of what she might have said.

"Anyway, I'm sorry, babe, that I kept it from you."

"I'm sorry that I wasn't there for you…"

He was sorry for so much more than that. But couldn't figure out how to make any of it right.

One thing he'd learned a long time ago—life didn't give a guy do-overs.

"We promised ourselves that we wouldn't let regrets from the past eat up our future," he reminded her—even knowing that thinking they were going to get through this together was a pipe dream.

"I know."

"You need to get some rest."

"You, too. Are you going to be okay?"

"Yes." He'd been managing his nightmares on his own for more than a decade.

But for the second night in a row, Pierce took a sleeping pill before he climbed under the covers.

WHEN ELIZA'S PHONE rang while she was in the shower Saturday morning, her heart leaped and she rushed out to answer it. She'd left her cell on the bathroom counter, just in case.

But the ring was coming from the landline.

Dripping on the carpet, grabbing yesterday's clothes up to her body, she answered, only to find that the shuttle was going to be half an hour later. Taping had been moved back half an hour due to an issue at the studio, and as an apology for the inconvenience, the hotel would be sending breakfast up to her room.

Once she was over the initial letdown, she was slightly relieved that the call hadn't been from her son. She needed to focus on cooking for the next few hours.

She would have liked to hear from Pierce, though. Would have liked for him to call her rather than wait for her to call him. It was a routine they'd established, that she call him. And it made sense since she was the one coming and going. But she wished anyway...

Still, the reprieve was nice. Breakfast was nice, too. A bit much, with two kinds of eggs, pancakes, toast, bacon, coffee, juice, a muffin and fruit, but she ate what she could of it. Mostly it was nice to have a few extra minutes in her room to compose herself. From Pierce's injuries to the revelation of her baby secret, it had been a tough week. She hoped it was the toughest one they'd face.

But she knew they had some difficult days ahead.

Not impossible. Just difficult.

As difficult as getting a spot on *Family Secrets*. And then winning one of the competitions. And she'd managed to do both.

Feeling better than she had all week, she went down to meet the shuttle ten minutes early. As was also her routine. As she exited the elevator and rounded the corner into the lobby, she expected to see some of her fellow contestants. The twins, at the very least.

Five minutes later she was still the only one in the lobby. And started to get a bit uncomfortable. Her phone rang, and Eliza grabbed it up. She'd already talked to Pierce, having called to tell him about the change in the day's plans. He'd wished her good luck, just as he had each week…

The call was from a number she didn't recognize.

All other thoughts fled as Eliza pushed the button to answer.

"Hello?"

"Eliza?" The voice on the other end of the line was feminine.

"Yes?"

"This is Angela. We got the message you left about driving yourself in today, but it's getting late. Are you okay?"

"What? What message?" Dread weighted her chest. She looked around the busy lobby as though someone would appear to help her. "I didn't leave a message. What about the shuttle? The issue at the studio? No one else is down here yet, but…"

"Everyone's here, sweetie. Taping starts in half an hour. There was a message on the show's answering machine telling the shuttle not to wait for you, that you had your own ride this morning…"

*Oh no.* "I didn't leave a message!" she was running now, back to the bell desk. "I need a cab!" she said, and then, into the phone, "I'll get there as quickly as I can…" And prayed they'd wait for her.

"There are no cabs out front, Mrs. Westin. We can call you one if you'd like."

She nodded. Thanked him. And went to the rental car desk at the same time. She was only ten minutes from the studio. She'd never driven it before, but after so many back and forth trips, she was pretty sure she knew the way.

In the end, the rental car was quicker. She

was belted in and on the road before the cab pulled into the drive.

Another catastrophe averted.

She could do this.

And later, she'd figure out what in the heck was going on.

One thing was for sure. Pierce's assurance that the previous mishaps on the set weren't personal to her no longer held weight.

Clearly, this was personal.

Very personal.

Someone was out to get her.

She just had no idea who. Or why.

## CHAPTER EIGHTEEN

PIERCE WAS UPSTAIRS vacuuming guest rooms when his phone buzzed against his hip. Off the job for another week at least, he knew it wouldn't be work. But it could be Jamison or one of the other guys checking up on him.

He almost let it go.

It just wasn't in him to do so.

*Eliza!* He saw her name on the screen and turned off the vacuum.

"What's up, Liza?" She was supposed to be in the green room. Ready to go on stage for taping.

His heart started to pound as she told him that the change of plans had been neither official nor legitimate. He hated her driving in such a hurry on unfamiliar roads. Hated that she was all alone. Hated that he couldn't get to her quickly and easily.

He hated that he didn't have a clue what was going on. And most of all, he hated that he hadn't taken the previous incidents more seriously.

Insisting that she stay on the phone with him until she'd arrived and was safely in the green room, Pierce wished her luck. Told her to have fun cooking and they'd worry about the rest later. He told her he loved her.

He hung up.

And was on the phone with Palm Desert police before she would have had time to put her phone away.

BY THE TIME Eliza called him after the show, Pierce had done all he could do for the moment. He'd been in touch with law enforcement, had opened an official report and had someone standing by to speak with Natasha, Eliza, Grace and anyone else they deemed necessary.

Maybe it was overkill, since there'd not even been a threat of personal harm, but he'd unabashedly pulled the cop card. Asked for a favor.

Questions would be asked. People put on alert.

*Before* any personal harm could happen.

He might have failed Eliza in a lot of ways, but he was not going to let her down on this one. Protecting her was his duty, and he was going to get it right.

He geared up to tell her so, to let her know about the police escort she'd have back to the hotel, but he didn't even get a word out before she said, "I won! Pierce, I won again. Can you believe it?"

He'd hoped. Wasn't surprised. Her fried vegetables were about the best thing he'd ever eaten. But he hadn't put a lot of stock in the win since she was already going to the final round.

It was clear that the further accolade mattered to her, though.

Surprised that he hadn't known how talented she was, he congratulated her. Smiled as she talked a mile a minute, telling him about the runners-up. One of the twins. And Grace again.

His news could wait a minute. Or even two.

"So, there were no problems on set?" he asked her when she finally slowed down. She was in a hallway outside the green room—as she'd been each week when she'd called to let him know how taping had gone.

"None," she said. "Natasha knows about my mix-up this morning, but she asked if we could keep it quiet until after the taping, and

I agreed." A note of unease had entered her voice, and he took the opportunity to let her know that the police were waiting to speak with her.

He half expected her to be upset with him. To tell him that she could take care of herself. Or that Natasha wanted to handle things her own way.

"Thank you, babe." Her words warmed everything cold inside him. "You have no idea how much better I feel knowing you've got my back."

"I always do, Liza. Always."

And if that was the best he could give her, at least there was that.

ELIZA WAS HALFWAY back to the hotel, with a police car directly behind her, when she started to feel the thump. It was like she'd run over something and it had stuck to her tire.

She'd been watching the road. It had been clear.

What would...

Red-and-blue lights started to flash in her rearview and side mirrors. The cruiser behind her was signaling her to stop.

She'd thought Pierce was being overprotective when he'd arranged her escort back to the hotel, but was glad he had as she pulled off.

What was wrong now?

And when was this all going to end?

Pulling to the side of the road, she waited for the officer to approach. And was more confused than anything when she heard that she had a tire that was severing. She called Pierce. Got in the police car as he instructed. And talked to him until she was safely in her hotel room.

They talked for hours that night.

About life. Vacations they'd always wanted to take but hadn't. About a guest she'd never met, an elderly gentleman who'd amused Pierce when he'd checked in. They talked about the show. The dishes others had made. The reasons the judges had chosen her dish. They talked about social hour, and she hung on while he made certain that Margie was okay doing it without him. They talked while he did all of the dishes afterward so their friend could go up to the room she was staying in that night so she could serve breakfast early in the morning and be on-site should anyone need anything.

They talked about a lot of things. But not

one that mattered. He told her he loved her. She told him back.

And meant it.

Still, when she got on the plane to go home the next morning, she was nervous about what the coming week would bring.

FOR ALL HER WORRY, the next days were almost eerily placid. As the week wore on with no emails or texts or phone calls from her son, Eliza started to realize that she'd built his one visit to the adoption agency months ago into something much bigger than it was.

Started to realize that she probably hadn't needed to tell Pierce about the boy at all. Hadn't needed to train-wreck her marriage or her husband's peace of mind.

Not that her marriage was falling apart. It wasn't. She and Pierce were as in love, as good to each other, as always. She needed him. He needed her.

But there was something missing.

The something that meant the most.

There was no intimacy between them. Off work for another week, at least, Pierce was around more. Tending to her, the inn, as much as he could. He was kind and thoughtful. Present.

He just wasn't *hers*. Not in the way he always had been.

An element of trust was missing.

A sense of ending had taken its place.

They didn't talk about their baby, the one that she'd given away.

He never asked if she got a call or email or text.

They didn't talk about the future—not even to discuss the painting they'd been planning to do in a couple of the upstairs rooms that month.

It could wait.

Pierce got his stitches out. He could stop wearing the elasticized bandage around his wrist whenever he felt comfortable doing so. His bruises had healed, and he'd been released to go back to work in another week.

They tended to their guests. They chatted with Margie. They got along.

And she practiced making her Bolognese sauce for the last competition. The final week's category was sauce, but the contestants were expected also to prepare whatever the sauce was meant to complement.

Her secret ingredients, other than dual meats and very little tomato, were cream and wine—something her grandmother had taught her. Bay leaves gave it an Italian flair. Thyme, sea salt and olive oil were finishing touches to the otherwise classic mixture.

Sea salt was one of Eliza's signatures, she'd been told by the judges the previous week. She found unique and different ways to use it. She hadn't realized it but could see that they were right.

The ocean, coming to Rose Harbor to be with her grandmother—they'd saved her life. She clung to them.

Loved them.

And incorporated her love for them in her cooking.

She wondered if Pierce loved the ocean and Shelby Island. A month ago she'd have been certain he did. Now, she didn't feel like she knew him well enough to be sure.

Was he just there because she'd been so rooted?

She wanted to ask him. But she didn't. They weren't that close anymore.

Instead, she made the sauce and spread it on pizza dough, timing herself, on Tuesday night.

And then made it again, timing herself, mixing it with pasta the next night.

Either base would be doable from ingredients stocked in the general pantry on the set.

Pierce preferred the sauce over pasta, he told her Wednesday night as they were eating a late dinner. Then, "I'd like to come with you this weekend."

In the beginning, she'd guarded her time in California as her own.

Because of her son—about whom he knew nothing.

And then later, too… She didn't know why. But she'd needed the space. To be focused on her task there.

Now, the thought of herself in that hotel room for another weekend felt…lonely.

She smiled at her husband. From the inside out. "Okay," she told him. Talked about her flight, the airline she was on, getting him a seat, maybe even getting them seats together. Talked about them renting a car for Friday afternoon and driving around the area. And arranging for Margie to have help at the inn.

Pierce listened. Smiled once. Let her go on until she was finished.

"I had a call from the Palm Desert police department," he said in response. A reply she felt like a slap in the face.

He wasn't deciding to join her because he

wanted to sit next to her on the plane. He wanted to come because of the unexplained attacks.

Still, it was something.

He had her back.

Eliza decided to be happy with what she could get.

## CHAPTER NINETEEN

PALM DESERT POLICE had traced the phone call to Eliza's room to a hotel house phone located in the lobby. And while there were surveillance cameras, there were none that covered that particular phone. Breakfast had been ordered from the same phone to be sent to Eliza's room and charged to her account, which was paid for by the studio. Police traced the call to the studio as having come from the hotel, as well. They picked up no usable fingerprints. And no one noticed anything unusual.

Six of her competitors were staying at the hotel. Technically, any one of them could have made the calls, or asked someone else to do so, and any of them could have had access to the kitchens. It took only a second to grab a bag of mushrooms or switch out a water bottle.

The question was, why Eliza? Starting before she'd even won?

"The thing that points away from any of your competitors," Pierce was telling her, not for the first time, as they waited for the rental car he'd arranged at the airport, "is the car. Your tire was slashed while you were on stage. None of them could have made it off set, outside, slashed a tire and then back on set without being noticed."

"Anyone but Grace could have done it," she told him. "There's a passageway between the kitchen pods for us to leave the set if we need to. The cameras just stay away from our kitchen while we're gone. Someone could have taken a kitchen knife, left to use the restroom, headed outside, slashed my tire and made it back on stage in less time than a commercial break."

"No one left the stage during last week's taping."

She wasn't just repeating what they'd already discovered. She hadn't actually been aware whether or not anyone had left. Natasha's stage manager had relayed the information to the police.

"Think, Liza. Who have you spoken to? Ignored? Has anyone said anything that made you think they were jealous? What about family members or friends who are in the green room during the taping? Have you talked to any of them?"

He'd already asked the questions multiple times that week. He was focused. And determined to protect her at all costs.

It would help if he knew what or who he was protecting her against.

He was avoiding the fact that he was entering territory where she was living her own life apart from him. As a successful, soon-to-be famous professional chef. And as a mother...

"Grace's friend Albany is the only person I've really spoken with. I could see building a possible motive case with her. She and Grace have been best friends since childhood—more than seventy years—and she knows this is probably the only chance Grace is going to get for something like this. But she's as sweet as can be, and she can't move without her walker. I hardly think she'd be able to get that outside to slash my tire without being noticed." He ignored the slightly droll tone in her voice.

She could be bored with the conversation. He couldn't be. He was watching for an unknown. They were the hardest kind of perps to catch.

No one who'd been watching the taping in the green room the week before had noticed anyone going outside. No one had noticed anything or anyone unusual in the green room. Their usual snacks had been delivered. They'd watched the taping. Albany had had to use the restroom a few times. She'd joked about it with the rest of them. In all there were five people in the room. The same five who'd been there the week before.

Pierce had already run background checks on all of them, turning up nothing.

None of them had ever been on the set.

In the car, with navigation activated, Pierce hardly noticed the flowered street corners and palm trees that Eliza had raved about. He didn't pay attention to the vast mountain ranges in the distance. He focused on traffic.

And keeping his wife safe.

"It only makes sense that someone on Natasha's team, someone from the studio, could be behind this," he said now. "Who else could have been on stage without standing out?"

"Anyone with access to the studio. There are several sets and stages."

"The *Family Secrets* section is locked when not in use."

"A lot of people have keys."

Again, more information they'd already covered. It's what they had to work with. Someone wanted his wife to suffer. He had to find that person.

"And someone on the show wouldn't have been at the hotel, making those calls," she reminded him.

Which brought him back to one of the contestants or a friend or family member of a contestant. All of whom he'd have access to, starting that afternoon.

"You go nowhere without me or the security escort Natasha has assigned at the studio," he reminded her. And then, with a sideways glance, he said, "Not to cop an attitude. I apologize for how harshly that came out."

Her grin turned his insides to mush. "It's okay, Pierce. I love you, too."

He nodded.

And squinted against the sun's blinding brightness reflecting off the fender in front of him.

ELIZA DIDN'T WANT to be on an investigation. Pierce was with her in California. He knew they had a son. She had nothing to hide.

And so much to show him.

She wanted them to use the weekend away as a chance to rekindle whatever had slipped away over the past few weeks.

They'd loved each other for too long, overcome too many odds, to lose each other, right?

Or was there just too much in their way? From the moment she'd introduced him to her parents when she was just fourteen, they'd disapproved. Then, days before her sixteenth birthday, when she'd conceived a child, they'd hated him. He'd left without a word to her. No explanation. Nothing to let her know that he cared.

She'd had a feeling, since the first day she'd finally heard from him after all those years apart, that Pierce could be taken from her again. Was theirs a love that had been doomed from the beginning?

Eliza didn't believe in such things.

She also didn't know how to make things good for both of them. She needed, desperately, to have their son in her life. And... maybe...for them to raise a child.

She wanted to win *Family Secrets*. To be a renowned chef. Not to give up Rose Harbor, but to be more than just an innkeeper.

He needed to work the streets and come

home to a quiet life. To have his time off be in a small, peaceful community. He needed a personal life that did not require him to be responsible for, or a role model to, an impressionable young person.

*There was compromise...and then there was impossible.* Her father had said that to her once, in the early days of her pregnancy, when she'd been begging them to find a compromise. A way for her to finish school *and* meet the potential her father insisted she meet, but still keep the baby she and Pierce had created together.

She'd eventually allowed herself to be convinced that her father was right...

Pierce didn't go straight to the hotel as she'd expected. He took her to downtown Palm Springs instead—to the famous shopping district. Patiently walked with her from designer to designer, telling her to pick out whatever outfit she wanted for the show the next day. Trying to throw herself into the mood, she settled on a black Lycra jumpsuit with a white silk belt and white silk trim around the cuffs and pockets. He bought the wedge shoes that were shown with it.

Took her for an early dinner at one of Palm Springs's famous eateries.

And then back to the hotel to meet with the other contestants in the lobby. He was polite. Attentive. Charming.

And becoming a stranger.

HIS CONTACT WITH Palm Desert police, Ernie Ryan, was going to let Pierce sit in with him on Saturday as he made the rounds of everyone associated with *Family Secrets*. Since they weren't looking at murder here, only possible intent to harm, there'd been no point in calling everyone in to the station or spending the man-hours to seek them out at home.

Still, the attacks on Eliza were escalating, which indicated the possibility of future physical harm, as well as a host of other minor crimes, so they were taking the situation seriously. More security cameras had been installed around the studio—both inside and out. More security was on-site, including an officer whose sole duty was to remain on guard in the green room. And after the taping, everyone associated with the show was being asked to stick around until Officer Ryan had had a chance to speak with them. He'd been given a soundproof room down the hall for his task. A recording studio.

Eliza had been invited to sit in the sound

booth upstairs and listen in. She'd be able to watch the questioning on a television monitor—not a requirement, just something that was possible due to the studio's technology and so had been offered to her.

It was costing Natasha Stevens a lot of money for the show to go on, but she'd stand to lose a lot more if it didn't.

"Everyone's so on edge," Eliza told him, waiting for a call with him standing beside her. He'd walk her to the edge of the stage, and then she'd be on her own.

"Is there anyone here who seems to you to be acting out of character?" he asked her. He'd never been on a television set before. Should have been fascinated.

All he could think about was keeping her safe. And figuring out who'd tried to sabotage her to begin with.

It was all he could let himself think about. Anything more and his thoughts started to scramble. There was no good to come of indulging in what-ifs. He'd fought a long, hard battle after combat to find out who he was, to find peace with himself and his place in the world.

He wasn't going to lose all of that now.

"There's a lot more nervousness," she said,

"None of the usual camaraderie. Yet everyone's as close as always."

He'd noticed the closeness already. Felt like an outsider in a family Eliza had joined without him. Figured he could be jealous. But knew he wasn't.

He gave her a hug before she went on stage, but no kiss. He didn't want to mess up her makeup. He wished her good luck.

Grinning, she left him with a nod and a little skip. But no "I love you."

Pierce watched from the green room as Eliza and her competitors cooked. More, he watched those watching. He took in everything, the food on the sideboard, the drinks, even the tea dispenser. When he grew restless, he walked to the side of the stage and watched what he could of the proceedings from behind the scenes.

Nothing felt out of place except him.

He was there when participants plated their food for the judges. And when Natasha took her microphone to the middle of the stage and announced that the second runner-up was Grace Hargraves.

Natasha talked. Grace talked. Clearly excited. And it was time for the first runner-up. Pierce didn't realize he'd actually been holding his breath until he heard Jason Wright's name called. His sauce had been some warm chocolate, banana and liquor mixture that he'd served over ice cream. Something his father had taught him to make, apparently.

And then it was time for the winner. Natasha went into her usual bit of rhetoric, and Pierce tuned it out, as always. He didn't need any suspense.

Couldn't allow himself to get caught up in it.

That afternoon, it caught up with him. As badly as he wished they could just turn back the clock, that Eliza was home, fulfilled and gloriously happy without needing a son or chef accolades, he really wanted her to win.

Because the truth was, he'd had only thought she'd been gloriously happy before. She was a woman who found the good in everything, who found glory in every day, who made the best of what she had.

But all of the time he'd been with her, there'd been a part of her that had mourned for her son. Yearned for him.

And a part of her that hadn't been content as keeper of her grandmother's inn. Because she knew Pierce appreciated the peace and beauty of her small island home?

As her father had said, she had potential. He was not going to keep her from it…

"Today's winner is…Eliza Westin!" Pierce heard the ocean. He heard his wife squeal. Heard other contestants call out congratulations as they clapped. He felt deeply, deeply proud of her.

Completely in love with her.

And totally out of place.

Hands in his pockets, he slipped down the hall to the room where he and Ryan would be conducting their interviews. Eliza's studio escort would see her upstairs when she was ready.

## CHAPTER TWENTY

ELIZA KNEW THE interviews had been scheduled to start the second that taping stopped. There'd been a list—those who were least involved in the show would go first. No one wanted to hang around for hours. They all had lives. And Officer Ryan had assured them all their time with him would be short.

She'd known that Pierce was determined, to the exclusion of all else, to make certain that the culprit was found and she'd be safe.

Still, she'd run off stage the second that she'd heard "cut," eager to land in his arms. She'd won again! She couldn't believe it! And finally, she didn't have to stand there alone to be congratulated. She had someone there with her, her person, to celebrate with her.

She'd needed, more than anything, to share it with him.

She'd run off stage. And felt like a fool. Pierce wasn't there. He hadn't waited for her. She'd run to the green room just to make sure. One of the runners in charge of shopping was there. The woman had already had her time with Ryan. She told Eliza that Pierce had been in there.

In there. Not out with her.

The writing was on the wall.

AS PEOPLE WALKED into the room, Pierce studied them. Intently. He was trained—not so much by the police force, but through combat—to assess and render judgment. Was this person safe, or was death imminent?

Not a skill that was probably necessary in today's task, but one that he'd never learned to shut off. His radar had been honed. Which was why he'd been the one chosen to go in that day in the Middle Eastern desert.

Techies came and went. Lighting. Camera. Sound. Runners. Show employees. Contestants. He watched. Listened. Occasionally he asked a question. As always, he gave the possible suspect a full dose of radar.

And he was coming up empty.

Felt empty.

He wanted Liza. The girl he fell in love with back in high school. The woman he'd thought he'd been living with all these years.

A woman who didn't exist.

"CONGRATULATIONS ON YOUR WIN." Tamera, the security officer assigned to Eliza for the day, spoke for the first time in ten minutes as the two women sat alone in a sound booth, watching a small television monitor and listening to Officer Ryan question people employed by Palm Desert Studios or Natasha Stevens Productions.

As she'd escorted Eliza upstairs, the woman hadn't said anything. When they'd taken their seats in the empty room, she'd asked her if she wanted something to drink. A few minutes later she'd asked if Eliza was comfortable.

And now…this. Congratulations.

"Thank you," Eliza said, still feeling a hint of the thrill. But only a hint. How had life gotten so out of control? It was like her car had careened off the roller coaster.

Because she'd received a letter that she hadn't been able to let go. She'd started all of this. Put it in motion. Seeing mention of the *Family Secrets* audition. Taking that as a sign. Signing up for it. Winning. Seeing that as another sign.

Somehow she'd missed some signs along the way.

She was losing Pierce.

Was no closer to knowing her son.

And now someone was sabotaging her, trying to get her off the show at the very least. But last week, even that had escalated to possible physical danger. She could have crashed the car, driving on a sliced tire. Been rear-ended. Stranded.

"Nothing happened today," she said aloud. She didn't know how much Tamera knew, but figured it was everything. Plus, she was hearing all of the same questions Eliza was hearing.

*Do you have access to the stage? Have you ever been on the stage? What is your access? When were you last on the stage during the first week of taping?* Then specific times and dates. *Where were you during the taping of show three? Were you there the entire time? Where else were you? For how long?*

*Have you ever been to the Monteleone Hotel?*

*Do you have anything against Eliza Westin?*

*Had you heard of her, or ever had anything to do with her, before her appearance on* Family Secrets?

The interviews went on and on. Quickly.

Interviewees came in and out at a pretty impressive rate. The questions didn't change.

Nor did the answers.

"With all the detail everywhere, it would've been pretty hard for anyone to do anything today," Tamera, a lean black woman, said from her seat between Eliza and the door. She'd been watching the interrogations, but watching the room, as well. Not that there was anything there but equipment.

Still, Eliza felt safe with her. The woman seemed to be aware of every speck of their environment.

By "detail," Eliza figured Tamera meant the extra security guards and cameras. And maybe Pierce. He'd certainly made his presence known.

"I'm guessing that knowing the police were going to interview everyone today would have been a deterrent, as well," Eliza said. She didn't know Tamera at all. But sitting there with her, she felt like she did.

Or maybe she was just desperate to have someone to talk to.

"Having the police involved, period, could have put an end to it," Tamera said. "It's one thing to do little things that you think can't be traced back to you, things that aren't an obvious crime. But to slash tires…that's upping the ante more than maybe a win on this show would warrant."

"You think it's about more than the show?" Pierce did. But he worried about her…

Ryan was talking. A cameraman was answering. Same questions. Same answers.

"Nah. Trying to make you miss the show last week made it pretty clear that it's about the show. The whole shuttle thing took a lot of maneuvering, and if it had worked, the only outcome would have been you missing the competition."

Pierce had said the same thing. But then there'd been the slashed tire. It was the escalation that had bothered him, the police and consequently Natasha. It fit a profile of someone getting more upset, more determined, perhaps more desperate.

Angela, Natasha's stage manager, entered the interview room. She was open, concerned, intelligent. Not the least bit defensive. And had absolutely nothing, that Eliza could see, to give them.

"I'm guessing your win today will either end things, in that it's pretty much a given you've taken home the prize, or it will escalate them," Tamera said. "If the person who's behind this still has a chance to win."

"You think it's one of the other contestants." They knew it wasn't. No one had left the stage during the time her tire was slashed.

"Or someone connected to them. Someone who knows something the rest of us don't."

If it continued, it would have to be someone connected with Grace.

Either that, or someone who just had it in for her and didn't want her to win.

The only person she could think of who might be threatened by her win was Pierce—if he thought she'd let fame go to her head and want to leave Shelby Island—and clearly he wasn't their saboteur.

Nor did she want to leave Shelby Island. Rose Harbor was as much a part of her as her arms and legs. She just wanted to be more than an innkeeper. Like she had more than arms and legs. She wanted to be whole. Arms, legs, brain, drive…and full heart.

Like maybe Rose Harbor could be the inn that a famous chef owned. Guests would come to her not only for the beautiful accommodations so close to one of South Carolina's best-kept beaches, but also because her cooking drew them…

A young girl entered for her interview. Camille. Eliza had spoken to her a time or two.
Each time a *Family Secrets* six-week segment
began with new contestants, Natasha chose
two kids from the local high school to intern
on the set. Camille had filled snacks in the
green room a time or two. One time when
the TV star wannabe, Kaylee Newcomb, had
dropped a carton of eggs, Camille had rushed
in to clean up the mess.

In her *Family Secrets* T-shirt and jeans,
she looked nervous as she sat down. Eliza felt
sorry for the kid. She'd been given an excit-
ing opportunity and had ended up being in-
terrogated by the police. While Ryan toned
himself down a little bit, his questions were
basically the same. Her answers were the
same. She didn't know anything. Hadn't seen
anything. Hadn't heard anything. As he had
in all of the interviews, the officer turned to
Pierce and asked if he had any other questions to add. Sometimes he did. Sometimes
not. He took a moment to answer. But in the
end, had nothing.

Ryan looked over his pad again.

The girl looked like she might be sick. Or
burst into tears. Eliza tried to imagine how
she'd have felt at sixteen, in an interrogation

room with two intimidating cops. And wondered why her parents hadn't been there with her. She knew from Pierce that notices had gone out about the day's plans and that parents of minor interviewees would have had to allow the questioning.

Eliza wished they'd just let the girl go.

And then they did.

"I heard someone say today that she's a foster kid," Tamera said, watching the monitor. "That her foster parents weren't going to be here. Doesn't seem right…some kids having to go it alone like that…"

The door downstairs opened. Closed. Camille was gone.

But she'd left a mark on Eliza's heart. Eliza had never thought about fostering. But there were so many kids out there needing the love of a parent who really cared.

She had so much love to give.

Pierce made a comment to Ryan, and Eliza gave herself a mental shake.

She'd consciously made the choice to marry a man who couldn't be a father. While she hadn't known his inability to have kids was more than just biological…she *had* told him, before they'd married, that she'd rather have their family of two than not have him.

She still felt that way.

She didn't want to lose Pierce. So what was she supposed to do with all of this heartache bubbling up inside her?

A young man entered the room next. She recognized him. Daniel, the other intern, who'd run for their porcinis the first week. He was alone, as well.

Eliza hadn't seen as much of him as she had Camille, but he'd been around. Usually on the side of the stage. She'd seen him talking to Grace a time or two. He'd been there to congratulate the older woman the week she'd won. Had brought her a bottle of water once when she'd been sweating under the lights…

"He's a senior. The other one there, she's a sophomore," Tamera said. Eliza wondered if the security officer had any kids of her own.

But didn't ask. Was loath to get into a kid conversation at the moment. Felt kind of like an alcoholic walking into a bar. She was fighting feelings that were unraveling her life. No need to make it harder on herself to move on.

Officer Ryan asked his questions. The kid answered. His replies were straightforward. Sitting up straight in his *Family Secrets* T-shirt, he looked both men right in the eye, without arrogance.

Eliza was glad to see there were still good kids in the world. And when she started to wonder if her son was anything like Daniel, she turned away. She wasn't going to do this. Wasn't going to see her boy in every male teenager with whom she came into contact.

She'd been through that already. When her son had been a baby. And then a toddler. She'd looked, everywhere she went, thinking she might get a glimpse. Thinking that a mother would have some kind of sixth sense to know if her child was near. That she'd recognize him.

She'd looked at other babies and imagined her own son experiencing the same phases. Exhibiting the same behaviors…

"There's something you aren't telling us." Eliza's head shot back as she heard her husband's voice—in a tone he'd never used in her presence before.

Daniel frowned. Shook his head. "I swear, I have no idea who's behind this. I'd do anything I could to help you. I just don't know anything."

"I don't believe you." Leaning forward,

his eyebrows drawn together, eyes narrowed, Pierce looked menacing.

Daniel, his blond hair respectably short, shook his head. "I'm sorry, sir. I'm telling you the truth."

Eliza looked at Ryan. His gaze moved between Pierce and Daniel. She couldn't tell what he was thinking. Whose side he was on.

Had Pierce sensed something? He had some very special skills. Jamison had talked about them to her when Pierce was in the hospital. Not long after she'd asked him if he thought Pierce had a death wish.

But Daniel was a nice kid. His nurturing of Grace that week...

Grace.

The only contestant she'd be competing against for the win.

Was Daniel somehow associated with her beyond the show? A grandson? Or friend of a grandson? Someone in her family who stood to benefit if the older woman's recipe was mass-produced? An heir, perhaps?

Her mind flew with possibilities.

But... Daniel?

He had alibis for the times in question. Maybe not for when the mushrooms went missing, as no one knew for sure when that had happened. But the water and vinegar—Daniel hadn't been on the set since the previous week. When the calls had been made from the hotel the previous week, he'd been on set helping a techie with some wiring. He'd also been stage left the entire show the previous week, so he couldn't have slashed her tire during the taping. There were numerous people who could back up his story.

"I've been asking myself since the second week, with that minute amount of vinegar added to a water bottle, who could have done it. Trying to remember everything I've seen. Last week, I swear, I was watching the whole time." The boy gave a self-deprecating smirk. "I thought maybe I could be the one who— I had this stupid idea that I might figure it out, and then..."

"You want me to believe that you only want to help?" Pierce asked, not relenting. Which Eliza didn't understand at all. It wasn't like they were talking about murder here. Or even a felony—unless someone pressed charges for the sliced tire and attached an intent-to-harm accusation to it.

Why was Pierce being so hard on the boy? If his alibis didn't check out, Ryan could always pick him up. Bring him back for further questioning.

Did Pierce know something Eliza didn't?

"It's the truth, sir." Daniel said. "I swear to you."

Pierce didn't look ready to back down anytime soon. "I don't know who you think you're dealing with, but…"

"Okay," Ryan cut Pierce off. "We're done here. You can go, son."

Heat spread up Eliza's body, suffusing her face. That poor kid…

Expecting Ryan to ask Pierce to leave for the remainder of the interviews, she didn't respond when Tamera said, "Wow, your man really went after that one. What's up with that?"

Ryan didn't kick Pierce out, though.

One by one, the current roster of *Family Secrets* contestants came in. Grace first. The older woman was flustered. She stumbled over her answers.

But Eliza didn't think for one second Grace had anything to do with the mishaps. She'd been too upset by the missing mushrooms. Of course, that could have been an act…

But…no… Grace would not want a win by ill-gotten gains.

There'd been that restraining order her own daughter had filed against her...

No. She wasn't going to think such things.

She liked Grace. A lot.

Didn't blame her for being flustered.

Pierce didn't seem to blame her, either.

He had no questions for the older woman at all.

## CHAPTER TWENTY-ONE

PIERCE PAID CLOSEST attention to the contestants. They were the ones who had the most at stake. A mass-produced recipe could make someone millions. It might not, but it could. And a *Family Secrets* win would give a chef star status. If he or she didn't get his own show, the winner could certainly expect to be called on to appear as a guest judge on other shows, to take part in television food channel special functions.

They'd all had access to the stage for a mushroom steal and water bottle change-out. All but Grace were guests at the hotel, would have been there when the phone calls were made and fully capable of making them without drawing attention.

The only thing he couldn't directly pin on any of them was the slashed tire on Eliza's rental car.

She'd rented the car at the last minute. Was it possible the tire had already been sliced?

And had just taken a while, with driving, for it to start to unravel?

The contestants all knew that Eliza had rented cars from the hotel lobby in the past. Was it too far-fetched to think that one might have slashed the tires after making the phone calls, and before leaving on the shuttle for the studio?

She'd had the same car each time. As they waited for the next contestant, Kaylee Newcomb, to join them, he leaned forward so he could speak privately to Ryan.

"We need to check the rental fleet. To see how many cars they have. What was the chance that Eliza would get that particular car? I'm assuming there'd have been a report if more tires than just hers were slashed."

"Already ahead of you, bro," Ernie Ryan said. "They have three cars parked on-site. The other two weren't tampered with. And Eliza's wasn't tampered with on-site. It's under video surveillance, and I've already looked at the footage."

Clearly he should already have been on it, too. He was slipping. And that was unacceptable. "I didn't see that in the report." Not that Ryan owed him anything. This wasn't his investigation. The Palm Desert police were just being respectful by letting him be involved at all.

"I was just there this morning," Ryan said. "After you'd already left to come here."

So he hadn't been so far off—and he and Ryan had both been right in their assessment that the tire had been slashed on-site at the studio.

"Don't you wonder why it was just the one tire?" Ryan asked then.

What was taking Ms. Newcomb so long?

"I'm guessing whoever did it got spooked. Or they wanted Eliza to be out on the road before she noticed anything. They didn't want her stranded at the studio."

"If they got spooked, we might be able to figure out why. I'll see if there were any deliveries to the studio that afternoon. Any reason someone might have been in the parking lot that we don't already know about. I can check footage from the traffic camera at the corner…"

If they didn't want her stranded at the studio, that likely meant they wanted her stranded somewhere else.

As a warning?

Or because they'd hoped for harm to befall her?

Each time he had the thought, Pierce's blood ran cold. He could imagine living his life without Eliza, if that's what she wanted, but he couldn't imagine a world without her in it.

Ms. Newcomb came in and took her seat.

Ryan ran her through the questions. Pierce listened but didn't expect to get anything from the woman. She was too self-centered to have noticed anything that didn't directly affect her.

And she exuded no defensiveness at all. No sense of feeling invaded by an interrogation.

Only one person that day had put out that sense to him.

"Can you think of any reason someone would vandalize Mrs. Westin's rental car?"

"Maybe to scare her off?"

"Do you know anyone who would want to do that?"

"To scare her off? No. If you're asking if I've heard anyone talk bad about her, then, no again." She smiled at both of them.

Ryan nodded at her. "Have you heard anyone talk about the things that have been happening to her? The vinegar in the water bottle, for instance?"

"Sure. Everyone's talking about it. It's kind

of blowing some of the fun of being on the show, you know? This is a once-in-a-lifetime experience for some of us, and we've gotten to be friends. It's wrong what's being done to her. Eliza's sweet. She wouldn't hurt a fly."

Pierce was ready to wrap this up. To grab Eliza and get out of there. Wondered if they could get on an earlier flight and make it home that night. If she'd even want to do that. She'd just won the competition for the third time. She might want to celebrate with her new friends, as Kaylee Newcomb had just described them all. She deserved to celebrate with them.

"So you don't think one of your fellow contestants could be behind this?"

Ryan was liking someone close to Grace. The missing mushrooms could potentially have hurt her chances, too, but the key was that they hadn't. They could just as easily have been a ploy to distract eyes away from Grace being involved.

"Not unless they hoped the pranks might get them some more on camera time, you know, like, sabotage adding suspense to the show."

Pierce focused. Had she just given them a motive?

"You think Ms. Stevens should have let the home viewers know what was going on behind the scenes?" he asked.

Kaylee shrugged. "It's a reality TV show. This is reality, right?"

Ryan looked at him. He answered the silent probe with an affirmative.

Pierce knew Kaylee's history, her purpose for auditioning for *Family Secrets* in the first place—to try to get noticed. He knew because Eliza had told him. Ryan would have no way of knowing that.

"So you'd like it if, say, during next week's final round, Natasha talked about the odds that Eliza has been up against?" Officer Ernie Ryan asked the question. Pierce couldn't have done it better.

"It's too late now, don't you think?" Kaylee said. "I was just saying someone might have thought it would add some, you know, drama. At least it might have made people curious and draw in more of an audience. Give them a reason to follow along, to tune in each week find out what happened."

She had it well-thought-out.

And next week would indeed be too late, if the plan was hers. Because she wouldn't be there the following week. Ms. Newcomb was headed home for the last time—a loser.

ELIZA DIDN'T WAIT for them to finish with the twins from New Orleans. With Tamera trailing behind her, watching her back, she headed down to the green room to collect her things and wait for Pierce.

Of all the contestants, she knew the twins the best, having shared cocktails with them in the hotel lobby a couple of times. She most often sat next to them in the shuttle, too. There was no way she'd believe they had it in for her.

Unless… They were the ones she'd talked to the most that first night—the only ones she'd really gotten to know at all—before the mushrooms had gone missing.

No. Maria and Micha were lovable, funny chefs who had no reason to wipe out the competition. They were each other's competition!

After Kaylee's testimony, Eliza had just wanted to be done. It wasn't up to her to find out who wanted to hurt her chances at winning. Or hurt her. She just couldn't think about it anymore.

It got to a person, constantly feeling like you had to watch your back, like you couldn't trust anyone you liked, or even your own instincts as to whether or not you should like them.

Maybe this was what being out in the world was like. Maybe she was happier than she'd thought on Shelby Island—protected from vandals, and...

The house next door to hers—an acre over—had been vandalized the previous summer. And a woman had been killed on the island a couple of years before. The police had thought the woman's ex-husband did it but had never arrested anyone for the crime.

There were crimes on the beach every summer. Thefts. A stolen car or two. Robberies. Usually small stuff.

But bigger than missing mushrooms and slashed tires.

Kaylee was just heading out the door as Eliza pushed into the empty green room. The younger woman congratulated her again. Told her she'd be in the audience watching the next week. Said goodbye, and left.

Eliza proceeded to her locker. She used the combination she'd been given and pulled it open.

She reached her hand in before she'd had a chance to look and stopped as she noticed the white index card bent and jammed under her purse.

As though someone had crammed it through a ventilation slat on the bottom of her locker. There was black writing on the card in stick-on letters. She couldn't read what they said but didn't want to touch the card.

"What's wrong?" Tamera was beside her in seconds, though Eliza hadn't made a peep.

Eliza pointed.

"Oh—" The expletive the woman uttered was not one Eliza had heard often. "Back away," she said next, putting an arm gently between Eliza and the locker, guiding her beyond the tile and onto the carpeted side of the room while with her other hand she pulled the radio off her hip and called for help.

PIERCE WAS OUT of the interrogation room, a few doors down the hall from the green room, before Ryan could excuse them to Micah Donaldson. He still wasn't the first person to answer Tamera's call. Another security guard, one employed full-time by Natasha Stevens, was there first.

Natasha, Pierce knew, was in her office in another part of the studio, waiting for a report from Ryan and to hear any instructions he had for her, her team or the studio. Not because he'd told her she had to stay, but because she'd insisted on doing so.

The guard was using a paper towel to reach for the card. He handed the towel to Pierce instead.

The card was bent up pretty good. But Pierce could still read it before he'd even fully dislodged it from the locker.

You've been warned. Don't come back.

"Has Kaylee been through here?" Pierce barked to the room at large. He'd taken in Eliza, standing at the other end of the room with Tamera when he'd first entered.

"She just left," Tamera said.

He was out the door, leaving the card hanging out of the locker for Ryan to bag.

"I CAN'T BELIEVE they didn't hold her." With a rare glass of wine in her hand, Eliza looked at Pierce, sitting across from her on the private balcony off her room. Up on the fourteenth floor, they had a great view.

One she hadn't bothered to enjoy until that night. Something about being out on a balcony all alone hadn't appealed to her the previous weeks she'd been a guest at the hotel.

"They have nothing to hold her on," he told her now, speaking of Kaylee Newcomb.

Eliza was sure now that she was the culprit. "She's from LA, Pierce. That's only an hour and a half away, depending on traffic. She could easily have had any friend of hers slip onto the back lot and slash my tire. The rest of it, we already know any of the contestants could have done. She's desperate enough to be a star that she auditions for a cooking show when she doesn't even like to cook. Plus, she practically told you she'd done it. She told you why, to get buzz going for the show…and she called everything that's happened 'pranks.' Natasha Stevens doesn't think they're pranks. If whoever did this had been successful, they could have hurt the show."

She didn't want to talk about *Family Secrets* anymore. About mushrooms and vinegar, phone calls, shuttles and tires.

She was tired of it all.

She wanted to enjoy her wine with the man she loved.

She wanted that man back.

"Unless her fingerprints turn up on that card, or anything else points to her, the most she can be is a person of interest in a case where no one has even been hurt." Pierce reminded her.

"Tamera said that card was a direct threat. That means whoever is behind this is crossing into felony territory."

"She's right. And believe me, Ryan is going to be checking every step Newcomb has taken since the show began. He's got other leads he's following up on, too. That's all he can do until he gets some concrete proof."

She'd already spoken with Natasha. The woman had asked her what she wanted to do about the final round the next week. If she wanted to continue.

Technically, with the releases Eliza had signed, the show wasn't responsible for any losses incurred if Eliza backed out. But Natasha had offered to reschedule the taping for an off week later in the spring if Grace would also agree to the change.

Eliza had told Natasha she was fine to be there the following week. If they postponed the finale, it would be a hardship for Grace to get back. There was no telling whether the woman would even agree, and part of Eliza didn't want to find out if she wouldn't.

She also didn't see much point in putting

off the inevitable. If someone was trying to get Grace a win, that person could just as easily do so a couple of months from then.

Pierce had disagreed with her decision. He'd wanted Ryan to have more time to figure out who was behind the threat and other mysterious happenings.

Eliza couldn't bear the thought of living on the precipice upon which she'd been balancing these past weeks for much longer. She needed this whole thing done.

She also needed to finish it. That was the one thing about all of it that she and Pierce had agreed on.

Not just because it was wrong to let the bully win. Not even because, with all of the added security—it would be more than doubled for the final round, including electronic screening of audience members—there would be little chance of physical harm to Eliza. But because she had to live like the professional chef she was. Most particularly with three wins under her belt. Most everyone thought that her win the next week was inevitable.

She sipped her wine. Watched while Pierce jiggled his glass of iced lemon water, knocking the cubes against the sides of the glass.

She'd suggested he have a beer. He enjoyed one occasionally with guys from work.

He'd declined the beer, saying he never drank when he was on a job. Implying that he was on the job, then? Thinking of the response, her feelings were hurt all over again.

"You were awfully rough on Daniel today."

"He's hiding something."

What was it with him?

"He's just a nice kid looking out for an old lady," she said now, taking another sip of wine.

"He's hiding something. I can feel it."

"And these feelings, they aren't ever wrong?" She softened the question with a smile that would have been personal if he'd been on the receiving end of it weeks ago.

"Not often."

"Maybe this is one of the few times."

"It's not."

He was copping that attitude again. And she was tired. Tired of carrying the weight of the world. Of feeling guilty for needing so desperately to meet her son. And feeling guilty for giving him up in the first place. For lying to Pierce about him, and about the fact that the letter from the adoption agency was the reason she'd auditioned for *Family Secrets* to begin with.

She was tired of wondering which of her new friends might be sabotaging her.

Tired of trying not to cry every single time she was in a room with Pierce these days.

She missed Rose Harbor. Her guests. Margie.

And her own bed.

"You were too hard on him, Pierce. Even Officer Ryan saw it. To the point that he cut you off…" She couldn't pussyfoot around this anymore. "It's because he's a kid, right? A boy. And you just can't be impartial when a young man is involved."

He'd nearly gotten himself killed because of his inability to think rationally enough to follow protocol when the other kid had been in trouble two weeks before. Whether he'd saved the boy's life or not, he'd taken a huge risk that could just as easily have had tragic consequences.

"I need to know what happened to you, Pierce. I need to understand."

She'd promised herself she'd never ask. That if Pierce ever needed to tell her about his time in the Middle East, she'd listen attentively, but that she'd never force him to do so.

She'd made a lot of promises to herself that she wasn't keeping.

His gaze was deep, dark, shadowed, as he looked over at her.

And nodded.

# CHAPTER TWENTY-TWO

"I WAS ON my second tour." Pierce's voice cut into Eliza as he started to speak. It lacked the warmth she'd always associated with his deep baritone.

It didn't sound like him.

She wasn't sure what she'd asked for. Wasn't sure she was up to it.

But dropped to the floor at his feet, her arms on his knee, as he looked out beyond the aesthetically lit pool and gardens below to the shadows of the mountains looming in the distant dark.

"It's okay, Pierce," she told him, suddenly realizing what she'd asked. He was in the desert, reliving an experience that had taken place in the desert.

She should have known, been more aware.

Any other time she would have been.

That was the moment when she realized that Pierce had been right to think that she'd been pulling away from him. Leaving him, he'd said. She'd thought he meant literally—as in walking out on him, and maybe he had.

She had no intention, even now, of divorcing Pierce, or even of separating. But these past weeks, she had been slowly leaving the part of Pierce who'd trusted her always to be there.

The man who couldn't bear to be a father. Of any kind.

He looked down at her, and she could tell that it was taking him a second to break out of his mental world and back into the one in the hotel room in Palm Desert.

"I'd been there a year for my first tour," he said, looking her in the eye as he spoke. If he felt her touching him, leaning on him, he didn't let on.

With gentle fingers, she rubbed the back of his calf. The inside of his knee. "I had a knack for reading situations," he said. "I'd made a few comments, been overheard, and been right…"

"You were more aware than any boy—or man—I'd ever known, Pierce. I told you that…"

He blinked. Touched the top of her head. She wasn't sure if that was a ghost of a smile touching the corner of his mouth—or a twitch.

"It wasn't long before I was called up to take on jobs that relied solely on precision and composure for successful execution."

"You didn't lose it," she said. She didn't know why she was interrupting. But felt that she had to. That she needed to keep him with her.

And was ashamed that she wasn't sure if she was doing it for him or for herself.

"I didn't panic," Pierce said. And then gave a dry harrumph that might have been meant to be a chuckle. "Funny, when now I can't even talk about kids without having a nightmare."

"You had only one." This time around.

"I've been taking the sleeping pills the doctor gave me."

Her heart dropped. More secrets. More things they should have shared. Something she should have known even if he hadn't told her. She should have noticed…

"Every night?"

He shook his head. "A few times at home. And here, last night."

She didn't even know he had them with him. They shared a toiletry bag. A suitcase…

"You have one for tonight?"

He nodded. And she understood why he wasn't drinking that beer she'd offered him. She didn't want the wine she'd left on the table by her chair, either.

She'd thought things couldn't get any worse, and they'd already been worse than she'd known.

"It's bad," she said. Stating the obvious, and yet asking him to prepare her.

He nodded.

"I was sent on this particular mission during my second tour. Chosen specifically."

"They wanted your opinion?" she asked, proud of him even as she was hating *them*, whoever they were. Hate wasn't an emotion Eliza felt often.

Pierce had never had a strong male influence in his life. She'd trusted the army to take care of him. Not use him up.

"I scored at the top of my class for shot accuracy," he said. Something else she hadn't known. He was a good shot. Jamison had made mention of that, too. But…

"They wanted you for frontline battle." She probably sounded like the complete ignoramus she was when it came to such matters.

"There were insurgents. Their leaders were

meeting in a key village, all together for what we believed was the first time ever, to finalize plans to launch a war that would most certainly have changed the world. We'd been sent over to infiltrate in any way we could and take them down. Every one of them. If one was left standing, our mission failed."

Didn't seem like one man could do all that.

"Why not just take them prisoner?" She'd understood that to be the American way.

"Intel said that the group was armed with enough chemical warfare to take out a country. And that they had means to get it to the United States. The problem was, no one could figure out how. But they believed the threat was real. This group, they'd been around. They'd made other threats, seemingly impossible ones, and they'd carried them out successfully every single time."

Her stomach ached. Every muscle in her body ached as she sat there, stiffly, listening. Afraid to move.

As though if she took too deep a breath, Pierce's world would explode.

"It was believed that no one outside the key leaders at that meeting knew the details of the plan. If they died, the plan died with them. The thought was that they wielded their power by not making what they knew known to others. Information is power. As soon as it falls in another's hands, even if the other is a friend, it weakens your power."

She heard his words. Couldn't really comprehend the scope of what he was telling her.

Or maybe she just didn't want to believe that the world's problems were really that critical.

That the power held by those she believed protected her was that fragile.

"We believed the group didn't know we knew about the meeting. Or that anyone knew they'd all be together. I was sent in with three other guys. Supposedly on a peaceful mission to tend to some business in the village. I was to assess the situation and report back."

She waited. Eager to hear about his success. There'd been no country wiped out by chemical warfare.

Pierce's success was a foregone conclusion.

"Ten minutes after we got to the village, I knew that we'd been made. A young boy we'd befriended told us. His father was our real contact. He used the boy to talk to us. He said the leaders knew why we were there.

They knew what we knew. And they knew my mission."

Oh. God. No.

He'd been captured. Tortured. In ways that didn't leave physical scars all over his body. She'd heard about some of the horrible things they did to prisoners over there. Unconscionable, unimaginable things that no human being could live through and come out of normal. And the more someone withheld information, the worse it got...

No one knew better than she that Pierce was one of the best there was at keeping his information to himself.

But wait...he'd said that they knew everything he knew...

"Pierce?"

His expression had gone vacant. He didn't even seem to notice shoving Eliza aside as he lowered his head to his knees, burying it beneath his arms.

She had no business doing this.

Why had she thought she and Pierce could get through this alone, without professional help?

"Pierce?" She called to him because she didn't have any other answer. Because her heart was calling to him.

"Pierce?" she said a second time. More firmly.

He lifted his head. Looked at her.

"We retreated," he said. "Made ourselves scarce as quickly and quietly as we'd come in, telling the little boy to let his father know we'd send an army back."

Good. Okay. This was good. Pierce was talking. He was going for help. The village, the warfare, were no longer his sole responsibility.

He looked at Eliza. For a long time. His lips started to tremble. "But I knew..." The words were a whisper.

"I knew how they knew about us. And I knew why we knew about them, too."

Her heart pounded. It was Saturday, past nine in South Carolina. She had no idea whom to call. Either there or here.

She thought about calling the local hospital. Needed some kind of professional help on standby.

Not because she didn't trust Pierce. But because she was afraid.

From the very beginning, the things she and Pierce had faced, an adult love so young, her father's disapproval, a baby...it had all been too big for them to handle on their own.

They'd failed.

Every time.

"They were our intel, Eliza. The father. His eight-year-old son…" He broke off. Moisture in his eyes now, but no tears breaking free. Nothing close to such a cleansing.

"I'm not sure how much the boy knew, but his father was the group's imam, so they trusted him."

She was cold and wanted to go inside. To lock the doors. Shut the curtains.

To hide in the bathroom where there were no windows.

"How can you be so sure that they knew why you were there?"

"Because of a word the boy used. It was code for the leader of the group. I'm certain he hadn't meant to say it. I suspect he didn't know he did."

Pierce whispered the word. It wasn't anything she understood.

"He said it that day when he'd been referring to his father. The man we thought was their imam—their religious consultant. He was, instead, the insurgent leader."

"So they weren't really having the meeting?"

"They were, but they knew American intel-

ligence had infiltrated a portion of the group's
hierarchy. They knew they didn't have much
time. And so they played us. The boy came
to us on behalf of his father, whom he told us
was the village imam. He had much to tell.
Information that panned out. A smaller group
of insurgents were taken as prisoners. This
continued for over a month. Until they could
trust that we trusted them. The boy and the
father. They called us to the village that last
day and when the boy uttered that one word,
I knew we'd been had. His father wasn't a
religious man, he was a leader of bad men.
When they sent us away, I knew we had to
go back. Fast."

"Didn't they know you'd be back?"

"Yes, but they thought they'd have the time
it would take us to go back and get our 'army.'
When we returned, they'd be long gone and
we'd be walking into a death trap. They didn't
just want the handful of us. They planned to
use the chemical warfare on the entire unit—
to show the world what they could do. That
their threat was real. And that we couldn't
stop them."

Pierce was still there. It hadn't ended the
way the insurgents had planned.

"Couldn't they have just bombed your camp?"

"Not without risking authorities possibly knowing who they were. And bombing would have come with a high risk of failure—they'd have to get to us without getting caught. And be able to get enough gas out to do significant damage before they were stopped. They wanted to lure us to them. To show us that they'd infiltrated the highest rank of our intel without us knowing. And to massacre all of us on the spot. But only after they'd left. They had helicopters close by. And if my men and I had left, they'd have been on those helicopters. By the time we got back to camp, it would have been too late. Their 'bombs' would have been dropped, and we would have walked into torturous deaths."

"Wait. You said you left."

He nodded.

"I knew we didn't stand a chance of getting them if we left that village. That we might never have another chance with all of the key figures together. I couldn't risk another possible 9/11. Or any version of it. We circled back. We were all trained snipers, and the leaders were all in one place, gathering their things together to head in one caravan to the make-shift airfield. We took them out one by one."

Okay. It was horrible.

But...good.

"There were two left, the father and the son. I faced them, head-on, with villagers all around us at that point, fearing for their lives. These weren't men who could die for their cause. If they died, their cause went with him. The man pulled his son in front of him. The boy held a small black box. It had enough chemical in it to wipe out the village. His father said if I didn't let them go, the one I didn't kill first would detonate the bomb.

"The boy was crying. His eyes begged me not to hurt him..."

No. No more. She'd heard enough.

"I had one shot, one chance, to kill them both. I saw the shock in my little friend's eyes and watched him die. Watched them both die..."

Tears poured down her face. She was sobbing and couldn't stop.

Even then, Pierce sat before her, dry-eyed.

"You want to know the rest?"

There was more?

She didn't nod consciously. It just happened.

"They didn't really have a chemical weapon. They'd been ruling by fear. If we'd exposed them they'd have been prosecuted by their own people... When this became known, we knew we had to keep silent, or risk a furor of fallout. My men and I...we made a pact not to tell anyone what happened that day..."

He broke then. In his way. He didn't sob. Or make any sound at all. He just sat there, tears streaming down his face.

Eliza went to him and held him. She cried for a while. And when she eventually calmed, she still held on.

He hadn't touched her. Hadn't moved. But a glance at his face showed her he was still grieving. She could see the glistening of wetness on his cheeks.

Eliza had no idea how long they sat there. Pierce moved eventually. Pulled her up onto his lap. Into her arms.

"There was no real threat. Just the power of possibility. Of fear. I didn't have to do it, Liza," he said to her in the darkness.

"You did what you believed you had to do," she said, believing the words with all of her heart.

At some point, she shivered. He was concerned for her. She took the chance to convince him to climb into bed with her. She brought him a glass of water. Asked him where his sleeping pills were. He pulled a small vial out of his concealed carry holster.

She watched him put a pill in his mouth. Swallow.

And then she lay down beside him. Determined to hold him.

No matter what life brought them.

# CHAPTER TWENTY-THREE

PIERCE HAD EXPECTED his entire world to be different when he awoke. Eliza's image of him had been forever changed. Their connection had ended.

Truth was, it had ended a long time ago. When she'd given up their baby and chosen to live as though he'd never existed. And when he'd looked in the face of a crying and frightened eight-year-old child and executed him.

Both acts, however justified, had changed them.

He and Liza had been living a lie all these years. She didn't say much as they ordered room service before heading down to catch their ride to the airport. She didn't eat much, either.

But she fussed over him like he was a bird with a broken wing.

He let her. Because it was easier than talking.

They would eventually. He was certain of that.

But not until they were home. Not until they'd both had time to rest. Process.

Not when the pain was so raw. Not many good decisions came out of reaction to pain. You chose the easiest way to rid yourself of the pain, which usually meant a quick fix that worked only in the moment.

Margie and the new check-ins were waiting for them when they got back to Rose Harbor. The hot water heater had gone out. Which sent Pierce to Charleston for a replacement. He had to rent a truck to get the hundred-gallon monster back to the island.

By the time he got home, the old one had drained. It was ten o'clock that night before the water was hot again.

He fell into bed, with Eliza beside him, and slept.

Without pills.

The rest of the week passed quietly. Busily, but quietly. Eliza was focused on her guests. Taking back the inn, she said once. He started to ask her what she meant by it but stopped. He didn't want to go there.

Didn't want to open a door that would force them to look at their future.

Or even to talk about having one.

Right now, he needed her. She seemed to need him.

And that was enough.

For the moment.

THE FINAL ROUND category was casserole. Eliza knew what she was going to make. She just wasn't sure about her timing. It was a dish her grandmother had called the all-in-one. It was delicate and classy, yet down-to-earth enough for less cultured tastes. It was great for an occasional dinner meal served at an inn because it pleased most palates. It was her all-in-one.

And in her mind, the sure dish to please gourmet chefs and the child judge at the same time.

The only problem was, she had to shave half an hour off the cooking time. She used canned beans instead of soaking dried ones overnight. The dish called for two meats— one pork, one poultry or lamb. Normally she browned one meat, and then in those drippings, the other, then browned her onions, added the celery, garlic and wine and boiled it until the wine reduced before adding the chicken stock, tomato sauce and beans. Now she cut down part of the time by cooking both meats at once and then combining their drippings to do the vegetables. She sliced off another ten minutes by letting the wine reduce while already in the company of the broth and sauce.

She just wasn't sure how it was all going to taste. But to be safe, on Thursday night, when she served Margie and Pierce with her finished product, she used twice the butter-rubbed croutons—big chunks made out of a day-old baguette—for the top of the casserole. She panicked for a second when she couldn't remember if she'd ordered the day-old baguette for the show, but then remembered that she had.

It had been like that all week. She'd been fine. And then she'd panicked. Fine and then panic.

It was as though everything rested on the win. If she won, her life would be okay. If she lost, everything was going to fall apart. She was being irrational. She knew that. And yet it felt real. If she won, she'd have something to start with, to build upon. She'd be somebody good no matter what else fell apart in her life. She'd have something to hold on to if everything else disintegrated.

She'd have the sense of self-worth that she'd been lacking her entire life.

Her son hadn't called. He hadn't texted, emailed, contacted her on social media or shown up at her door. As far as she knew, he hadn't even been back to the agency, asking for her. The one thing they'd been able to do for her was inform her if he was in possession of her current information.

She'd hadn't heard from them.

"I heard from Ryan this afternoon," Pierce told her while they were packing Thursday night. It was the first time they'd been alone together since they'd gotten up that morning. Pierce had gone back to the precinct the day before but wasn't officially starting back to work until Monday.

He'd said there was no way he was sending her to California alone.

"What'd he say?" Hard to believe that she'd been so consumed by the pranks that had happened at the studio. By one warning to stay away.

"They couldn't get an ID off the card prints."

"With so much forensic stuff on TV, you'd have to be pretty dumb not to know to wear a pair of gloves if you're going to threaten someone. We're still probably just dealing with an amateur." She was shocked to hear her world-weary tone. Had she grown that disillusioned in such a short period of time?

Pierce was quiet, so she glanced his way to find him grinning at her.

"There were prints on the card, Liza. Just no match in any database."

"Oh." Most of the contestants weren't in police databases. Pierce had already told her that.

"Nothing turned up with Grace or Daniel," he told her—the first hint of a real conversation between them. It was his treatment of Daniel that had prompted him finally to confide in her about his past.

A tragic, horrible, unfair past. Difficult choices that had irrevocably changed him…

"I knew they wouldn't," she said softly. She wanted to help him. But what could she do that professionals over ten years had been unable to do? She knew full well that there were just some things that changed you irrevocably.

"He's hiding something."

Pierce's comment took away another vestige of what little hope she had left. Even knowing his issues, he couldn't let go of the boy. She let go of the conversation.

Chose the red patent leather shoes she wanted to go with her dress. Went to her jewelry box for the big red enamel and gold-plated button earrings and matching necklace...

"At this point, they're just going with the increased security measures for the final week. And the scanning of everyone entering and exiting the studio. Are you okay with that?"

"Of course." She stopped. Looked up at him. "Are you?"

His answer mattered to her. Cooking mattered. Packing mattered. And Pierce mattered.

"Yes." He nodded again.

And she was satisfied.

THERE WAS NO gathering of contestants in the hotel Friday evening. Eliza was the only contestant staying there. As far as they knew, none of the others were flying in for the final round. Still, Pierce was glad to know that the hotel staff had been alerted by police to report anyone asking anything about her. They weren't to give out her room number for any reason. And nothing was to be delivered to her without either her or Pierce personally requesting it. If they requested by phone, the order would be delivered only after a call back to the room to verify that it was they who'd ordered.

They were proceeding with more caution than might be necessary.

He fully approved of the plan.

He'd approved the police escort that drove them to the studio the next day, and insisted, with Eliza's permission, that Eliza be on the premises in a room of her own an hour before the doors opened to the public.

He just wasn't sure what he was supposed to do with his beautiful wife for the almost two hours they were going to be sitting there, staring at each other, before her call.

"I've got hair and makeup artists coming in half an hour," she said after several minutes of silence.

She'd been playing a game on her tablet. He'd been watching her.

She'd need to feel beautiful, she'd said when she'd chosen the short red dress two nights before. He hadn't felt like he had a right to argue. Hadn't wanted to test the waters on that one.

"You look beautiful just as you are," he said. And knew before the words left his mouth how inane he sounded. She wasn't wearing any makeup at all. And even he knew that the bright lights on stage would make her bare skin look washed out.

She was wearing her hair down but was having it lifted on top and curled around her shoulders. He knew because he'd heard her talking to someone from the studio about it on the phone that morning.

She went back to her game. He went back to watching her.

She'd had him wear black dress pants, a white shirt and a red tie to match her dress. If she won, he'd be called up on stage with her. He'd shaved twice.

"You can turn on the television," she said.

He had his tablet, too.

"I'm fine," he said.

Who knew how much longer he'd have times like this, alone with her?

"You want something to eat?" he asked, getting up to see what snacks had been provided for them.

"No, thanks."

"A drink?"

"No."

He nodded. Sat back down.

"You think Officer Ryan's here yet?" she asked.

"No."

And so it continued. Stilted conversation. Criminal that it had come to this between the two of them.

But, esteemed cop that he was, Pierce couldn't seem to find a way to solve the problem.

FORTY-FIVE MINUTES before call, Tamera came to the room to tell Pierce that Ryan wanted to speak with him. Something had come up.

"I'm going out to meet Ryan for last-minute checks," he told Eliza, who was sitting in a chair with her hair done, waiting on makeup. "I'm going to be stationed with him during the show." She already knew that second part, but he told her anyway, so it would sound like everything was going as planned. He didn't want her worried about anything except cooking. This was her moment. Her time.

She looked at him. Needing more than he could give her.

So he gave her what he could. He leaned over. Kissed her deep and long. "I love you."

He didn't wait to hear if she could return the sentiment. He had to get to work.

ERNIE RYAN HAD a grim expression as he met Pierce outside the green room and led him down that hall to the soundproof room they'd used the previous week for questioning.

He opened the door and stood back for Pierce to enter.

He wasn't surprised to see Daniel Trevino sitting there, a manila folder on the table. The high school senior looked like a kid anyone would be proud of. Neat blond hair. Short-sleeved *Family Secrets* shirt tucked into clean jeans. Socks and deck shoes. A cell phone sticking out of the pocket of his shirt. He sat up straight, his hands on the table.

Looks were often deceiving. Especially with boys.

Pierce knew that Eliza didn't trust him to know what he was doing where Daniel was concerned.

But his instincts had kept a lot of people from dying in the Middle Eastern desert. They'd told him that another boy was lying to him.

"What's up?" Pierce asked, choosing to stand rather than take the seat that Ryan indicated.

Ryan pushed the folder toward Pierce and,

directing his comment to the boy, said, "Tell him what you told me."

"I found those this morning under the passenger seat of my car," Daniel said.

Pierce studied the boy and then opened the folder.

There wasn't much inside. A couple of index cards. And some sheets containing small black stick-on letters...with pertinent letters missing.

Pierce spelled "You've been warned" and "Don't come back" with the empty spaces. And stared at the boy.

"Why?"

"Why what?"

"Are you somehow associated with Grace?" he asked. Why couldn't he nail the boy? He'd bet his life on the fact that Daniel was hiding the truth.

"I didn't do it," the boy said, his tone even. "But I think I know who did, and I have no idea what else she might do."

"The girl," Ryan said. "Camille. She rode with him to the studio last week."

"And you didn't notice her carrying these out to your car?" Pierce tossed the folder back down on the table. Eliza was due on stage in less than an hour. If there was going to be a problem, they needed to find out what it was and stop it from happening.

"She was already in the car by the time I got there. You questioned her first, and I gave her my keys so she could go out to the car to wait for me while I was being questioned."

Which would have given her time to stick the note in the locker. He was a smart kid. The questions the previous week must have made him nervous.

No decent guy hung his crime on a girl.

"Where's Camille now?" Pierce asked Ryan, still watching Daniel.

"We don't know," Ryan said.

"I stopped by to pick her up this morning, but her foster mom told me she hadn't come home last night."

"And you didn't hear from her?"

"Only a text this morning." He pulled his phone out of his pocket and showed them the text.

See you at the studio.

"She plans to be here," Daniel said, wearing a worried frown as he glanced between

Pierce and Ryan. "I'm afraid of what she could have planned…"

Pierce had more questions for the boy. A lot of them.

But first, they had to find the girl.

"What happens if we don't find her before it's time to go on the air?" Pierce asked after Ryan told Daniel to stay put and they left the room.

Ryan shook his head. "We have an audience full of people, a live nationally televised show and what amounts to some concerning pranks."

And a warning. With no real threat attached, other than the fact that it was issued. *Don't come back.* No real threat of harm.

And yet…an implied threat.

"The studio's been checked," Ryan continued. "Natasha Stevens says the show goes on. The studio backs her decision. You have any idea how much money is riding on this? Advertising dollars alone are more than I make in a lifetime."

Pierce figured the guy was exaggerating a bit, but he got the point.

So, did he try to convince Eliza to back out?

Or did he go find the girl?

He opted to find the girl.

ELIZA HAD A rare moment alone in the room she'd been in all morning in a hallway she'd never been down before. Tamera had excused herself to the adjoining bathroom, and Eliza had been glad to see her go. She liked the woman; she just needed a second to compose herself.

To let her mind rattle off her recipe. To check herself on every detail of the day's dish. She ran through what-ifs. What if the meat didn't sear quickly enough? What if they had goose instead of duck? What if the baguette wasn't a day old?

What if Pierce left her when they got back to Shelby Island the next day?

No.

She couldn't go there. Not then. She was a professional chef. Her job was to cook.

The outer door opened and she looked up, hoping to see Pierce, hoping that he'd come back to wish her luck. Just to check to see that she was okay.

It was the girl, Camille, instead. In her *Family Secrets* shirt and jeans, her short brown hair perky as usual, she smiled. "Just checking to see if there's anything I can get you," she said, looking down the hall behind her and then back into the room. "Some water? Anything to eat?"

The last thing she wanted to do was eat.

And she didn't want to have to pee while she was on stage. "Thank you, but no," she said. "I really appreciate you thinking of me, though."

"Where's Tamera?" Camille asked.

Eliza nodded toward the bathroom door, expecting the guard to be out any second.

Camille got a funny look on her face, like she was unsure of herself, and then came fully inside, closing the door.

# CHAPTER TWENTY-FOUR

AS SOON AS Ryan got word out that they were looking for Camille, his radio started to buzz. Several guards had seen her on the premises.

She'd been seen in a back hallway. In the room where employees stored their personal items while they worked. She'd been spotted on the side of the stage, running a headset to one of the cameramen. And had gone to collect a red bulb to replace one that had burned out. As best they could tell, she'd been on the premises for half an hour or more.

One voice stopped and another started. Camille had been seen less than a minute before, at the door of Eliza Westin's dressing room.

Pierce bolted.

ELIZA GLANCED UP as Pierce rushed in. Tamera was beside her, talking on her radio, but all Eliza could think about was the young woman who'd slumped to her lap and was clinging to her so tightly it hurt—sobbing uncontrollably.

Camille had spoken a time or two, but the only thing Eliza had been able to make out was the word *sorry*.

Pierce looked her over. "You okay?"

"Fine." As in, she could handle the discomfort.

When Pierce spoke, the girl squeezed harder. Eliza could hardly breathe.

And then she was gone, pulled forcibly away.

"No!" Camille cried, still reaching for Eliza. "I'm sorry!"

"What's..." Stunned, Eliza watched as Pierce handed Camille off to another female officer.

"I'm so sorry, sir," Tamera was saying to him. "I just went in to use the restroom, and no one was allowed in the hallway unless they'd been screened..."

Eliza would not have wanted to be on the end of the look Pierce gave the woman.

Eliza stood up. "She wasn't trying to hurt me, Pierce. She's deeply disturbed by something. She needs her mother. Or professional help, maybe. She's just distraught..."

While the situation had been alarming, incredibly distressing, Eliza wasn't afraid. There was no reason for...

"She's the one who left the note, Eliza."

*Camille?* It made no sense. Nothing made sense anymore. "But...why? How did you figure it out?"

"Daniel."

"He was in on it, too?"

"He says not, but I'm sure he is."

So she'd been wrong about that, too.

As the police escorted a hysterical Camille down the hall, Angela came in. "You have ten minutes till call. You going to be okay to go on?"

"Of course." She had no idea if she was okay. But more than ever, she had to get that win.

It was the only way she'd have any control over her life.

"We're sending makeup and hair back in case you need any touching up," the stage manager said, shaking her head. "I'm really sorry, Mrs. Westin. No one saw it coming from her..."

Eliza nodded. Maybe someday she'd know why the girl had picked her, in particular, to target.

Maybe not.

"You think it's because of Grace?" she asked Pierce after Angela left. Eliza didn't want Grace to be involved.

"We can't find any connection between her and Daniel. Maybe once we look at Camille's past...who knows."

"You think it's guilt that set her off? Or fear of being caught because of all the questions last week?"

He shrugged. "We don't know, Liza. But you can rest assured we're going to find out."

A knock on the still-open door signaled the arrival of someone from the wardrobe department. Thankfully her dress was fine.

In the flurry of activity that followed, Pierce left.

He waved. Smiled.

He didn't tell her good luck.

"YOU KNOW MORE than you're saying." Ryan, seated directly across from Daniel Trevino, gave him a direct stare. Pierce, feeling somewhat detective-like in his dress clothes, stood off to the side, arms crossed, leaning against the wall.

Camille's foster mother had been called, and the girl was going to be taken to the police station for questioning once she'd calmed down. From what Pierce had heard, child services was involved since Camille was in foster care. He'd also heard that the girl had sworn that she hadn't done anything else after she constructed that note.

What wasn't yet clear was whether or not she'd been responsible for the earlier incidents. And whether or not she'd worked alone.

The other big question was why? Why these kids? Why Eliza?

Or was it just *Family Secrets* they were after for some reason, and Eliza had been a random target?

"I swear." Daniel shook his head. "I don't have any idea why she did this."

As it stood, they had no reason to hold Daniel. But Ryan was a good guy—he was giving Pierce a chance to go at the kid.

"You're sure you didn't help? Maybe just with the mushrooms? The vinegar?"

"No. I did not. I would not. Listen, Camille's a little…she's been through some tough stuff. She kind of leaned on me, and I wanted to be there for her if I could, but I'd never condone sabotage. I can hardly believe she did it. She's not a bad kid. She's just…off right now. Ask her foster mother. She'll tell you."

"You know her foster mother, then?"

"Just from, you know, picking her up and stuff."

"Have you ever heard Camille say anything about Mrs. Westin?"

"Never."

"She didn't have it in for her for some reason?"

"Not that I ever heard."

Pierce got an internal nudge, but it wasn't strong enough to act on.

"How about *Family Secrets*?" Ryan asked. "Could Mrs. Westin just have been a means to an end? Did Camille think she was getting a raw deal from Ms. Stevens? Or the studio?"

"No, she was pumped when she got the internship. She's the one who told me about it."

"How well do you know her?" Pierce asked.

Daniel shrugged. "Kinda well."

"How do you know her?"

"From school. And…around."

There. Pierce got that stab in his gut that told him something more was up.

"You two date?"

"What?" For the first time the kid showed a hint of losing his cool. "No way, man! She's a kid. And…no!"

Ryan looked at Pierce and asked, "Did she want to date you?"

"I don't know. I didn't think so. She's like…a kid sister."

"So, you met her in drama class?" From Ryan again.

"No, sir." The teenager looked over at Pierce and added, "Sirs."

Coming forward, Pierce pulled out the chair at the end of the table. Sat down and folded his hands.

"How did you meet?"

"I dated her older sister." Now they were getting somewhere. Whether or not it would lead to the attacks against Eliza, he didn't know. But he didn't want this kid out of his sight until he was certain that he hadn't been involved in targeting his wife.

And by then, someone should be getting a report from Camille.

"Dated. You broke up?"

Daniel's lower lip started to tremble, but the young man looked him in the eye as he said, "No, sir, she passed away. Six weeks ago. She was in a car accident. That's why Camille's so out of it and kind of hanging on to me. Her sister was all she had in the world."

The kid was too smart to lie about such a thing. It was too easily verifiable.

Pierce sat back.

They were done here.

ELIZA BROWNED HER MEAT. She talked to Natasha, explaining what she was doing. She moved quickly. Efficiently. Remembering to smile at the audience. She concentrated on her recipe and spoke to Grace, encouraging her as she went to the big refrigerator between the two kitchen pods.

During the regular competition Eliza and Grace were in the same pod. But Natasha had wanted each finalist to have her own pod, and since Eliza had more wins, she'd gotten first choice.

She chose to move, figuring it would be easier for Grace to keep the same kitchen.

She wanted to win. But she wanted her cooking to be the determiner. She didn't want the win because Grace was at an unfair disadvantage, like having to look for utensils that weren't where she expected them to be. Or getting turned around under the bright lights.

She watched the clock. Chopped onions and worried about Camille. She'd never witnessed a nervous breakdown but was pretty sure that was what she'd just seen. And she had no idea why.

Until, on commercial break, she heard a couple of techies talking on the side stage. She couldn't be sure but thought she'd heard one ask the other if he could believe that little Camille was the one who'd been responsible for all of the things that had happened to Mrs. Westin.

It made no sense. What had she ever done to Camille? Or to anyone who knew her?

Had the world gone totally mad?

Shelby Island, and her beautiful, professional kitchen in Rose Harbor, seemed like something out of another lifetime.

Thinking about her kitchen, her guests, her home, the bedroom she shared with Pierce, Eliza browned onions. She measured chicken stock, tomato sauce and wine. She blended and boiled and stirred. She chopped browned meat into chunks. Opened cans of beans and poured them into the sauce mixture.

Everything went together as planned.

She finished on time.

Had her food plated and ready.

And was ready to take the win.

DANIEL WAS TOLD he was free to go home, but the teenager chose to stay and finish out his internship. Pierce respected the choice. But he didn't like it.

He was equally uncomfortable when the boy positioned himself side stage, with a direct view of where both Grace and Eliza were standing, holding hands, while the judges told them what they liked about their final efforts.

Poised, ready to act on a second's notice, he kept an eye on the boy. On everything. If it was the last thing he did for her, he was going to be certain that Eliza had this moment. These moments.

Even if she went on to do regular television spots, there would never be another first time. These six weeks were it.

He listened to the judges praise her. Smiled when the little girl, Jasmine, told Eliza that she'd really liked her food and wondered if she could teach her mom how to make that dish. Fell in love all over again when his wife assured her that she'd be happy to do so.

Regardless of the years he hadn't had with Eliza, he was lucky, thankful, for the years he did have.

It was time then for Natasha to name the final round winner and recipient of, among other things, a nationally distributed packaged rendition of the winner's recipe.

Pierce didn't want to be there. With every second that passed, Eliza was moving further away from him.

And yet he was excited. Proud of her. Grinning as he watched her face, ready to see her expression as her name was called.

*"Grace Hargraves!"*

What?

"Are you kidding me?"

Pierce heard the words, softly spoken, but filled with disappointment, and turned to see Daniel Trevino walking away.

He noticed. But didn't watch the boy go.

He was too busy watching Eliza—standing proud, smiling, congratulating Grace.

He felt her pain.

# CHAPTER TWENTY-FIVE

ELIZA COULDN'T BELIEVE IT. She had to get off the stage. She wasn't sure she had the strength to walk the distance from center stage to the wings.

She'd *lost*?

Grace hugged her, and she hugged the woman back. Glad, in some part of herself, that the woman had won. And yet completely devastated at the same time.

She hadn't won. She wasn't an award-winning chef after all. She was the runner-up. The one who was not quite good enough.

Afraid she was going to embarrass herself further by passing out or having to be carried off, she saw Pierce waiting for her. And guilt gave her strength. She'd messed up their lives so completely. Put everyone out with her need to be a real chef. To compete on television.

It had all been for nothing. Because of some perverse selfishness inside her?

She'd been so revved up. So excited. So sure she'd had to pursue this chance.

Pierce pulled her into his arms. Held her close.

And she felt like the world's biggest fraud.

THERE WAS NOTHING more for them to do. Eliza had no desire to press charges against Camille, though the police could still choose to do so for the tire and the threatening note left in Eliza's locker.

Ryan told Pierce he'd keep him posted as things unfolded, and left him and Eliza to head back to her room.

Natasha popped into Eliza's dressing room as she was gathering her things, to let her know that there'd be offers of guest spots on shows along the way. Eliza nodded. Thanked her.

Pierce was happy for her. She was getting what she'd needed—recognition as a professional chef. He hated how unhappy she seemed. Like she hadn't just won three out of five episodes on a national cooking show. He needed to get her out of there. Off stage. Out of the eye of strangers. Where she could just be herself.

And feared that, even then, she'd be closed off. To him.

Where were they if Eliza couldn't even let him see what she was feeling? If she couldn't lean on him? Share with him? The moment solidified how much he'd already lost her.

A knock sounded on the door, and he felt like giving something a knock. Eliza had given them all she had. It was time to leave her alone...

She looked up at him, and he pulled open the door.

Daniel Trevino, looking like a worried rat, stood there. "I need to talk to you."

Pierce nodded, moved to step outside with the kid.

"To both of you," Daniel said, patting his hand against his thigh. "In private."

Pierce was wearing his weapon. And Daniel wouldn't be there if he'd had one. He'd come through electronic screening, and all employees had been hand-patted, too, at the request of Natasha's attorneys.

"What's going on?" Eliza was at the door.

Opening it wider, Pierce stepped aside, letting the boy enter.

He'd give the kid a minute. No more.

He wasn't letting Daniel put anything else on Eliza.

The vision of her sitting with a hysterical teenager in her lap earlier that day, the distraught look on her face as she'd glanced up at him, was still fresh in his mind.

Too fresh.

Eliza was strong, incredibly strong. But emotional overload could happen to anyone.

Daniel paced between them. Patted his leg again. "I have some things to say. I don't know how to say them."

"You want to have a seat?" Eliza motioned toward the couch. Dropped down to an armchair. And gave Pierce *the look*.

She wanted him to sit down, too. To mind his manners and behave.

As if he'd ever done anything else around her.

But he knew what she was asking. She needed him to suck up his issues long enough to be decent to the kid.

Daniel sat. Rested his elbows on his knees, bouncing the tips of his steepled fingers against each other, again and again.

He looked at Pierce and then down at the floor. He looked at Eliza and just kept staring.

"I…"

Pierce sat back. Took a deep breath. Not sure how long his patience was going to last.

Looking over at him, Daniel asked, "How long have you two been married?"

"Seven years," he answered. The answer seemed to please the boy. And that's when he knew what Eliza had known the week before. His instincts were on the fritz.

Daniel's blue gaze turned back on Eliza.

"If you've got something to tell her, get it over with," Pierce said, thinking he was helping the boy along.

Truth was, impatient as he felt, hearing the reasons behind the sabotage, would be good for Eliza.

It would be good to have the issue settled before they went home. To have questions answered. It would give them closure on this particular episode in their lives.

Not that he kidded himself into thinking the issues the episode had inadvertently brought to light would be disappearing.

Ever.

Daniel took a deep breath. Sat up straight. Gazed at Eliza with the strangest look in his eyes, and said, "I'm your son."

Pierce felt like he'd fallen into one of his nightmares.

He watched from afar. Hearing the ocean in the distance.

Eliza sat in her chair. Staring.

"What did you say?"

"I'm him," Daniel said, his voice squeaking on the second word. "I'm your son. The one you gave up for adoption. You told the agency you were okay with me contacting you."

"You're…"

Eliza didn't move. Pierce had the strangest urge to get up and help her. To lift her from her chair and take her to the boy.

She looked back at Pierce, a question all over her face.

He didn't know the answer.

But he nodded at her.

"You're… *Oh my God!*" She screamed so loud Pierce prepared himself for authorities storming the door. Before he remembered all the rooms in the hallway were soundproof.

"I can't…" Eliza jumped up. "Oh my God, Pierce." She looked at him and then at Daniel. Dropped to her chair and burst into tears.

Reaching across the space between them, she took Daniel's hand between both of hers, stared at it. Like she was trying to imagine it as it had been when she'd given him away.

She rubbed her fingers back and forth across his hand.

Pierce felt her pain. He felt her shock.

What he couldn't feel was her joy.

He looked at the boy—his boy—though he was pretty certain Daniel didn't know that yet—and all he felt was…shame.

He couldn't do it.

Couldn't face the boy.

Not even for Liza.

He didn't think. He didn't decide.

He just left.


"WHAT'S WITH HIM?"

They were the first words her son said to her with them being mother and son.

Eliza felt like every word from here on out would be forever etched on her memory. In a special book in her mind, reserved for second chances.

She shook her head. There was a lot Daniel would have to know.

Eliza wasn't in a state of mind to tell him. To do justice to the story. Or to Daniel's father.

She needed Pierce. Felt his absence like a slice to her heart. He wouldn't go far. Would he? Wouldn't leave her stranded there…

It wasn't the first time he'd walked out. He'd done so at home recently when he'd gone down to the beach.

And any other time his emotions got the better of him. He left before he reacted and did something he'd regret. She knew this. Reminded herself.

And knew, even if Pierce didn't, that he needed her help in the moment.

Daniel was as much his son as he was hers. Until Pierce could parent him, it was up to her to do so for both of them. Whatever that meant.

"He didn't know about me, did he? Didn't know that you'd had a son before you two married or that you'd given a child up for adoption?" Daniel said. "I thought about telling you separately. Planned to, actually, but when I saw how close you two were, and... well... He's kind of scary, you know. I just figured he'd be less likely to ban me from your life if I included him and told you both at the same time. Especially since you gave permission for me to contact you and all. I figured you wouldn't have done that if you had family...stuff...to take care of."

This young man was the heart of her heart. And Pierce's.

"He knows about you," Eliza said, smiling. And crying, too. Soft tears that trickled down her cheeks. She wiped them away. More came.

She sniffled. And Daniel reached for the tissue box on the side table, handing it to her.

There were so many questions. Not enough answers.

Too much pain and not enough joy.

Her son had just handed her a tissue.

Her son.

He was healthy. And sweet. And kind.

And sitting right in front of her. She couldn't believe it. Was in a crazy, inexplicable fog. Hanging on for dear life.

Yet for the first time in many, many years, Eliza felt…complete.

PIERCE WENT LOOKING for Ryan. He wasn't sure why.

The other man had already left.

As far as he could tell, other than security and some techies who were doing what they did after television shows, everyone had gone.

The theater was empty. Only half an hour before, the place had been full. The lobby was empty. The green room was empty.

He was empty.

While his family—

*Family.*

His *family.*

They were only steps away. Without him.

He couldn't be a real father to the boy, wouldn't be an example to him because he wouldn't be responsible for leading him wrong, but he was still Eliza's husband. And had created the boy.

What kind of parent walked out on that?

The thought propelled him.

A parent like his own mother, like the father who'd dived into a bottle of alcohol and had never come out. Those were the types of parents who did that.

Not him.

At a run, Pierce took the hallways, bruising his shoulder against the corner of a wall as he entered the hall leading to Eliza's dressing room. His dress shoes didn't give him the best traction. He didn't let them slow him down.

If he was too late...

If they'd left without him...

He'd been gone only five minutes.

Ten, tops.

He'd find them.

He was a cop.

Had friends in the local department.

He'd find them.

Grabbing the handle on Eliza's door, he fumbled in his haste. Pushed before he'd turned. When the door opened, he half fell inside. Expecting to see them gone. Promising himself he'd find a way to make it up to them.

"Pierce!" Eliza jumped up, grabbed at his arm as though to steady him.

"You're still here." He wasn't out of breath from the run. But he sucked in air. Rapidly.

"Of course we're here. Where would I go? You're my ride."

He was her ride.

Right.

He was hers.

She could have ridden off with the boy.

Had she thought of that?

"Okay," he said. Nodding.

Facing the situation head-on. "We have to get to the bottom of this," he said, clasping his hands together. And then not sure what to do with himself.

He should sit. Standing over them wasn't appropriate in this situation. He didn't need to intimidate.

Sit where? On the couch?

No, the boy was there.

On the arm of Liza's chair?

Looking behind him, Pierce grabbed a straight-backed chair from the little table for two in the corner, pulled it over not too far from his wife.

Daniel and Eliza were both watching him, and it occurred to him that he had no idea what they'd already said. What they'd been talking about. What they already knew about each other that he didn't know.

What *was* clear was that they were now both looking to him to make the next move.

"So, Daniel," he bowed his head as he said the word, and then glanced up at the boy. Aiming for the eyes. Landed on the forehead. It was high.

Like Pierce's dad's.

And his, too.

So, if that was the only thing the kid got from them…

The kid's eyes were blue. He'd noted that earlier, when he'd been just a person of interest. Because he noted details about everything.

Liza had brown eyes. Big brown eyes.

Pierce's were blue. He'd been told his mother's eyes were blue.

The kid probably had his eyes.

But not the mirror into his soul. No, the boy's soul would have to mirror Liza's. There just wouldn't be any other way about it...

"Pierce?" Liza's voice was soft. Like it was just the two of them in the room.

But it wasn't. Couldn't she see how, in the space of seconds, everything had changed? Irrevocably.

The boy, Daniel, he was there. In between them.

Where he was going to be for the rest of their lives.

This was it. The wedge that was going to split him and his wife apart.

## CHAPTER TWENTY-SIX

ELIZA'S STOMACH TWISTED. A knife's blade tore her insides. *Be careful what you ask for.* Her father's words came unbidden. Really? Her dad intruding on a moment that would never have been if not for him.

She watched her husband. Daniel would be uncomfortable. Maybe even scared. But in that moment, Pierce needed her more. She could only imagine the struggle inside him. And needed him to know that he didn't face it alone.

She would always be there.

Wherever he'd let her be.

Another strike of the knife. *Would* he let her be?

"Pierce?" she said again. Calling him back to them. Out of the darkness and into her dressing room. She glanced at Daniel briefly. Long enough to send him a reassuring smile.

"Why don't you tell us what you know."

Sounding perfectly normal, polite albeit distant, Pierce addressed Daniel.

Her son. Her baby boy. Sitting right there. She couldn't wrap her mind around it. Couldn't believe...

"I'm sorry, sir. I don't understand."

Daniel looked straight at Pierce. Just like Daniel's father would have done...

"About Camille. About what went on here. Obviously you're involved. The first order of business is to find out what we're facing. I need to know what you know about all of this."

Tears sprang to Eliza's eyes, and she blinked them away. She loved her husband so very, very much. Could feel his restraint.

And his fear.

And he still thought Daniel knew something...

Daniel looked at her.

And her heart sank.

"I honestly didn't know she was behind the vandalizing until this morning."

Eliza believed him immediately.

But tensed as she watched Pierce.

"What do you know about her?" Pierce said. And then, "And I want to know everything this time."

"Yes, sir." Daniel nodded. Licked his lips. And sent a look to Eliza that seemed almost apologetic.

"I don't know why she'd do those things," he said to Pierce. "I can't understand that part, either." He looked at Eliza, "But she knows you're my mother."

Eliza froze. Mother. She was a mother. Of course, she'd known she was. But...for so long she'd been forced to deny that part of herself...

*Mother.* Her.

"What reason would she have for wanting to hurt your biological parent?" Pierce asked.

Daniel shook his head.

"I asked for the whole truth." Pierce's tone maintained its kindness, but it was also clear he wasn't fooling around.

The teenager turned to Pierce. "I've known Camille only about a year. My girlfriend, Molly, was her older sister. Molly's been in foster care since she was little. She and Camille were split up. About a year ago, her family services worker told her that her sister was having some emotional issues and they thought it might help if Molly met her. Molly didn't even know she'd had a little sister. She was beyond ecstatic about the whole thing."

"Did Molly know you were adopted?" Eliza had so many questions. And needed answers so different from the ones Pierce was seeking. She needed to know about his parents. That he grew up loved and adored and happy.

He was a great kid. Everything she'd want him to be. His parents had done a great job...

"Yes," Daniel said, glancing at Eliza. "It was one of the things that drew us together..."

He broke off. Couldn't meet her gaze.

"How so?" she asked.

In her peripheral vision, she saw Pierce frown. She wanted to reach for his hand, but it was too far away.

"My...adoptive parents...divorced when I was eight," he said. "They both remarried, had families of their own. I was welcome in both homes. They were great to me. Included me. Always came to my baseball games. But... I was the odd one out, you know? When I was at Dad's, I was the one with family at Mom's. When I was at Mom's, I was the only one who also had family at Dad's. On Christmas, both families, my half brothers and sisters, would all each have all day at home, while I spent part with one and part with the other..."

Her eyes filled with tears again.

"And when you met…Molly…with her being in foster care, the two of you had something in common," Pierce said. Kindly.

And yet like a cop.

"Yes, sir."

"And then she met Camille."

"Yes, sir."

"Did they hit it off?"

"Yes. Absolutely. But…like they said, Camille has some emotional issues. She'd, like, call Molly in the middle of the night, tell her she was thinking about killing herself, stuff like that. She'd talk about cutting…"

"How did Molly handle that?" Eliza wanted to know everything about every aspect of his life. All the things a mother would know.

"She was great. Molly was…she was the motherly one at school. Always taking care of everyone…" His voice broke, and Eliza wanted to pull him into her arms.

And had to remind herself that she was still a stranger to him. That another woman had mothering rights where he was concerned.

That he'd grown up loving another woman as his mother. And clearly still did love her.

But he'd sought Eliza out.

She needed to know why. In the worst way.

"So…what happened with Molly…when… How did…"

"Camille had called her late one night. Said she had to see her. Molly called me. I told her she shouldn't go. That she needed to call Camille's foster mother. That she needed to let their parents do their jobs. She said she would, but next thing I know, Mom's waking me up to tell me there'd been an accident." He broke off as he teared up again. And Eliza went to him. Put an arm around his waist and held on.

She was holding her son. For the very first time. He'd lived within her for nine months, and she'd never even been allowed to hold him.

She filed away the moment. Right then, it couldn't matter.

"I'm so sorry," she said, her heart in her throat. She glanced at Pierce, needing his help. He was watching as if from a great distance.

"She was hit by a drunk driver," Daniel said, wiping his eyes and sitting up straighter.

He was more man than little boy.

Eliza gave him space, but she didn't leave the couch.

"I'm assuming Camille then attached herself to you," Pierce said, his gaze intent, but... impersonal, too.

"Yes, sir."

"Let's back up a minute," Pierce said. "How did it come to be that you and Camille happened to be working on the *Family Secrets* set at the time that your biological mother was a contestant?"

Finally, a question she'd have asked.

Looking down, Daniel picked at the skin on one finger. He shrugged. Then glanced at Eliza, looking embarrassed.

"I...went to the agency last fall..."

Before Molly was killed. It just hit Eliza. He hadn't yet been hurting and feeling alone when he'd sought her out.

"Did she know?"

"Of course. We told each other everything. She...um...was the one who suggested it. The whole idea was hers."

"Whole idea?" Pierce sat forward.

"To find my...her," he said, nodding toward Eliza. "The information was decades old, but over Christmas break we did a ton of research and found out that the person who lived at the address we had had worked at Rose Harbor Bed-and-Breakfast..."

Eliza nodded. Smiled through a new spate of tears. She just couldn't seem to turn off the waterworks.

"Molly was into these cooking shows… always watching them because she said she wanted to be the kind of cook I'd always want to come home to." He blinked. But looked at Pierce and continued.

"When she saw that one of the upcoming contestants on *Family Secrets* was from Rose Harbor, you could have heard her scream all the way in Hawaii, I'm pretty sure." He grinned. And then sobered. "She said there were no coincidences, that this was our chance…"

"Your chance?" Eliza asked.

Turning his head toward her, he nodded. Rubbed his hands together as he leaned forward on his knees. And then gave his attention back to Pierce.

"She did some checking and found out that the show took interns, two of them, from local high schools, each segment. Camille was in good with our drama teacher—some kind of counseling thing for her, to work out her emotions through theater—and she got us in."

"So she was the one who brought you and Eliza together?" Pierce was nodding.

"Yes. Which is why it never occurred to me that she'd do anything to hurt her." He nodded toward Eliza again.

Eliza wanted to know why he hadn't told her the very first day who he was. She remembered him just standing there on the side of the stage, watching, when she'd discovered the mushrooms were missing.

He'd been watching her, she now realized, not because he knew anything about the mushrooms, but because he'd been getting his first look at his biological mother.

What had he thought? What did he think now?

That she'd abandoned him?

Shouldn't he have asked by now why she gave him up? She had so much to tell him.

But the story wasn't just hers. It was Pierce's, too.

"I think it's pretty safe to assume, given the circumstances, that when Camille saw you with your birth mother, she felt threatened," Pierce was saying. "Either because you would have contact with a biological parent, which would leave her alone in her fosterhood, or because she somehow thought that if you had a chance to get to know Eliza, you'd leave her, too. At the same time, she knew this was what Molly wanted, so she'd wanted to be supportive. Maybe she hoped that when you saw Eliza, she'd somehow be a disappointment to you, or you'd take an instant dislike to her and that would be that."

When Daniel's gaze narrowed, Eliza glanced at Pierce. He really did have a gift for...

"She did talk a lot about how much she hated her parents for abandoning her and Molly," he said now. "Like, every time I saw her as though she wanted me to identify and feel the same way about my biological mother. I just thought it was because she was missing Molly so much..."

"She wanted to please Molly, but she wanted the meeting with Eliza to go badly."

Eliza expected Daniel to nod again.

He didn't.

"There's more," he said.

He looked at her. There was something in his gaze. Despair. Determination. A mixture of the two.

And that was when Eliza knew that she'd stepped into far more than she'd ever imagined.

More than she could make right.

*I GOT THIS.* Rolling up the sleeves of his white dress shirt, Pierce adjusted the tie that matched his wife's dress and faced the boy.

"I asked for the whole truth," he reminded Daniel. He'd been in the room twenty minutes. Was doing fine.

He'd surprised himself. And imagined his wife was pretty surprised, as well.

He couldn't be a father, but he could be in the room with the boy. Could take care of business.

When the young man in front of him appeared to be having difficulty continuing, Pierce thought back over the interview. Looking for what hadn't been said.

*The whole idea was hers. This was our chance.* Daniel's words came back to him.

"What idea did Molly have when she suggested you intern?" he asked slowly, watching the teenager for any sign of subterfuge. "*Family Secrets* was your chance to do what?"

Meet Eliza? He could have kept researching. He'd have found her.

But…

"Why did you choose now to search for your mother? What made meeting her so important all of a sudden?"

Daniel flinched. Pierce was onto something. Finally.

They'd get their answers. Go home.

And figure out what they did with what was left between them. You didn't just walk away from a love like theirs. They'd remain friends. At the very least.

*I can do this.*

"Like I said, it was Molly's idea," Daniel said. He gave Pierce a pleading glance. A first. Pierce wasn't at all sure what to do with it.

"I need to hear the idea." He went with his instincts. He'd questioned kids before. Did it all the time on the streets. *What you got in your pocket, boy? Did I just see you take that candy bar off that shelf and walk out the door with it?*

"Molly was pregnant." His chin lifted as though daring Pierce to make something of it.

"I'm assuming the baby was yours?"

"Yes, sir. Of course it was. Molly wasn't like that. We were in love…"

He'd heard it before.

Coming out of his own mouth.

He faltered. A major brain blip. His kid

didn't even know him from Adam and he was already following in his footsteps.

It stopped right now.

"We were talking about her idea."

"We're both seniors, and we'd both hoped to go to college," he said.

"You wanted to give up the baby for adoption, and she wanted to talk to me and see if, all these years later, I still thought giving you up was the best decision?" Eliza blurted. Pierce worried about her. She looked far too fragile all of a sudden.

"No." Daniel swallowed. "She knew there was no way I'd consider giving up any child of mine," he continued. "I'm sorry," he nodded toward her. "But after the way I grew up, never being fully part of either family, knowing that I was the only one who wasn't really related to any of them…I swore to myself that when I became a father, that's when I'd have a family of my own. My own family," he said.

Sniffling, Eliza raised a tissue to her face and nodded. She didn't speak. Pierce suspected that she couldn't.

"You were telling us about the idea," Pierce said again.

He could do this. Be strong where Eliza

wasn't. Handle the situation. Get them home. Figure out where they went from there…

He had his part down.

"Molly wanted to keep the baby, too, but said I had to have a chance to go to college. Especially when I got the scores back on the entrance exams. She said that I had the potential to be whatever I wanted and that I had a right to that chance. She said that there was someone in the world who owed me that right. The person who'd robbed me of the chance to grow up being part of a real family. She said that it was karma, how I had the chance, now, but needed some help to make it all work out right. She said my biological mother was older now and should take responsibility. Just until we could get through college."

Pierce didn't move. The entitlement should have appalled him. Except that he came up against the same pretty much every day. Kids nowadays grew up thinking that it was all about them.

And yet, mixed up in there, this kid was trying to do the right thing.

Unlike Pierce, he'd had the goal to provide

for his child. To be there for him. To give him a solid, loving family...

He swallowed a lump in his throat.

But then Molly had been killed. The baby had died, and...

"So why, after Molly was killed, did you still want to meet me?" Eliza asked, her voice wobbly with emotion. "I'm so sorry, Daniel. I never meant... If I'd known... Giving you up was the last thing in the world I wanted to do."

Daniel looked more like a young kid than an almost-adult as he looked at Eliza.

Pierce was uncomfortable now. Had to get things back on track.

"Why did you continue with your plan to meet your biological mother after Molly and the baby were gone?" he asked. Because this wasn't about him. Daniel hadn't sought out his father. Only his mother. Pierce had to assume that was for a specific reason.

"He's not gone." Daniel looked between Pierce and Eliza with wide-open blue eyes. "Bryant Nathaniel is very much alive, and I need your help. That's why I'm here. I was hoping, like how Molly thought, that you'd get to know me over these weeks and be more willing to help than if I just contacted you out of the blue. But, either way, we, my son and I, need your help."

Pierce felt like he was going to puke.

# CHAPTER TWENTY-SEVEN

SHE HAD A *GRANDSON*? She and Pierce were…

Her gaze flew to the love of her life. He sat straight, his hands on his thighs, immobile. He was looking in her direction but wasn't blinking.

It was as though he was in a trance.

Recognizing the signs, she watched him.

"What's up with him?" Daniel asked. The kid was obviously feeling the effects of emotional overload. His voice squeaked. His heel bopped up and down. He was pounding one thumb against his thigh.

What was she going to do?

Her men were falling apart on her. She'd just found out she had a third little guy who was someplace without them, and she had no clue whom to tend to first.

"He suffers from PTSD," she told Daniel. "He's having what he calls mind blips. They're emotionally based. He can feel them coming on and generally gets himself outside, or even just turns around and focuses on something else and…"

They'd never been this bad. Usually it lasted a second at the most.

Pierce blinked. She knew the second he'd focused on her that he was okay. For the moment.

"You ready to go?" he asked her.

Of course she wasn't. None of them were.

"Let's all go back to the hotel." She looked at Daniel. "That is, if you have time?" They were in town until the next day. If she'd won, there would have been after-show taping to do as well as a congratulatory dinner with the judges scheduled for that night.

"I've got time." The young man seemed to have regained his composure almost completely. "I can follow you."

The fact that Pierce didn't argue was a testament to the level of his distress.

"I'M FINE TO DRIVE," Pierce said when they reached their car. The boy had gone to an employee lot to get his Ford Ranger, white, he'd said, and would be coming around to meet them. He also knew a shortcut to the hotel where they were staying. He'd said that if Pierce wanted, he'd lead the way.

Pierce wanted time alone with Eliza. However that had to happen.

"You're sure?" Eliza's concern made him feel like a wimp—and comforted him at the same time.

"Positive."

She studied him for a long minute, but then nodded and climbed into their rental sedan.

"You scared me back there, Pierce. Are you sure you're okay?" she asked again as he started the car.

"I'm fine." Where was the boy?

"Has that ever happened before?"

*Not since you've been back in my life.* "Yes. A couple of times. Before I learned to recognize the warning signs. And learned how to prevent it."

He hated how telling that statement would be. And then figured it was for the best. "I told you, Eliza. I cannot be a father." Could it be any clearer?

"Is that what your doctor told you?"

Which one?

Didn't matter. None of them had said so. Brain blips were treatable. Most particularly when they were emotional-stress-based, as his were. He could walk into burning flames and be cool as a cucumber.

But put him in a room with a kid needing a father...

"Did you hear what he told us?"

Did she think he was deaf as well as soulless?

"We have a grandson, Pierce."

Was she nuts? Putting him right back in the fray?

"I'd rather not talk about it."

She nodded. Rubbed the back of his neck. "I love you."

He loved her, too. But he wasn't going to use it to hold her to him.

To prove it, as soon as they got back to the hotel, before Daniel had joined them, he turned to her.

"You and the kid talk. Figure out what it is you need to do. We can talk in a bit. I'm going upstairs to rest."

"He doesn't know you're his father, Pierce."

Relief flooded him. He was pretty sure she noticed. He nodded. "Good." And then, "Thank you."

He kissed her. Clung to her. Said goodbye to something he didn't deserve.

And went upstairs to call his shrink.

FEELING BEREFT WITHOUT her husband, Eliza couldn't have followed him if the world had been crashing down. Their son needed her. Now that she knew that, there was no force that could keep her from him.

She finally got why people sometimes said that having children broke up marriages. How on earth did a woman choose between the man she loved and the child they'd created together? The child she'd borne?

Daniel didn't seem to share her grief in Pierce's absence. She suggested that they sit out by the pool. It was seventy degrees, too cool for guests to be swimming. They'd have the place to themselves.

She chose a round umbrella table with a view of the hotel door. She could see the lobby. If Pierce came down looking for her, she'd see him.

Taking her cell phone out of her purse, she laid it on the table beside her.

Precise, thoughtful moves. It was as though she were outside herself. Later, when she was alone, she'd come back together and deal with it all.

Daniel started to speak the second they sat down. "The whole reason I…"

She stopped him with a hand on his arm. "Do your parents know where you are?"

He shook his head. "They never do on

weekends. I'm pretty much on my own. I crash at one or the other's house. They're fine with it. I'll be eighteen soon, a legal adult, and…"

"You just turned seventeen, young man," Eliza told him. She named the date. And threw in the time, too, though she felt a little immature about that.

"Do they know you've been in contact with me?" she asked next.

And was relieved when he nodded. "I talked to my dad about the idea when Molly first suggested it. Both he and mom, and the steps, too, for that matter, were adamant that we give him up for adoption. Molly has no family other than Camille and her foster parents, who are already dealing with new families. My dad tried to prepare me for the fact that I was only going to get hurt. He told me the chances of you being willing to take in a child for four years and then give him back were pretty much nil. Talked about you probably having a family of your own now, too. But in the end, he agreed that if I still needed to try, then he would support the decision."

Eliza liked the man, whoever he was. Mr. Trevino, she supposed. And wondered what he did for a living. What kind of home his wife kept. If he played with his kids.

"So that's your plan? Yours and Molly's? To ask me to keep your son for four years?"

He nodded, looking slightly sick.

"What about your mom?" Mentally she tripped over the word. But she made herself say it. She was not Daniel's mom. She'd given up that right. And couldn't think about his plan yet. She was having her own mind blip.

"She pretty much thought we were nuts. But she supported my need to find you. To know who you were. She thought it would help me come to terms with giving up my own child for adoption. You know, to help me realize how much better a life I had with them than I would have…"

He stopped. It wasn't the first time she'd felt the knife-sharp pain of his words.

"Daniel, I want you to be honest with me. This situation…it's tough. For all of us. But I'm to blame. You are not. You had no say whatsoever in choices that were made for you seventeen years ago. They affected you, those choices. They were all about you. Shaped your whole life. Obviously you're going to have your own set of feelings associated with them. And we can't even hope to build a relationship—" she hoped so desperately that that was what they were doing "—if you can't be honest with me."

He nodded. "Just sounded kind of cruel, you know, when it came out…"

She told him then. About her and…his father. About being just shy of her sixteenth birthday when she'd gotten pregnant…

"Wow," he interrupted her. Grinned way too much like the old Pierce would have done. "So, like, you're only thirty-three and you're a grandma!" His chuckle died off quickly.

And she continued telling him about the complicated circumstances that had led to his birth. Leaving out one key factor.

The identity of his father. She couldn't tell him. Not without Pierce's permission.

And yet…she'd just told him that they had to be honest with each other.

Feeling like her heart was being pulled in half, she waited for his question.

Oddly enough, it didn't come.

He didn't *want* to know who his father was?

Didn't he want to know that young man who'd left for the army and been coerced by her father never to contact her again, and had done so anyway? Because their love had been calling to him since the day he'd left town?

"So...you and Mr. Westin, do you have any kids?" There was the question. Fifteen minutes later than she'd expected. And coming in a different door.

She wanted so badly for Daniel to know what a great man his father was. She wouldn't build their relationship on lies.

"Pierce was injured in the Middle East. He's unable to father children." She felt like she was walking in a minefield but moved ahead anyway. Trusting that she had it in her to be a good mother.

"So he was in the military, too?"

It took her a second to realize that the "too" referred to his biological father. She'd told him he'd been conceived the night before his father had left to go to the army.

"Yes," she said. "He's a cop now, in Charleston."

He nodded. "I know. Officer Ryan told us when they had us all in for questioning last week. He's kind of a serious dude, isn't he?"

"Officer Ryan?"

Daniel shook his head. "I guess he'd be Officer Westin, not Mr., huh?"

Or Dad.

"So…" She didn't know how much longer she should leave Pierce up there alone. "Tell me about your son." Did he seriously want her help raising the baby?

Her heart palpitated at the thought. She couldn't see how a baby would fit anywhere in her life. And knew she'd do whatever it took to make it happen.

"That's why I did this." He nodded. "I never even thought about looking you up before all of this."

His words hurt. But she couldn't blame him.

Really, in a sense, she was glad. He'd have needed her only if he'd felt the lack of a mother's love. While he didn't like being an in-between—which she fully understood—he was a lot more secure and loved than he probably realized.

"And that's why I don't get Camille trying to sabotage the whole thing. She knows why meeting you was so important."

He pulled his phone out of his pocket and started scrolling before turning it to her.

The breath caught in her chest and wouldn't move. In or out. She could hardly make out the small form in the bassinet with tubes protruding from nearly every part of his body. Her eyes were filling up again.

"Oh my God," she said. Smiling. And crying, too.

She'd just lost her heart again. In a way she'd never have believed possible. She'd never even met the little one, and she'd give her life up for him.

No matter what.

"It's a miracle he's alive," Daniel was saying, a tone of pride in his voice way beyond his years.

Her baby had his own baby. Was more of a parent, already, in the six weeks his son had been alive, than she and Pierce had ever been.

Daniel had been talking for fifteen minutes straight about Bryant Nathaniel. Talking about physical challenges and the special care the baby was going to need for some time to come, once he was released from the hospital. He knew it all. And spoke with a sense of responsibility that broke Eliza's heart. And did it good, too. She was so proud of him. But couldn't take any credit for the young man he was.

"What's his prognosis?" she asked, alarmed as she listened to the battles being taken on by such a tiny body.

"Perfect, they tell me," Daniel said. "It's mostly premie stuff. He wasn't hurt in the accident." He broke off.

In the next instant, she could swear she was looking at Pierce. A more modern version of him—as in, the Pierce she knew now. Daniel's face had twisted, his eyes hardened. Not in meanness. Just...with foreboding.

"Molly didn't die because of injuries she sustained in the car accident," he said. "The seat belt caused her to go into early labor. She died giving birth to him." There was no emotion in his voice now. And out of nowhere, Eliza knew a fear she'd never felt before.

Hopelessness.

"I was there," he continued. "Mom had taken me to the hospital as soon as she woke me up. Molly wanted me in the delivery room with her. It was touch-and-go, and she was so weak. She was bleeding too much. Then something happened, something about birth fluid going into her body because something had perforated."

He blamed himself. The fault wasn't his, but he blamed himself. The truth was clear to Eliza.

And suddenly, in the midst of all the pain, she understood.

Things happened for reasons. Everything, not just some things.

Pierce's choice to join the army had led to the day he'd faced that young boy. Killing the boy, which he believed at the time would have saved countless lives, had taken a piece of his soul. And now here was his son, with his own piece of soul missing.

Somehow she was supposed to do something with all of this.

She had absolutely no clue what to do. How to do it.

She just knew that she was a wife. And a mother.

And she had to find a way to be both.

## CHAPTER TWENTY-EIGHT

PIERCE DIDN'T LIE DOWN. He knew he wouldn't sleep. Knew he didn't want to. The exercise would be a nightmare in waiting. He had things to work out.

Within himself and with others.

Sitting on a balcony identical to the one he'd shared with Liza the week before, he thought about the conversation he'd had with the department psychologist he'd been speaking with for the past couple of years.

He was on track. Doing the right things. Taking responsibility for his own mind. Taking charge. He could have a prescription if he wanted one. They both knew he didn't.

The only way he was ever going to be able to get over his aversion to being a father was to forgive himself.

It was a battle only he could fight. Only he could win.

There was no pill that would do it for him.

*There is no right or wrong here, Pierce.* He'd

been told again that afternoon, during phone counseling, but many times in the past, too.

It didn't matter that he'd been a great soldier, wouldn't matter if the President himself gave him a Purple Heart. If he couldn't forgive himself, the demon wasn't going away.

He couldn't forgive himself. Lord knew, he'd tried. Tried to find some way he could understand what he'd done in a different way.

His mind wouldn't let him.

And no one else could make it happen; it was between him and his psyche.

And now there was a grandchild. A grand-*son*.

One who needed Eliza.

He was going to have to let her go.

ELIZA TOLD DANIEL that she had to speak with Pierce. The boy nodded, his gaze serious. Not hopeful. But not lacking in hope, either.

She wanted to hug him. To pull him to her heart and never let him go.

He needed more than hugs.

She couldn't make promises to him without Pierce's input. Without him knowing. He was her husband.

"I am not going to give you up a second time." She looked him straight in the eye as she made the one promise she could in that moment.

He seemed to understand. Wise beyond his years. His gaze moistened, though there were no tears. He nodded. Stood.

"I have to get to the hospital. I like to spend more time with him on Saturdays since I can go for only half an hour before school, and then in the evenings," he said.

She nodded. Had seen pictures of Daniel holding his tiny son. And had sobbed right there at the pool, too.

"Is it okay if I join you there later?" she asked him, also standing. Her grandson was just a few miles away.

"That'd be awesome." Daniel nodded. Kind of smiled. And then, leaning over, he gave her a loose hug. All in all, it was a little awkward. Arms not sure what to do and a lot of distance between their feet.

For Eliza, it was all the impetus she needed to do what had to come next.

And balm to a very pained heart, too.

PIERCE DIDN'T WANT to interrupt Eliza's time with Daniel. He had some things to say to the boy. But they could wait. He needed to take care of his wife first.

He needed to free her to take care of the children…

Yet when he heard her key in the door, he knew he wasn't ready.

Grabbing the keys, he met her at the door. "I was just heading down," he said. A complete fabrication.

A sign of what was to come? The two of them speaking in platitudes instead of truths?

"Are you sure, Pierce? Did you rest?"

He told her about his phone call. Or rather, that he'd made it. And that he was okay.

"In that case, I need you to drive me to the hospital," she said.

His first thought was that she was in physical distress. And then it hit him… "To see the baby." He understood. Knew, too, that she'd worded her request the way she had on purpose—to make it about her. Not him. Or anyone else. She didn't expect any more out of him, wasn't asking any more out of him, than a ride there and back.

Watching him, she nodded.

He wanted to give her the truth. "I can't see him."

"I understand."

She took his hand. Squeezed it. And then kissed him.

ELIZA HAD TOLD herself that she was not going to meet her grandson for the first time without Pierce present. They'd missed their only child's babyhood. Separate and apart. They would begin their second chance side by side.

Just as they'd found out Daniel was their son. The two of them. Side by side. Together.

That couldn't have been a mistake.

She took Pierce to a family waiting room just down the hallway from the NICU. Daniel had told her where to come, to text him when she got there and had said he'd come get her. The room wasn't big. Daniel had told her it was usually used for families in crisis.

She didn't ask what that meant. Her imagination filled in those blanks.

And yet, if ever there was a family in crisis, it was theirs.

They'd passed the larger waiting room, with children's toys and activities, magazines and a couple of couches, closer to the elevator. "I should wait down there," Pierce said when she turned into the vacant room.

She shook her head. "He said this one would be more comfortable," she said.

He nodded. Squeezed her hand. And let her go.

Tearing up again, Eliza slipped out the

door, closing it behind her as Daniel had told her—except that he'd told her to wait on the inside, where Pierce thought he was waiting for Eliza to be done. The closed door indicated to hospital personnel that the room was in use.

She hoped she was doing the right thing. Knew she was taking the risk of her life.

Because she had no other choice.

She texted Daniel. Told him she was there.

And then she walked down the hall.

Sent one more text.

And prayed.

It's a matter of life or death, Pierce. Talk to him. For me.

Pierce read the text once. And then twice. It came in under Eliza's number. She was the least dramatic person he knew. Yeah, she'd been emotional that day—who wouldn't be?—but even on the way to the hospital she'd been calm. Nurturing.

It was Eliza's nature.

He didn't know what she meant. She wasn't asking him to join her in the unit. Wasn't asking him to see the child.

Her request made no sense.

Until Daniel walked in the room, stopping when he saw Pierce there.

"Where's...she?" the boy asked, frowning as he looked around.

In what appeared to be a hospital paper gown over the jeans he'd had on at the studio, the boy looked more like a young doctor than a seventeen-year-old kid. He had a surgical mask resting against his throat as if he'd just pulled it off.

*She.* He didn't know what to call Eliza.

The awareness shouldn't have surprised Pierce. He was good at tuning in. At knowing what people were hiding. Even with this kid, he'd known when he was hiding something from them.

But that was...before.

Everything that had taken place before those irrevocable words, *I'm your son,* would be forevermore the before in Pierce's life.

*It's a matter of life or death, Pierce. Talk to him. For me.*

"Come in," he said.

It became clear suddenly that Eliza needed him to tell the boy he was his father. She was asking him to let her off the last hook of loyalty to him.

It was a fair request.

One he'd already planned to honor. He was not his old man. He would not turn his back on his own son.

He respected the boy when he shut the door behind him and stepped forward, his shoulders square, his head high. He was as tall as Pierce.

They met eye to eye.

"Eliza asked me to speak with you," he said.

Daniel's lips pursed, his chin puckered. He nodded. "She's not here, is she?" More accusation than question.

"What? Of course she's here. She's Eliza. There's no way she wouldn't be here." He slowed as he realized the boy had no way of knowing what type of woman his mother was.

And the crime in that truth cut through him.

"Your biological mother is the most nurturing, kind woman I've ever had the honor to know," he said, not caring that he sounded like the sap he was where his wife was concerned.

Just as Daniel wouldn't suffer for the father who'd created him, he deserved to benefit from the mother who had.

Daniel crossed his arms. Still facing Pierce head-on. "So, what's this about?"

"I expect she needs me to talk to you about your biological father…"

What? *"She needs me to tell you that I'm your biological father"* was what was supposed to have come through.

"You know about him?" Daniel's blue eyes were narrowed. Pierce could have been looking in the mirror. Another kick to the gut.

One he withstood. He had a mission to see through. And then he'd be done.

"When she didn't mention him, you know, back at the pool when she told me the truth about giving me up, about her father and all… she only said she was in love with my father. She didn't say anything else, except that he left for the army and that her father had told him to stay away from her. I…thought maybe…you know, he hurt her pretty bad by doing that, and she didn't know for a long time that it wasn't his fault. I thought maybe it was too painful for her, so I didn't ask. Do you know who he is? Is he still alive?"

Pierce felt the blip. He blinked. Reminded himself of his mission. Of the goal—doing the right thing. Being a man. Loving Eliza with action.

"I do know him. And yes, he's alive," he said. Blipped. Blinked. Blipped. Blinked. "He's standing right in front of you."

ELIZA TRIED TO hang out in the family waiting room. She didn't make it five seconds. Too many sweet children. Young mothers. Worried grandparents.

She walked instead, and ended up by the elevators, sitting on a window seat in front of a half wall of windows.

Using all her focus, she sent Pierce her energy. Her love. Tried to show him his self from her perspective.

And she saw herself, too. A girl who'd always disappointed everyone. Her parents. Her son. Her mom and dad would be seeing the show soon. They'd asked her not to call them ahead of time to tell them she'd won. They wanted to watch it themselves. Get it all firsthand.

She hadn't won. She hadn't wanted it badly enough. What she'd wanted badly enough, the only thing she'd wanted badly enough since she was fifteen years old, was a family with Pierce.

She'd brought this to be.

Yeah, she'd told herself she'd needed to be

the best at something, to receive the ultimate recognition as a professional chef to feel like she'd reached her potential. Because she'd known she was good enough as a cook. But her heart hadn't been about the show. It had been consumed with finding her son. Cooking was allowed. It was something no one would fight her on. Her son had been forbidden on many levels.

She realized something else, too, as she sat there raw and open, where honesty was the only thing she had left.

It wasn't her father she was worried about disappointing. It had been herself. She'd disappointed herself when she hadn't fought hard enough to keep her baby.

But seeing him now, seeing the young man he'd become with the love of two sets of parents devoted to him, she wasn't disappointed in her decision anymore. She'd have been a great mother. But not at sixteen. She wouldn't have been able to give Daniel all of the advantages, the stability, that his adoptive parents had given him.

She thought about the choices he was making—determined to find a way to keep his son in his life while he did what he had to in order to become an adult who would one day be a great parent, able to provide all of the things that a child deserved.

And she knew something else, too.

She'd come full circle.

There was another baby. Just down the hall. Her flesh and blood. She had a chance to be the mother he needed.

And she had to face the prospect of doing it without Pierce.

## CHAPTER TWENTY-NINE

"You're my father."

Daniel had fallen down to one of the couches. Pierce took the other. Sitting back, arms along the back of the couch, he was open to answering the boy's questions.

Or blipping.

Either way, he'd get the job done.

"I fathered you, yes. But I'm not father material, Daniel. That has to be understood right from the beginning."

"I get it. You don't want me."

"No!" Pierce stood up. Sat back down. Left his arms at his sides. "You don't get it. I am fully prepared to support you financially in any way you will ever need. With everything I have. I will pay for college. Give you a down payment on your first home. Buy you a car."

"You want to buy me off so I stay out of her life."

"No." He crossed his arms. Then spread them out. "Listen, Daniel, had I known about you, I would have moved hell and high water to make it back to you. To your mother. It's not a matter of wanting you…"

"You don't want my kid, my son."

"I…"

Daniel stood, turned as if to leave. "That's why she's not here. She didn't have the heart to tell me you said no. You're here to break it to me." He was heading toward the door.

"Hold it right there." Pierce couldn't remember ever using that tone.

Daniel froze. Turned back to him.

"Eliza does not need me to speak for her. And if you think for one second that she would let you down, that she'd let that baby down, you are grossly mistaken. I forgive you for thinking so only because, through no fault of your own, you don't know her. But when you do get to know her, if you ever disrespect her that way again, I will…" He stopped. What was he doing?

Daniel threw himself down to the couch. Stared up at him, a slightly belligerent look on his face, and a curious maturity, too.

"You just said you wouldn't be a father." The belligerence was out in full force, mixed with a hefty dose of accusation.

"That's right. But not because I don't want to be. Because I can't."

"I don't get it."

Pierce had known this wasn't going to be easy. He just hadn't expected it to be quite so hard. Or thought that he'd be able to sustain the conversation without walking out the door if it had been.

"Look, what you're doing…looking for a way to keep your boy with family while you do what you need to do to prepare for fatherhood…it's exactly what you should do. It's noble and decent. It's right. You are a tribute to the family who loved and raised you, Daniel. You're one of the good ones."

"Yeah, right." Daniel's tone had changed completely. "You want to know what I am?" he asked, jumping up. "I'm a murderer, that's what. A damned murderer." He was crying. Raising his voice. Pacing.

Pierce stood, too. Strong and able where the boy was weak.

"What are you saying?" he asked, cop and more, as he stood there. What had the boy done? He couldn't help him out of it until he knew the details.

But he'd help him. He could pull strings. Have him watched over until they could sort it out. He knew attorneys. Or would find one…

"Molly. If I hadn't gotten her pregnant, she'd still be here…"

Pierce didn't move. He watched the boy and had to take a second. It was like watching himself. He'd had a similar thought just weeks before.

If he hadn't gotten Eliza pregnant, her whole life would have been different. She wouldn't have wasted it pining for a child she could never have back. For a life she'd wanted more than any other, that she'd never have…

"No," he said aloud. "That makes you human," he said. "Maybe you should have been more careful. She should have, too. But when you found out what had happened, you stood up to it. You're still standing up to it…"

As Pierce was doing. Right then. Standing up. For Eliza. For the boy. Because it was what a man did. Even when he wasn't capable of being all that they needed. Even when he knew that giving them each other meant losing what he had. Losing Eliza. Their life.

Most especially them.

"You don't get it. It's my fault," Daniel said, shaking his head. Pacing. Still crying.

Grieving, Pierce figured. He recognized

the wail. Had been through something similar himself. When he'd first gone into counseling.

Daniel sat again, dropped his head to his knees and sobbed.

Pierce recognized even that. The pain. The helplessness.

The hopelessness.

The guilt that was weighing down an honorable young man. And shouldn't be.

He'd been faced with an untenable situation.

Pierce sat down without thinking. Put his hand on the boy's back. His neck. Rubbed his hair. Because he remembered needing to feel Eliza's comforting touch when he'd been sitting in a stranger's office, trying to find a way to endure the rest of his life with the weight he carried.

"You told Molly you would find your mother. You promised yourself you wouldn't give up your son," he said. "And today, when you could have walked away, you stayed. You asked the toughest question ever. You asked complete strangers to love your son.

"When a good man is faced with tough choices, no clear right or wrong, and no time to think, he keeps his word." He wasn't sure he'd ever heard the words before. Didn't think he had. Didn't remember them. But they came to him.

And he recognized their truth.

ELIZA HAD NO idea how long she sat on her window seat, staring out at mountains that had managed to sustain all of the trials and tribulations of millions of years of life. From battles to lightning fires. Population, drought, earth shifts, four-wheelers and quakes might have changed them through the centuries, but they endured. Stood tall enough to reach the clouds. Gifted the world with glorious beauty, proof of incredible strength and the will to live.

She had no way of knowing if Daniel and Pierce were even still talking. But until one or the other of them contacted her, she wasn't moving. She'd put them in the same room together. The rest was up to them.

They found her there. Sitting in that window seat. Looking out at the sun setting over the mountains in the desert. Quietly crying.

"Come," Pierce took her hand, pulling her up. She stumbled. Her foot was asleep after sitting for so long.

Daniel was there. Taking her other hand.

They started to walk.

"Where are we going?"

Pierce looked at Daniel. He looked at Pierce. Neither of them said a word.

Could a boy become his father in the space of an hour?

They reached a door that said No Admittance. Daniel took care of getting them admitted. He showed them where to get gowns and hats and helped them put them on, tying Eliza's while Pierce tied his own.

And then they took her hands again. She was afraid to move. To look.

Afraid she'd fallen asleep in that window seat and was going to wake up alone. Lonely. Heartbroken.

Incomplete.

They entered a room. A long room with four glass-encased little beds. But she couldn't say if there was anything in any of them. There were no other adults in the room. She heard some swishing. An occasional light beep.

"Mother, Father, meet Bryant Nathaniel." Daniel let go of her hand, picked up the tiniest body Eliza had ever seen in person, swaddled him in a blanket like a pro and handed him to her.

Her arms were shaking, but she took that tiny bundle, watching his tubes as Daniel instructed, cradled him close to her heart and cried, too.

It had been seventeen long years. Years of grief. Of longing. Of trying to give up on what could never possibly be.

And there she was, Eliza Maxwell Westin, holding the baby who was flesh of her flesh. And flesh of Pierce's flesh, too.

Her heart, like the mountains, had endured. She'd remained open to hope and love even after having lost everything. That open heart had brought Pierce back to her.

And now, in one day, they'd become both parents and grandparents.

That's when it occurred to her that he was still standing there. He wasn't blinking. Or blipping.

Daniel was at his shoulder while Pierce stared at the baby.

"In tough situations, a good man keeps his word," the teenager said. Eliza didn't understand.

But apparently her husband did. He nodded.

"If you blip, we're right here," Daniel said, sounding so much like Pierce it was eerie.

Eliza caught on enough to move closer to Pierce. "Come on, Grandpa, he needs to feel you, too," she said and then, still holding the baby, rested her arms against Pierce.

They could do this in baby steps.

His arms came up. They cradled Eliza's. He nodded.

Daniel was grinning. And crying a bit, too.

"We're going to make one heck of a family," he said. Then, with a quick word to Eliza, he walked with his father out to the hallway to get some air.

"YOU'RE SURE YOU'RE okay with this?" Eliza looked at Pierce in his gray suit with the sedate gray tie. He'd insisted on buying new clothes so he'd look respectable enough.

"We've been given a second chance, Eliza. Only a fool turns his back on that."

"But..."

With a finger over her lips he said, "Shhh. We'll get through the rest, Liza. One step at a time. If I have a problem, I take a breather. If I have a nightmare, we'll get through it. I may never have another. This could be it. I may have them for the rest of my life. Either way, we go together."

It was all she'd ever wanted. She didn't

need a millionaire. She didn't need five-star hotels or the best schools. She needed what she'd needed since she was fourteen years old. Pierce Westin. By her side.

"Sorry." Daniel, in jeans and a Harvard sweatshirt, came running up the hall. He looked at the baby carrier hanging on Pierce's arm. "I can't believe how bad I had to pee…"

He'd put on a little weight. All muscle. Playing baseball as a freshman at his mother's alma mater. It had been a crazy six months since Eliza had appeared on *Family Secrets*. She was worried sick about him.

Pierce kept telling her to cool it. Their son was fine. He'd let her know if he wasn't.

"You're sure you want to do this?" she asked him anyway.

"Ma…" They'd settled on the term rather than the *Mother* he'd started with. *Mom* would always be his adoptive mom. Thankfully his adoptive parents had been happy to welcome Eliza and Pierce into their family.

They'd already decided that the baby had to be adopted out. And while they'd been sad to lose Daniel to the East Coast, they'd known he'd be going away to college.

"I told you," Daniel said, "I'm fine with this. I know it's different than what Molly and I originally planned. But she's gone. She won't be here to take him back. And I think I'll make a much better big brother than a father to this little guy. I'm not even eighteen yet."

Double doors opened in front of them, and a woman in a blue suit stepped out. "The judge will see you now."

Pierce, with the baby carrier on one arm, slipped his other arm through Eliza's. Daniel held her up on the other side and, as a family, they went in and got the job done.

Bryant Nathaniel became a Westin.

\* \* \* \* \*

*Be sure to check out the first book in Tara Taylor Quinn's FAMILY SECRETS miniseries, FOR LOVE OR MONEY, available now from Harlequin Heartwarming.*

*And look for the next FAMILY SECRETS story from Tara Taylor Quinn, coming in 2017!*

# LARGER-PRINT BOOKS!

## GET 2 FREE LARGER-PRINT NOVELS PLUS 2 FREE MYSTERY GIFTS

*Love Inspired*®

### Larger-print novels are now available...

**YES!** Please send me 2 FREE LARGER-PRINT Love Inspired® novels and my 2 FREE mystery gifts (gifts are worth about $10). After receiving them, if I don't wish to receive any more books, I can return the shipping statement marked "cancel." If I don't cancel, I will receive 6 brand-new novels every month and be billed just $5.49 per book in the U.S. or $5.99 per book in Canada. That's a savings of at least 19% off the cover price. It's quite a bargain! Shipping and handling is just 50¢ per book in the U.S. and 75¢ per book in Canada.* I understand that accepting the 2 free books and gifts places me under no obligation to buy anything. I can always return a shipment and cancel at any time. Even if I never buy another book, the two free books and gifts are mine to keep forever.

122/322 IDN GH6D

Name _____ (PLEASE PRINT) _____

Address _____ Apt. # _____

City _____ State/Prov. _____ Zip/Postal Code _____

Signature (if under 18, a parent or guardian must sign)

Mail to the **Reader Service:**
**IN U.S.A.:** P.O. Box 1867, Buffalo, NY 14240-1867
**IN CANADA:** P.O. Box 609, Fort Erie, Ontario L2A 5X3

**Are you a current subscriber to Love Inspired® books
and want to receive the larger-print edition?
Call 1-800-873-8635 or visit www.ReaderService.com.**

* Terms and prices subject to change without notice. Prices do not include applicable taxes. Sales tax applicable in N.Y. Canadian residents will be charged applicable taxes. Offer not valid in Quebec. This offer is limited to one order per household. Not valid to current subscribers to Love Inspired Larger-Print books. All orders subject to credit approval. Credit or debit balances in a customer's account(s) may be offset by any other outstanding balance owed by or to the customer. Please allow 4 to 6 weeks for delivery. Offer available while quantities last.

**Your Privacy**—The Reader Service is committed to protecting your privacy. Our Privacy Policy is available online at www.ReaderService.com or upon request from the Reader Service.

We make a portion of our mailing list available to reputable third parties that offer products we believe may interest you. If you prefer that we not exchange your name with third parties, or if you wish to clarify or modify your communication preferences, please visit us at www.ReaderService.com/consumerschoice or write to us at Reader Service Preference Service, P.O. Box 9062, Buffalo, NY 14240-9062. Include your complete name and address.

LILP15

# LARGER-PRINT BOOKS!

**GET 2 FREE
LARGER-PRINT NOVELS
PLUS 2 FREE
MYSTERY GIFTS**

*Love Inspired*
# SUSPENSE
RIVETING INSPIRATIONAL ROMANCE

## Larger-print novels are now available...

**YES!** Please send me 2 FREE LARGER-PRINT Love Inspired® Suspense novels and my 2 FREE mystery gifts (gifts are worth about $10). After receiving them, if I don't wish to receive any more books, I can return the shipping statement marked "cancel." If I don't cancel, I will receive 4 brand-new novels every month and be billed just $5.49 per book in the U.S. or $5.99 per book in Canada. That's a savings of at least 19% off the cover price. It's quite a bargain! Shipping and handling is just 50¢ per book in the U.S. and 75¢ per book in Canada.* I understand that accepting the 2 free books and gifts places me under no obligation to buy anything. I can always return a shipment and cancel at any time. Even if I never buy another book, the two free books and gifts are mine to keep forever.

110/310 IDN GH6P

| Name | (PLEASE PRINT) | |
| --- | --- | --- |
| Address | | Apt. # |
| City | State/Prov. | Zip/Postal Code |

Signature (if under 18, a parent or guardian must sign)

Mail to the **Reader Service:**
**IN U.S.A.:** P.O. Box 1867, Buffalo, NY 14240-1867
**IN CANADA:** P.O. Box 609, Fort Erie, Ontario L2A 5X3

**Are you a current subscriber to Love Inspired® Suspense books
and want to receive the larger-print edition?
Call 1-800-873-8635 or visit www.ReaderService.com.**

* Terms and prices subject to change without notice. Prices do not include applicable taxes. Sales tax applicable in N.Y. Canadian residents will be charged applicable taxes. Offer not valid in Quebec. This offer is limited to one order per household. Not valid for current subscribers to Love Inspired Suspense larger-print books. All orders subject to credit approval. Credit or debit balances in a customer's account(s) may be offset by any other outstanding balance owed by or to the customer. Please allow 4 to 6 weeks for delivery. Offer available while quantities last.

**Your Privacy**—The Reader Service is committed to protecting your privacy. Our Privacy Policy is available online at www.ReaderService.com or upon request from the Reader Service.

We make a portion of our mailing list available to reputable third parties that offer products we believe may interest you. If you prefer that we not exchange your name with third parties, or if you wish to clarify or modify your communication preferences, please visit us at www.ReaderService.com/consumerschoice or write to us at Reader Service Preference Service, P.O. Box 9062, Buffalo, NY 14240-9062. Include your complete name and address.

LISLP1

## WESTERN WP PROMISES

**YES!** Please send me **The Western Promises Collection** in Larger Print. This collection begins with 3 FREE books and 2 FREE gifts (gifts valued at approx. $14.00 retail) in the first shipment, along with the other first 4 books from the collection! If I do not cancel, I will receive 8 monthly shipments until I have the entire 51-book Western Promises collection. I will receive 2 or 3 FREE books in each shipment and I will pay just $4.99 US/ $5.89 CDN for each of the other four books in each shipment, plus $2.99 for shipping and handling per shipment. *If I decide to keep the entire collection, I'll have paid for only 32 books, because 19 books are FREE! I understand that accepting the 3 free books and gifts places me under no obligation to buy anything. I can always return a shipment and cancel at any time. My free books and gifts are mine to keep no matter what I decide.

272 HCN 3070 472 HCN 3070

Name _____ (PLEASE PRINT)

Address _____ Apt. #

City _____ State/Prov. _____ Zip/Postal Code

Signature (if under 18, a parent or guardian must sign)

### Mail to the **Reader Service**:

**IN U.S.A.:** P.O. Box 1867, Buffalo, NY 14240-1867
**IN CANADA:** P.O. Box 609, Fort Erie, Ontario L2A 5X3

* Terms and prices subject to change without notice. Prices do not include applicable taxes. Sales tax applicable in N.Y. Canadian residents will be charged applicable taxes. This offer is limited to one order per household. All orders subject to approval. Credit or debit balances in a customer's account(s) may be offset by any other outstanding balance owed by or to the customer. Please allow 4 to 6 weeks for delivery. Offer available while quantities last. Offer not available to Quebec residents.

**Your Privacy**—The Reader Service is committed to protecting your privacy. Our Privacy Policy is available online at www.ReaderService.com or upon request from the Reader Service.

We make a portion of our mailing list available to reputable third parties that offer products we believe may interest you. If you prefer that we not exchange your name with third parties, or if you wish to clarify or modify your communication preferences, please visit us at www.ReaderService.com/consumerchoice or write to us at Reader Service Preference Service, P.O. Box 9062, Buffalo, NY 14240-9062. Include your complete name and address.

WPBPA16R

# LARGER-PRINT BOOKS!
## GET 2 FREE LARGER-PRINT NOVELS PLUS
## 2 FREE GIFTS!

**HARLEQUIN®**

*super romance®*

## More Story...More Romance

**YES!** Please send me 2 FREE LARGER-PRINT Harlequin® Superromance® novels and my 2 FREE gifts (gifts are worth about $10). After receiving them, if I don't wish to receive any more books, I can return the shipping statement marked "cancel." If I don't cancel, I will receive 4 brand-new novels every month and be billed just $5.94 per book in the U.S. or $6.24 per book in Canada. That's a savings of at least 12% off the cover price! It's quite a bargain! Shipping and handling is just 50¢ per book in the U.S. and 75¢ per book in Canada.* I understand that accepting the 2 free books and gifts places me under no obligation to buy anything. I can always return a shipment and cancel at any time. Even if I never buy another book, the two free books and gifts are mine to keep forever.

132/332 HDN GHVC

| Name | (PLEASE PRINT) | |
| --- | --- | --- |
| Address | | Apt. # |
| City | State/Prov. | Zip/Postal Code |

Signature (if under 18, a parent or guardian must sign)

Mail to the **Reader Service:**
**IN U.S.A.:** P.O. Box 1867, Buffalo, NY 14240-1867
**IN CANADA:** P.O. Box 609, Fort Erie, Ontario L2A 5X3

**Want to try two free books from another line?**
**Call 1-800-873-8635 today or visit www.ReaderService.com.**

* Terms and prices subject to change without notice. Prices do not include applicable taxes. Sales tax applicable in N.Y. Canadian residents will be charged applicable taxes. Offer not valid in Quebec. This offer is limited to one order per household. Not valid for current subscribers to Harlequin Superromance Larger-Print books. All orders subject to credit approval. Credit or debit balances in a customer's account(s) may be offset by any other outstanding balance owed by or to the customer. Please allow 4 to 6 weeks for delivery. Offer available while quantities last.

**Your Privacy**—The Reader Service is committed to protecting your privacy. Our Privacy Policy is available online at www.ReaderService.com or upon request from the Reader Service.

We make a portion of our mailing list available to reputable third parties that offer products we believe may interest you. If you prefer that we not exchange your name with third parties, or if you wish to clarify or modify your communication preferences, please visit us at www.ReaderService.com/consumerschoice or write to us at Reader Service Preference Service, P.O. Box 9062, Buffalo, NY 14240-9062. Include your complete name and address.

HSRLP15

# READERSERVICE.COM

## Manage your account online!

- Review your order history
- Manage your payments
- Update your address

> *We've designed the*
> *Reader Service website*
> *just for you.*

## Enjoy all the features!

- Discover new series available to you, and read excerpts from any series.
- Respond to mailings and special monthly offers.
- Connect with favorite authors at the blog.
- Browse the Bonus Bucks catalog and online-only exculsives.
- Share your feedback.

*Visit us at:*
## ReaderService.com

RS15